When Sarah got to the dock. Sh was reminded of  and Alison's house when she told him about their night together.

That had been bad. Awful. So why did she feel like this—hearing from Reilly that he was getting back together with Paula—would be so much worse?

But really, would it be worse? It'd just put them right back where they'd been two weeks ago. Reilly with Paula and close friends with Sarah. It would be nice to get back to the way things had been between them.

Wouldn't it?

The uneasiness she felt about the real answer to that question had her barking out to Reilly once she'd caught up with him on the dock.

"Okay, okay, what do you want, Reilly?"

"A do-over," he said, turning to face her.

The harbor glittered behind him, almost causing a halo around his angelic white ringlets. Sarah shook her head, trying both to dislodge the image and to understand his words.

"What?"

"You asked what I wanted. That's it. A do-over."

"A do-over?"

"Yep." He put his hands on his hips, almost challenging her to ask. She wouldn't. She knew.

"You're crazy," she said, and turned to head back to the parking lot. Back to her car. Then to her shop. Give Maya her salad. Head to her studio and work on the custom candle for Alison.

Forget Reilly and this nonsense.

She was almost to the grass when she heard Reilly call, "Bwoooock."

She stopped dead in her tracks, then looked over her shoulder at him. Sure enough, he had his fists in his armpits, flapping his elbows to give it the full effect.

"Bwoooock," he repeated. He dropped his hands, and she didn't even have to hear the word he spoke next. She could read it on his lips.

"Chicken."

OTHER TITLES BY MARA JACOBS

The Worth Series
(Contemporary Romance)
Worth The Weight
Worth The Drive
Worth The Fall
Worth The Effort
Totally Worth Christmas
Worth The Price
Worth The Lies
Worth The Flight
Worth The Burn

Freshman Roommates Trilogy
(New Adult Romance)
In Too Deep
In Too Fast
In Too Hard

Anna Dawson's Vegas Series
(Romantic Mystery)
Against The Odds
Against The Spread
Against The Rules
Against The Wall
Against The Grain

Romantic Suspense
Broken Wings

Contemporary Romance
Instant Replay

Countdown To A Kiss
(A New Year's Eve Anthology)

WORTH the BURN

The Worth Series, Book Eight

MARA JACOBS

Published by Mara Jacobs
©Copyright 2019 Mara Jacobs

ISBN: 978-1-940993-06-5

All rights reserved. No part of this book may be reproduced in any form or by any electronic or mechanical means, including information storage and retrieval systems—except in the case of brief quotations embodied in critical articles or reviews—without permission in writing from the author at mara@marajacobs.com. This book is a work of fiction. The characters, events, and places portrayed in this book are products of the author's imagination and are either fictitious or are used fictitiously. Any similarity to real persons, living or dead, is purely coincidental and not intended by the author.

For more information on the author and her works, please see www.marajacobs.com

For My Mother. Always

Prologue

Twenty-two years ago
Age seven

SARAH RYAN SAT NEXT TO HER MOTHER IN THE CHURCH, waiting for the service to begin. Last night, her mother Yvonne had explained to her what would happen, but seven-year-old Sarah hadn't quite grasped it all.

All she really knew was the father she adored had died. He wouldn't be buried today, though. People weren't buried in the middle of winter in the Copper Country—the northwest tip of Michigan's Upper Peninsula.

Thoughts of her father in his casket, just lying around *somewhere* until spring had softened the ground, had kept Sarah up all night. That and the sound of her mother crying.

"Come on, Sarah, they need us to step out for a moment," her sister Melanie whispered to her, jamming her elbow into Sarah's side.

Mel was one of Sarah's two older sisters. Closest to Sarah in age, Mel was seventeen, halfway through her junior year at Houghton High School. Carla, the eldest sister, was twenty-four and had been gone from the house since Sarah could remember. Carla was six months pregnant and had her two-year-old son Carter dangling on her hip. Her husband Billy was currently deployed somewhere overseas that Sarah couldn't pronounce.

There was no way he could get back in time for the funeral. As it was, Carla's flight in from North Carolina had been delayed because of bad weather, and she'd only arrived that morning.

Carla was leading their mother through a door to a smaller room at the side of the church. Mel followed them, and Sarah followed Mel, desperately wishing that Mel would wait for her, take her hand. Something—anything—so Sarah wouldn't feel so alone. But her sister, like Sarah, was in shock. Mel seemed to remember her and waited for Sarah, even reaching out her hand. Just as Sarah went to grasp it, Carla handed a squirming Carter off to Mel, filling her arms with the little boy, and turned to put her arm around their mother.

The door closed behind Sarah, and it was just her little family—what was left of it—the minister, and Mrs. Glenn, the woman at their church who made everything happen, in a small room. Reverend George, who had baptized Sarah in this very church, looked at them all with compassion in his eyes. Maybe if Sarah stood next to him, he'd reach out and hold her hand?

"We ask the family to leave while we lower the casket lid. It will only be a moment, and then we'll begin the service. The music you've chosen is beautiful, Yvonne. I'm sure Peter will be smiling down upon us today."

That thought freaked Sarah out. Was her dad really up there looking down on them? She wanted to believe that, liked the thought of her father up in heaven, as her mom had explained it the other night. *Always* looking down on her? Sarah was a pretty good kid, but even at seven, she knew she didn't want an eye in the sky on her every move going forward.

Reverend George continued to talk to Sarah's mother as Sarah wandered around the small room. Upon closer examination, it seemed like this was the reverend's office, small and cramped as it was.

Her parents' office at the insurance company they owned was three times the size of this tiny room. Sarah was sad for her mother all over again when she thought about her having to go into that office and work alone. Most days, either her mother or father would pick Sarah up from school and bring her back to the office, where Sarah would read or do homework until the office closed at five.

Sometimes she hated it, wanting to be off doing sports or clubs, like Mel did. Other times she reveled in the added attention, the time alone with her parents.

Time with her father she'd never have again.

There was a soft knock on the door, causing Sarah and her mother to jump. Carla placed a hand on Sarah's shoulder to steady her. Wanting to bury her face into Carla's taller body, Sarah turned to her, careful around the growing baby in Carla's belly. But her older sister was already moving with the rest of the group toward the door back to the church.

They were led to the front row. Behind them were her father's brother, Uncle Dan Ryan, his wife, Aunt Ellen, and her cousin Petey, who was a big-deal hockey player in his freshman year at Michigan Tech.

Uncle Dan's face was pale and drawn. Sarah had never seen him so expressionless. He and her father used to laugh and argue and watch hockey together at least once a week at their house. Neither of them had been quiet men, which Sarah had loved about them both. Aunt Ellen clasped her husband's hand, both white from the pressure of the grip.

Sarah was reminded how many people were hurting today from the untimely death of Peter Ryan. It wasn't just she who had lost a father. Mel and Carla had as well. And her mother had lost a husband. Uncle Dan, a brother and best friend.

"Psst, Squirt. How ya doing?"

Sarah looked up at her giant cousin Petey, who stood in the second pew next to his mother.

Sarah nodded to her cousin, trying to convey the composure her mother and sisters seemed to exude. She knew it was all an act, but it was more than she'd been able to muster.

"It's okay to cry," Petey whispered as she walked past him in her pew. "I do it all the time."

She looked back at him, her mammoth cousin, major tough guy. He winked at her and started to whisper something else, but was cut off by his father clearing his throat—a clear warning for Petey to behave himself. Petey rolled his eyes in Sarah's direction.

It helped, being in on a small thing like an eye roll. But as the Ryan women sat and the service began, even the bit of warmth she'd received from her hulking cousin wasn't enough to warm Sarah.

And how did she happen to be on the end of their little group? She longed to be next to her mother, but Carla took that spot, with an arm around their mother. Mel was next to her, Carter sitting in her lap. Why didn't her mother know how much Sarah needed to be hugged, coddled, even just have her hand held? Small things to think about while Reverend George was beginning the service and talking about how many lives Peter Ryan had touched. Sarah knew that Carla was probably what their mother needed right now. She was able to say soothing things to Mom, whereas Sarah would probably only start crying. Sarah could tell Mel was trying hard not to cry as she bounced Carter gently in her lap.

So Sarah sat, chilled, on the hard wood of the pews and listened as Reverend George went on about her father and what a good man he'd been.

She tried not to look at the casket, now closed. It wasn't really her father in there, anyway. The body that she'd seen yesterday at the funeral home and this morning in the church was only what remained of her boisterous, loving father. It wasn't really…*him*.

The service went on, a hymn was sung. Although Mel held the hymnal low for Sarah to see, she didn't join in the singing, her eyes unable to focus on the words.

Uncle Dan got up to speak, talking about how much he admired his older brother. So much so that he'd named his only child after him.

There were other speakers and another hymn. It seemed to Sarah to last longer than a regular Sunday church service—which were agonizing enough. At least during those she didn't have to avoid making eye contact with the long, gray metal box that held what had formerly been her father.

The wood pew was too hard, the church air too cold. Sarah knew she only had seconds before she would absolutely lose it and crawl over her nephew, her sisters, and even Carla's pregnant belly to get to her mother. It would cause a scene she didn't want, but she saw no way around it.

And then a warm hand slid into hers, clasping tightly. Had Petey snuck around the side of the pews and joined her? But no, the hand was too small to be her hockey-playing cousin's.

She looked down and saw the hand was not much larger than her own, with uneven nails with a little dirt under them, though it looked like perhaps they'd been recently scrubbed to remove some of the grime.

Glancing up from her held hand, she saw the frayed cuff of a suit jacket, the too-short blue dress shirt underneath. It could only be one person.

Reilly Turkonen. A boy from her class, and one who lived in her neighborhood, a few streets away. They'd known each other since the first day of kindergarten and had always been friendly. What was he even doing here? None of her other classmates had come. Too young, her mother had explained.

But Reilly had come.

She met Reilly's blue eyes, and finally she felt like she might just make it through this awful day—and this never-ending service—without standing up and screaming at the top of her lungs.

Reilly nodded at her, mouthed, "I'm sorry" and squeezed her hand tighter. His blond curls clung to the side of his head, still wet at the ends. His sister Tessa would have made him clean up for the service, which Sarah knew was no small task. Only Reilly could have fingernails with dirt and earth lodged underneath them in the dead of winter, when the ground was buried under five feet of snow.

He was always finding things and showing the other kids his treasures—most of them squirmy and alive—in grubby hands. Most times Sarah peered with curiosity, sometimes squealing with fright if whatever Reilly had found chose that moment to come to life and jump at her. But now, today, sitting in the church as they said nice things about the father she loved, she had never been so grateful for Reilly's dirt-stained hand.

The wind howled outside, and Sarah clenched Reilly's hand tighter. Clouds must have moved over the sun, because the huge stained-glass windows darkened, as if the scene they portrayed had a curtain drawn over it. Which would have been fine. Sarah hated the one on the side of the church they normally sat. Somebody holding someone's severed head. It had always freaked her out, and now, as she thought about her dad in the closed coffin, her thoughts wandered to whether her father's head had been cut off in the accident. Had they just shoved it back on for the little time the casket was open for visitation last night and this afternoon?

A nasty howl of wind blasted the windows, and the power went out, leaving the sanctuary in near darkness. There was some light trying to make its way through the stained glass, but it was late afternoon, in early January, and cloudy.

The thought that her dad—the man who cuddled her and called her his favorite surprise when he tucked her in at night—would be in darkness like this forever made Sarah start to tremble.

"It's okay," Reilly whispered beside her. "It's only dark. I'm still here."

It wasn't enough. She could hear men walking quickly down the aisle of the church. She thought Reverend George said something to the congregation, but her head was swimming and she found she couldn't quite hear.

She was about to scream, or cry, or lunge toward the altar and her father's casket, but she was jabbed in the side by Mel's elbow.

"Here, take them," Mel said, passing something to her. Sarah blindly took what Mel handed her. "Give one to Reilly," Mel instructed when Sarah did nothing. She passed one of the small objects to Reilly, and then the light dawned. Literally. Mel tilted her lit candle to Sarah. "Let me light yours," Mel said. Sarah could hear the irritation in her older sister's voice. Whether it was from Sarah's lack of understanding or just the crappy circumstances, she wasn't sure. But then, as Mel lit Sarah's candle with her own, the light showed Mel's face softening as she looked at Sarah. "Now light Reilly's. You know, just like on Christmas Eve."

Right. She could do this. Just like Christmas Eve a couple of weeks ago. That was probably why the candles were so easy for the men to get to and pass out. They'd probably still been in the box in the vestibule where everybody had dumped theirs on the way out on Christmas Eve.

Sarah loved the Christmas Eve service, especially the very end when they turned off the lights, everyone lit their neighbor's candle, and they sang "Silent Night" in the dark. It was beautiful and all, but she loved it because it signaled the end of the service and they'd soon be going home to open two presents. That was their Christmas Eve allotment—the rest would be the next morning.

Holding the candle again so soon seemed wrong. There would be no reason to rush home after the service today.

She lit Reilly's candle, watching the shared glow reflect upon his curls as his head bent close to hers.

There was no "Silent Night." Reverend George continued on. It should have been worse, listening to the kind words about her daddy with just spooky lights throughout the congregation. But it wasn't. It was soothing, the soft glow of candlelight. She bent her head down and watched the play of flame from her and Reilly's candles, both being held by their free hands on their laps, near their held hands. She dug her thumb along the side of the candle, liking the pull of wax that came off under her nail. Taking a deep breath, she let the smell of warming candle swirl around her, giving her as much comfort as Reilly's hand.

"It's pretty, right?" Reilly whispered, and Sarah nodded.

She took another deep breath and stared at her candle through the rest of the service.

Finally, it came to an end, and they all stood. Sarah knew most of the people would be coming back to their home. She and her sisters had spent the morning helping their mother get the house ready. Sarah had been responsible for putting all the silverware they owned on the dining room table, opened to its fullest length to accommodate all the food that would be arriving after the service.

Her mother moved into the aisle, Carla following, then Mel. When Sarah walked by Petey, he reached out and placed his big hand on her head. It was warm and strong, and though it didn't feel as good as Reilly's hand in hers, it helped.

"See you at your house," he said, and Sarah nodded. Uncle Dan had been at her house almost nonstop since her father's car accident five nights ago. He had consoled her mother and talked through funeral plans with her. He'd even come up to Sarah's room and talked with her before he left each evening. Petey had been away playing hockey until yesterday, so this was the first Sarah had gotten to see him.

Her dad took her to all of Tech's home games, even before her cousin was on the team. Having Petey emerge as Tech's star had just added to the fun she had with her dad at the games.

Would her mom take her to the games now? Would Uncle Dan? Would she even get to do the same things she always did?

"It'll be okay," Reilly whispered to her, seeming to know her thoughts. They were in the aisle now and walking to the back of the church. Sarah was aware that all eyes were on her family, looks of pity on the faces of everyone she walked past.

"It sucks. But it's not all bad," Reilly added, still hanging on to her hand, walking shoulder to shoulder with her through the church.

Reilly would know about life without a father. At least some of the time. His father and brothers packed up every winter and went to Florida, where they could get construction work. They returned for the summer months.

They passed the last pew, where Reilly's older sister Tessa sat alone. She must have brought Reilly, for which Sarah was immensely grateful. Tessa nodded at Reilly, then stepped into the aisle just after they passed, following them into the lobby, where it looked like they were lining up to greet everyone.

Uncle Dan, Aunt Ellen, and Petey were right behind Tessa. After a quick glance back into the church, Tessa knelt down to speak to Reilly.

"I've got to get back to work, Reilly. Do you want to stay with Sarah, go back to her house? Or do you want to come with me?"

Reilly looked at Sarah, allowing her to make the decision for him. She didn't even need to speak. Her misery must have been obvious. Reilly quickly turned back to his older sister and said, "I'm going to stay with Sarah."

Tessa nodded, stood, and looked at her watch. "Okay. Umm, let's see, I could—"

"I'll get him to you later," Petey said, joining their small group. "You're waitressing at the Commodore, right?"

Tessa looked at Petey and nodded. "I'm on until nine tonight."

"Okay. We'll see how the afternoon goes. If he wants to hang with Sarah after everyone leaves, I'll make sure he gets to you at the Commodore before nine. That work?"

Tessa looked grateful, but she couldn't have been as grateful as Sarah felt knowing that she'd have someone at her side—holding her hand—as she navigated this horrible day.

"That okay, Reilly? Sarah?" Tessa asked. Both Sarah and Reilly nodded. Tessa knelt again and put her hand on Reilly's arm, giving it a squeeze. Then she wrapped Sarah in a big hug that Sarah returned. Her mother had hugged her plenty over the past five days, as had her sisters, but today everybody had seemed in their own space, nursing their own pain. Sarah disentangled her arms from around Tessa's neck when she felt the woman start to rise. Right away, Reilly reengaged his hand with hers, clasping tightly.

"We've got this," Petey said to Tessa, who seemed reluctant to leave Reilly and Sarah. Petey moved behind Sarah and Reilly and placed his big hands on both their heads. "Young Turk and I will look after Sarah. Isn't that right, Young Turk?"

Reilly looked up, his scrawny neck no match for Petey's mammoth hand. He nodded. "She's my best friend."

This was news to Sarah, but she nodded as well.

"Yeah, we got this," Reilly added.

Tessa nodded, said thank you to Petey, and then turned to Sarah's sisters and mother, making the requisite sounds of compassion before leaving the church.

"You guys don't need to be a part of this," Petey said, steering Sarah and Reilly away from the forming receiving line. "Aunt Yvonne, I'm taking Sarah and Reilly for hot chocolate. I'll bring them to your house in an hour."

Her mother looked at Sarah, then at Reilly's hand in hers. A confused look and then a sad smile crossed her face. "Thank you, Petey. Enjoy the cocoa, kids," she said to them.

At the coffee shop, the hot chocolate burned Sarah's tongue when she tasted it, and she started crying. Even she knew it wasn't the burn that set the tears flowing. Petey got her some ice for her tongue and handed her napkins as she cried.

Reilly—her new best friend—hung on to her hand the entire time.

One

SARAH HELPED HER MOTHER CLEAR AWAY THE DISHES from the dining room, leaving the rest of the Ryan clan to continue their discussion of the Red Wings' chances for the Stanley Cup next season.

It was only June. The Cup had just been decided a week ago, but already her uncle and cousin were debating who would win next year.

Loudly.

"It's so nice to have Petey back permanently and able to come to these dinners," Sarah's mother said as she brought another armful of dishes into the kitchen. As she neared the far end of the room, closer to Sarah, she added in a soft voice, "Even if all they do is argue with each other."

"At least they're speaking to each other," Sarah said. Her mother smiled in agreement and went back to the dining room for another load, while Sarah started rinsing and scraping the pile in the sink.

"I guess it's good they're talking, but my God, didn't the season just end?" Alison Jukuri said as she came into the room, holding two dishes. A clear escape tactic, which was obvious by the guilty look on her face.

"I mean, I love Dan. And of course, I love my husband, but..."

Sarah laughed. "It's okay, I get it. You've only had to come to these family dinners for months. I've had *years* to listen to those two."

Alison sighed. "And I have years to go."

Both women laughed. Alison offered to help Sarah, but Sarah waved her away. Alison propped a hip against the counter and stayed with Sarah, seemingly reluctant to go back to the dining room.

Sarah didn't blame her.

She loved the family dinners her mother hosted once a month, she honestly did. Uncle Dan had suggested the dinner five months after Sarah's father had died, and they'd been doing it once a month for the past twenty-two years. They'd been something that her mother, if not looked forward to, had at least made her get out of her routine of work, the girls, bed, rinse, repeat. Even if only for a day of grocery shopping and cooking.

The attendees changed, depending on which of the kids were in town, but it was always Uncle Dan, Aunt Ellen, and Sarah's mother.

Aunt Ellen had offered—many, *many* times—to take over hosting, but Yvonne had resisted, saying it was good for her to have something to plan that wasn't daughter or business related.

They'd been something to dread as a teenager, when Sarah wanted nothing to do with her family, except her NHL-star cousin who was always good for a few dirty jokes or off-color stories.

Now in her late twenties, Sarah had embraced the dinners and enjoyed getting to know her cousin again now that he was back in town permanently. And married.

"How's the shop doing? Good summer so far? Everybody looking for custom-made candles?" Alison asked her, probably desperate for anything that would keep her from having to go back into the dining room for the continued NHL talk.

"Pretty good, yeah. The shop itself is having about the same amount of traffic, but my sales here in Houghton at a couple of the gift shops have been quite a bit above my normal average for past Junes."

"That's great. Any reason that you can tell why?"

Sarah put the last dish in the dishwasher and dried her hands. "Not really. I've tried some new designs for this season, some new shapes. I think Yooper Treasures has been displaying them more prominently, which is probably some of it."

Her cousin came through the swinging door to the dining room with absolutely nothing in his big hands. "You guys hiding out without me?"

"Hiding out *from* you," Alison said.

Petey boomed a laugh and slung an arm around his petite wife, leaning against the counter with her. "Fat chance that'll work," he said.

"But I can still try," Alison said, causing Petey to laugh again and pull her closer.

A thought occurred to Sarah. "Hey, you haven't been buying up my stock from Yooper Treasures and the other shops in town, have you?"

Alison looked startled and looked up at her husband, puzzled. Petey didn't look puzzled, but he didn't look guilty either. "Nope. Should I be?" he asked.

"No," Sarah quickly said, holding up a hand. "Not at all. I was just telling Alison that my candles are jumping off the shelves in town."

"That's great, right?"

"Yes. I just want to make sure you didn't have a hand in it."

Petey gave a shake of his head. "Nope. Honestly, I didn't even know your shit is in those stores. I never go in those places."

"That's true. I can vouch for that," Alison said. "Besides, why would you think Petey would be buying them?" She looked from Sarah up to her husband. "You have some secret candle kink we need to talk about? And I'm not saying I wouldn't be into it, but..."

"Oh, hold that thought, Al. We are definitely going to discuss that at a later time, but no. No secret candle kink."

Alison looked back at Sarah, waiting for the answer that

Petey obviously wasn't going to give.

"When he'd be playing, and he'd have that long weekend off between camp and the season starting?" Alison nodded, and Sarah continued, "He'd come by my shop in the Harbor—it'd be a week or so before I'd close for the season—and buy out my entire inventory."

"You would?" Alison said "Why?"

Petey only shrugged. "Her stuff is good," he said.

"I know that, but why—"

"Because he was afraid I wouldn't make it otherwise. He was trying to help me out."

"Aww," Alison said, wrapping an arm around her husband's waist. Or around as much of his big body as her small arms would go.

"I knew you'd make it. I just liked your candles. They made good gifts."

"Yeah, that's what you said at the time. But I figured you were lying. Actually, I imagined my candles were either stacked in a huge closet in your house or strewn across the greater Detroit area. Parting gifts or consolation prizes or something."

Alison snorted, and Sarah remembered that the small woman was no longer just part of Petey's pack of close friends, but now his wife. "Sorry," she said.

Alison waved a hand. "Please. I, as well as anyone, know that Petey was a dog until we were together. You're not letting any cat out of the bag."

"*Was* being the operative word," Petey said, pulling his wife deeper into his side.

"Damn right," Alison said. She looked up at her husband, and they shared a smile that made Sarah turn to the sink and start rinsing dishes.

Seconds later, she heard a car pull up to the back drive, a door shut, and familiar heavy tread on the back porch steps. The screen door opened without a knock, and Sarah didn't even need to turn around. "You missed dinner, but help yourself to whatever's left."

"Sorry about that. I got here as soon as I could," Reilly said. "Hey, Petey. Alison."

"Young Turk," Petey boomed. He'd called Reilly that since Sarah could remember.

"Hi, Reilly. How's everything?" Alison said.

"Great, great," Reilly replied. Oh. She knew that "great, great," and it meant that everything was actually not so great.

She turned from the sink to Petey and Alison. "I've got this, you guys. There's not that much to clean up, anyway. And what is left, I'm sure Reilly can put away. You can go back and join the grownups."

"Yeah, that's what we're afraid of," Petey said. Alison nudged him in the ribs and stepped out of the circle of his arm. She looked from Reilly, who had taken up a chair at the kitchen table, back to Sarah. "Let's go, Petey. You can make nice with your dad for a little while longer."

"But—" Petey's words were cut off by the look Alison shot him. He looked at Sarah and shrugged, but with a smile, and followed his wife out of the kitchen, the door swinging with wide strokes from his force.

Sarah brought Reilly a clean plate and motioned to the leftover food. "You might have to nuke a plate. I'm not sure how warm everything is."

He nodded and spooned a glob of mashed potatoes onto the plate. Looking at the roast beef, he started to reach for the serving fork, but stopped. Resting his hands on the table, he said, "You know, I'm not really that hungry."

Definitely not "great, great," if he was turning down food. Wiping her hands on a dishtowel, Sarah sat down at the table across from Reilly. She folded the towel in half, set it on the table in front of her, and then sat back in her chair and waited.

"It's just that she knows how much I want to do this, you know?"

Ah, Paula. Reilly's girlfriend. She must have been on him about Reilly wanting to get into house restoration with a woman who was a ranger with him.

"I mean, Jess is taking all the financial risk for this first house, so I don't know what she's all freaked out about."

Because Reilly would be spending less time with Paula. But Sarah kept her mouth shut and just nodded. She knew the drill. She'd learned that lesson long ago.

"Yes, it's going to be a lot of work, but I'm not afraid of that. She knows that."

Again, Sarah said nothing. Reilly and Paula had been dating over a year. Sarah thought it would actually be hard to be with someone that long—living together—and still not have a basic understanding of someone. Paula didn't seem to *get* Reilly.

Or maybe she understood him but just didn't care.

Unkind thoughts. Sarah tried to turn her mind from them. Tried to listen as Reilly made his case for venturing into this new business with his friend Jess.

"... am I right?" he finished. She hadn't really heard the last part, but she knew what her answer would be.

"It's not about who's right, you know that," she said. "It's about finding the right compromise." Words she'd thrown out a hundred times, it seemed. Safe words. Words that wouldn't come back to haunt her from either Reilly or whatever girlfriend he had at the time.

Paula seemed to be sticking around. Had even moved in with Reilly. So it was important Sarah be cautious with her words so they wouldn't later blow up in her face.

"I'm not sure there is room for compromise on this one," Reilly said, pulling Sarah's attention firmly back to the conversation.

Hmm. That was new. She sat up in her chair and leaned her arms on the table. "So, what are you saying? Are you drawing a line in the sand with her?"

He looked down, playing with his fork in the cold mashed potatoes. His white-blond curls were longer than normal and fell in front of his face.

Sarah waited. She knew that most people thought Reilly was

a pushover, that the women he was in relationships with "wore the pants." They weren't wrong. Reilly liked to let his girlfriends take the lead in most things. But Sarah knew it wasn't because Reilly was weak. She'd always suspected that if there was something really important to Reilly, he'd speak up. Put his foot down. Take a stand.

At least she thought so.

The thing was, there just wasn't all that much that got Reilly worked up. He was the epitome of laid-back, which Sarah had always loved about him. Even though his name was Reilly, he never got riled up. About anything.

Except maybe this? The house-flipping thing?

The house-flipping thing was so new to him that it surprised her it would be the thing that made him draw a line. But maybe that was just what he'd been waiting for. Finding his passion.

His head came up, the curls settling. His face, once deceivingly cherubic, had hardened when they'd gotten deep into their twenties. As they neared thirty, his cheekbones and jaw became more defined. He was now handsome rather than the adorably cute he'd been when they were younger.

His ranger season had begun a month and a half ago, and though it wasn't hot yet, he'd gotten enough sun that his face was turning tan.

"I think I am. Yeah, I guess I'm drawing a line. This is something I'd like to at least try, you know?"

She nodded. "I think you'd be great at it."

"Really?"

Another nod. "Yes, of course."

He seemed surprised. Sarah's dislike of Paula jumped up a few notches. Reilly's doubt of himself was coming from somewhere, and it wouldn't have been from Sarah or Jess, or even his sister Tessa.

"Yeah, I think so too," he said. "Thanks, Ess," he said, using his nickname for her.

She nodded and waited for him to finish loading his plate

and dig into his dinner.
 Which he did.

Two

Nineteen years ago
Age ten

"WE BETTER GET CLEANED UP FOR DINNER," SARAH SAID behind Reilly. He looked up at the sun. Yeah, she was right. It had to be close to six. Looking over his shoulder, he noticed Sarah sitting on the ground with her back against the huge oak in his backyard, her head still in her book. His backyard was currently awash with more anthills than normal for this time of summer. A phenomenon that had Reilly lying in the grass observing with a magnifying glass most of the afternoon as Sarah read her book under the tree.

No closer to a reason on the ants' overpopulation, Reilly rose, walked to the tree, hoisted Sarah up with a hand, and walked to the back door.

"Wait," Sarah said just as they were about to enter the house. She began swatting at his knees, which he realized were covered with grass. So too were his shorts and T-shirt. Helping her with the task, Reilly also started cleaning himself off, shaking his shirt and swiping at his shorts. His bare feet looked okay from the top, but he knew they were probably filthy on the bottoms. Still, they wouldn't be noticed, and he'd be sure to run the tap over them while sitting on the edge of the bathtub.

"Hands," Sarah said, and Reilly held out his hands for her

to inspect.

She sighed, turning them over in hers. Her comparably lily-white hands. "Go directly to the sink in the kitchen. I'll go say hi to your mom."

He nodded, happy that Sarah was making the decisions on a game plan. His mind was still back on the ants. Had their soil changed so much over the winter that it was now a better breeding ground for them? Was there more food available this year?

"Reilly," Sarah said, pulling him out of the anthill in his mind.

"What?"

"Really scrub them. Lots of soap."

He pulled his hands from her. "All right. Sheesh. I know how to wash my hands, you know. We're ten, not two."

At that, he cut in front of her, entering the kitchen door first when typically he held it for Sarah like his sister Tessa had taught him to do.

"Real mature," Sarah said behind him, causing Reilly to smile. He headed directly to the sink and heeded her words.

As he scrubbed, he looked over his shoulder at Sarah, who was taking in the kitchen, her eyes wide. Reilly looked around the room himself, trying to see it through her eyes. She'd been in the kitchen a thousand times and had seen it messy before. But now Reilly realized that the kitchen was worse than normal. Things he never noticed were now standing out to him as he saw Sarah's eyes skitter over the crumbs on the kitchen table. Food left over from last night's dinner on the counter. The sink where he was scrubbing his hands was piled high with dirty dishes. Most of the cupboard doors were open, one hanging from only one hinge. Something his mother kept saying she'd get around to having fixed, but never seemed to do.

"I'll clean it up tonight," Reilly said quietly, turning off the tap and looking around for something to dry his hands on. The paper towel roll was an empty cannon of cardboard. The one towel that hung on the oven door handle looked like it might make his hands *dirtier.*

"I'm sure your mom's been busy," Sarah said, giving his mother an excuse that she didn't deserve.

"Yeah," he said. He flung his hands in the air to dry them, and Sarah came over holding hers out, waiting for his for inspection.

He laid his on top of hers, now closer to the same shade. But not quite. "Again," she said. "More soap. I'll go find a towel from the laundry room."

She was gone from the kitchen before Reilly could tell her that her search would most likely be fruitless. Tessa hadn't been down from the Harbor in several days. Which meant nothing had gotten done for that long.

He really needed to learn how to do laundry, he supposed. And dishes, though he already knew how to do those, yet probably not to Sarah's standards. But certainly better than the dripping pile that sat in the sink.

Guilt warred with shame in his mind. He could help out more instead of spending all day outside studying the bugs and plants around him. Sarah's mother ran a whole insurance agency by herself and still made Sarah (and lots of times Reilly) dinner every night. Their kitchen never looked like this. Having no father in the house wasn't really much of an excuse.

The guilt started winning the war as the feelings he had about his mother surfaced.

"I think you should come to dinner at my house," Sarah said as she came back into the kitchen. She was holding a small washcloth that was from the bathroom set. Probably the only clean thing that remained of the set. Reilly vaguely remembered drying off with a semi-crusty towel last night.

"My mom said she was making dinner tonight," he said, taking the small cloth from Sarah and drying his hands. "I need to stay here."

It didn't appear that his mother had started dinner yet. There were no signs that the kitchen had even been entered today. But when his mother had said goodnight to him last night, she had said today was a new day, and that she was going to "be good" and even make chicken for dinner.

But shouldn't a chicken already be cooking? He glanced at the clock above the sink, seeing it was six thirty.

"I think you should come to my house for dinner," Sarah repeated. Sarah and her mom had dinner late each evening, eating at seven. It gave her mother time to "unwind," she called it, after not getting home from work past six.

"I need to stay. My mom will be expecting me." He stuck his dry hands out for Sarah's approval, but she barely glanced at them, her eyes instead going to the floor.

"She's just getting a late start," Reilly said. "Probably had to work late." Though he couldn't think why there would be a need to work late at the paint store where Reilly's mother was a cashier.

"She's here already. Your mom. I saw her when I went to the bathroom for a towel."

"Oh. Well, see. Then she'll be down in a sec to start dinner. So thanks, but you can—"

"She's not going to be down in a sec. And I don't think she went to work today. I think…"

She didn't say it. She didn't have to. Even at ten years old, Sarah had come to recognize when Reilly's mom was passed out drunk. Not because she saw her that way all that often—Reilly made sure of that. But Reilly would sometimes walk the four blocks from the older, smaller side of the neighborhood to the newer, larger side where Sarah and her mom lived and show up on their doorstep when his mother wasn't able to make dinner for him.

Or when she didn't come home.

He made up excuses, of course, but the knowing look in Mrs. Ryan's eyes told Reilly that Sarah's mother wasn't fooled.

"I'll go wake her. It'll be fine. You can go home," he said, trying to keep his voice normal. Not wanting Sarah to hear the hurt in his voice. Or the fear.

She'd never missed work to drink all day. Not during the

week. Sometimes on the weekends when she didn't have to work, she—

He shook the thoughts from his head. No need to think about that.

"I'm not leaving you here," Sarah said. She looked around the kitchen and then found a piece of paper and pencil in the overflowing junk drawer. "We'll leave her a note in case she— We'll say you're at my house for dinner and will probably just sleep over."

"But what if—"

Sarah was already writing a note at the kitchen table, having to push that morning's cereal box out of the way to do it. She looked up as he spoke, but he didn't finish. Waving for her to continue, he went into the front of the house and locked the front door, grabbed a sweatshirt for later, and returned to the kitchen to find Sarah waiting by the door.

On the walk to her house, she slipped her hand in his and squeezed. He hung on to it the rest of the walk.

Mrs. Ryan didn't flinch when Reilly walked in with Sarah. She hugged her daughter hard and did the same with Reilly. He breathed her in, loving the soft and flowery perfume Mrs. Ryan always wore. It reminded him of her gardens that she spent most of her weekends tending.

"You need to check in with Emmy more often, Sarah," Mrs. Ryan said. "If you're going to be at Reilly's that long, she needs to know that."

"We lost track of time," Sarah said, giving her mother their standard answer. Emmy was a high school girl who stayed at Sarah's house during the day in the summers. Most days, Reilly came over and they played there. Some days Emmy even took them both to the beach. On the days like today, where they were in Reilly's backyard (they never played in his house, and not only because Reilly preferred being outdoors to anything in the world), Emmy would come over a few times throughout the day and check on them, bringing them lunch and an afternoon snack and juice box.

"She said that. And that when she last looked at five, Reilly was on his stomach in the dirt and you were reading a book under a tree."

"Ants," Reilly said, offering up what he figured was an obvious reason for him to be belly down on the ground.

"Of course," Mrs. Ryan said. "Well, go wash up, both of you. Dinner will be ready soon."

"But I already washed," Reilly said, holding his hands out for Mrs. Ryan like he had for Sarah.

"Pretty good, Reilly. Maybe one more spin at it?" She ruffled his hair, his curls spinning in front of his eyes until they landed back in place.

"Okay," he said.

"You take my bathroom," Sarah said. "I'll use the one down here."

Reilly complied, moving through the house and up the stairs to Sarah's bathroom.

When he came back down and held his hands out again, Mrs. Ryan barely glanced at them, only nodding. As he was about to turn toward the dining room, her hands snaked out and grabbed him, pulling him to her in a fierce hug. He wrapped his scrawny arms around Mrs. Ryan, not wanting her to think he didn't appreciate the hug. He caught a glance of Sarah standing behind her mother, looking guilty.

She'd told. She'd told her mother that Reilly's mom was passed out in bed and that was why Reilly had to come home with her.

He shot her daggers with his eyes while he still clung to Mrs. Ryan.

Sarah's look of guilt quickly turned to defiance. She crossed her arms over her chest and took a deep breath, letting it out slowly.

She'd done what she thought was best for Reilly. And she wasn't sorry.

"Okay, dinner's served," Mrs. Ryan, said, pulling away from Reilly.

When they were on dessert, the front doorbell rang, and Reilly thought for half a second that it might be his mother. Until he saw the look that passed between Sarah and her mother.

"Sarah, will you get the door, please?" Sarah slipped off her chair and dashed out of the dining room. Mrs. Ryan slowly put down her fork and turned to Reilly. "Honey, I called your sister. That'll be her. You're welcome to spend the night here, of course. And I told her that. But she wanted to come down herself."

"Tessa came down from the Harbor?" he asked, confused. His sister was a waitress at the Seafarer in Copper Harbor. She and several friends had rented a cabin there for the summer so they wouldn't have to drive back and forth for their shifts. She came down each Wednesday, her day off, and stayed until late on Thursday before heading back to the Harbor. But today was Tuesday. Wasn't it?

"Hey, kiddo," Tessa said as she entered the dining room. "Mrs. Ryan," she said to Sarah's mom.

"Yvonne, please, Tessa. Nice to see you again."

"You too. Um…thank you for calling."

"Of course," Mrs. Ryan said, her voice soft. Full of pity, Reilly realized.

"We need to get you home, Riles," Tessa said.

"Won't you join us for dessert?" Mrs. Ryan said. She pointed to one of several empty chairs at the large table. "It's not homemade, I'm afraid, but it's good."

Tessa stared at the pie on the table, a smile on her face. Reilly knew it was because the idea of having dessert served with dinner—even if it wasn't something *homemade*—was out of the Turkonen realm of normal.

Tessa thanked Mrs. Ryan and sat down to join them for pie. When they were done, Tessa thanked her again—as did Reilly—and they left, getting into Tessa's junker car and driving the few blocks to Reilly's house.

When they got into the driveway and Tessa cut the engine, she put her hand out to Reilly's arm, stopping him from leaving the car.

"I want you to know I'm not abandoning you here. To this. To her."

"I know," Reilly said. He was confused but didn't let Tessa know that. He loved his mother, but she and Tessa had long been at each other's throats. When their dad and brothers were in Michigan, there was a buffer, but they hadn't gotten back from Florida yet.

Tessa was twenty-four and had been out of the house for six years, rooming with girls and waitressing different places. Always in the Harbor during the summers.

But she always came to the house at least one night a week when his dad and brothers were gone.

"It might take a while, Reilly, but I'll figure something out."

"Okay," he said. He trusted Tessa but still wasn't exactly sure what she meant.

"I'll always take care of you," she said.

"I know," Reilly said.

As he fell asleep that night, he thought that maybe things would be okay. Yes, his mother didn't seem capable of taking care of him, but he had Tessa. And Mrs. Ryan.

And most importantly, he had Sarah.

Three

Reilly put his hammer down, listening. "Did you hear something?" he asked Jessica Chapman, who was across the living room from him, ripping up the carpeting.

Her head popped up, and she looked over her shoulder at him. "No. Just your hammer. Do you—"

There. A knock at the door. Jess shrugged and started to rise from her knees, but Reilly motioned for her to stay put. "I got it," he said.

"Who would even know we're here?" Jess said.

Reilly wiped his hands on a rag. "Maybe Zeke?" Zeke Hampton was Jess's boyfriend, a former Navy pilot who had returned to his hometown of Hancock and proceeded to sweep Jess off her feet.

"He's in Virginia Beach getting his belongings," Jess said to Reilly's back as he moved from the living room through the small house to the kitchen and back door.

He didn't ask Jess where Zeke's belongings would end up once back in the Copper Country, but he figured it would be in Jess's home in Eagle Harbor.

The two of them had moved at lightning speed since meeting last winter. Or, at least, it seemed that way to Reilly.

It might not be Jess's significant other at the door, due to him being in a different state, but it was less likely to be Reilly's girlfriend Paula.

She was in the area, but there was no way she'd show up at the house Jess and he had bought and were renovating. At least not during the demo phase they were currently in.

"Hey, I brought sandwiches," Sarah said when Reilly opened the door. She was wearing one of the loose, flowy top and skirt outfits that she wore when working at her shop, so she was either on her way to Copper Harbor or on her way back.

Reilly stood back from the door, allowing her in while he snuck a peek at his watch. Nearly six at night. Past their "noisy time" curfew. They hadn't even noticed, so engrossed were they in their tasks.

"Thanks," he said. Sarah was already setting the large tote bag she carried on the table they'd set up in the kitchen. Reilly had found the banged-up piece of furniture at a garage sale and figured it'd be needed for plans and meals at the house while it was being worked on. Jess had approved, and the next day, she'd shown up with a dorm-room-style mini fridge so they'd have cold drinks available.

"Jess," Sarah called. "Come take a break. I bring food."

"Well, when you put it that way," Jess said as she entered the room. Moving to the sink to wash her hands, she eyed Sarah's bag. "You're too good to us, Sarah. Or at least to Reilly."

Sarah laughed. "You're right. He's just the lucky beneficiary of me bringing you food and not wanting him to be left out."

Knowing the exact opposite was true, Jess smiled at Sarah as she dried her hands and then came to the table, pulling out one of the folding chairs Reilly had commandeered from the Seafarers' inventory. With Tessa's blessing. Sort of.

Reilly followed Jess's example and washed up then joined the women at the table, first nabbing some paper plates and plastic utensils that they kept in one of the cupboards. Cupboards that would be coming down in a couple of days if they stayed on target.

Sarah was unloading several Tupperware containers, and Jess was looking at them with desire. "Still no microwave?" Sarah said, looking around the empty kitchen.

"Didn't seem necessary," Jess said. "Do those need to be heated up?" There was almost panic in her voice, making Reilly chuckle. They'd knocked off for lunch, driving to McDonald's for a quick bite, but that had apparently been too long ago for Jess.

"No, they can all be eaten cold," Sarah said, pushing the containers toward Jess, who opened them all with sounds of delight. "Most of it is from Maya," Sarah said. Pulling the last item from her bag, she set a big globe candle in the middle of the table, then took a seat. Jess handed her one of the food containers after she'd put some of the food onto her plate, but Sarah shook her head.

"No, thanks. I'm having dinner with my mom tonight." She looked at her phone that she'd placed on the table. "In ten minutes, actually." She rose from her seat, just as quickly as she'd sat down.

Jess pointed to the candle in the middle of the table. "That's beautiful."

Sarah beamed, her face lighting up as it always did when she received compliments on her candles. "Thanks. Maya—the woman who works in my shop—said you guys needed to sage this place. To, you know… I don't really know why."

"I think it's like forcing out all the previous juju or something," Jess said, then dove into the pasta salad. After taking a huge spoonful of the stuff himself, Reilly reached for one of the sandwiches that was in a baggie. He tipped up the crust on the bread, knowing that Sarah would have put mustard on one and mayo on the other. She knew Reilly's tastes in condiments—had for years—and had asked Jess hers last week when she'd first shown up with a bag full of food.

He took the sandwich with mustard and passed the mayo one to Jess, who added it to her plate.

"I didn't have any sage, but I did have this sage candle in the shop, so I figured that would work. Anyway, burn it while you guys eat, do a little waving around, and call the juju good."

Jess laughed, and Reilly smiled at his friend.

"Okay, gotta go," Sarah said.

"Thanks so much," Jess said. "For the food and the candle."

"No problem. Reilly's always bringing a meal by the shop for me. Least I can do." One last wave and she was out the door.

"Got any matches?" Jess asked. "We can have a candlelit dinner."

Reilly got up, found some matches in his toolbox, snagged a couple of cans of pop from the fridge, and lit the candle as he rejoined Jess at the table.

"It almost seems like a shame to light it, it's so pretty," Jess said.

Reilly studied the candle as he took a big bite from his sandwich. Just the exact right amount of mustard.

He'd seen thousands of candles Sarah had made, so he'd become immune to the beauty of them, but Jess was right. Some of her designs were just way too nice to be burned.

And some weren't burned. Ever. Reilly knew that Sarah had customers who collected her candles with no intention of ever setting flame to wick.

The one now sending plumes of sage-scented smoke into the kitchen was round, with a scene of Lake Superior on it. The seams of different colored waxes blended so well where lake turned to sky that it looked more like a painting than a candle.

"She'd want us to burn it," he said. It was true. Flattered as Sarah was when she learned about collectors who refused to light up, she took more satisfaction in her products being used. She'd smile if they stumbled upon one of her candles, disfigured from use, at someone's home.

He and Jess ate in silence, finishing every scrap of food Sarah had brought them. It would save them some time, not having to take a longer break to go and get some dinner. "Want to keep going for a couple more hours?" Jess asked, echoing Reilly's thoughts.

"Yes, if you do. I hate to make you drive back to Eagle Harbor so late, though."

"It's okay. I like the drive. I usually call Zeke, and we chat until I lose reception."

"But then you have to come back in the morning. You know you're welcome to crash at my place on nights we're here late."

She smiled, but didn't look at Reilly. Instead, she stared at the small flame coming from Sarah's candle. "Not sure Paula would appreciate that," she said.

She was right. It would be a huge battle having Jess crash at his place, since Paula had moved in and it was *their* place.

"She'd get over it when she realized we were getting more work done that way," he said. Jess let out a soft snort. Yeah, Reilly had hit it on the head. He was damn good with a hammer—literal or figurative.

"Still. I feel like I'd be sleeping with one eye open. That she'd be sitting in the corner of the room, watching me."

He tried to stifle his smile, not wanting Jess to know that this time *she'd* hit the nail on the head.

Paula wouldn't be as bad as Jess made out, but there was no doubt that she'd have her antennae up if Jess was sleeping in their house.

Which was ridiculous on lots of fronts. Paula had nothing to worry about from Reilly—he wasn't the cheating type. Neither was Jess, who was now firmly in a committed relationship with Zeke Hampton. And if they were to mess around with each other, they had all damn day and a house with lots of empty floor space to do the nasty. Yet Paula had never shown up there at the little house they'd bought. Not even to see what he was working on. She said she'd come by when it was less dusty, but Reilly doubted it.

"If you wanted to crash in town, I'd make sure Paula left you alone," he said.

Jess smiled. "I know you would. Thank you for the offer. But I'm good driving home and coming back tomorrow. There won't be a lot of days where we can work back-to-back days like this, so it won't be a burden. Besides, I could probably stay at the Hamptons' if I wanted to. They've offered."

"Take them up on it," he said.

"I probably will. Just not tonight."

He let it drop. Jess was a grown woman, a few years older than him. She could make her own choices. He assumed, like he did with most of the women in his life, that she knew what she was doing and deferred to that.

"So, this is none of my business, of course…" Jess said, causing Reilly to stop piling up the used Tupperware to bring back to Sarah.

"But?"

"Why does Paula have a problem with me but not Sarah?"

Reilly barked out a laugh, the delusion Jess was under being so outlandish. "Who says she doesn't have a problem with Sarah?"

"So, she does?"

He nodded, cramming the containers back into the tote bag Sarah had left for just that purpose. "Big time. But she's learned to hide it."

"Like she hides her dislike of you and me working together?" Jess looked at him, and they both burst out in laughter.

"Yeah, like that. Except she's had longer to practice with Sarah."

"And she's better at it with Sarah?"

Reilly's laugh continued. "Not really."

"I mean, I get it. I might have a problem if Zeke's business partner was a woman."

Reilly rolled his eyes at her. "No, you wouldn't."

"No, I wouldn't. But maybe if his best friend since forever was a gorgeous woman who brought him food."

"Sarah?" he said, then felt bad. Of course Sarah was gorgeous, if he looked at it objectively. But he'd never been objective when it'd come to Sarah. To him, she was neither gorgeous nor plain. She was just…Sarah.

"Yeah, Sarah. Geez."

"Right. Right. Well, the thing is, I was pretty straight with Paula right from the start that Sarah was my best friend and that was not going to change just because we were dating."

"Yeah, I was upfront with Zeke about how things were going to be when we first got together too," she said.

"See? And that worked out okay," he said.

Jess smiled. "Well, yes, it worked out great. But it's the exact opposite of what I laid out at the beginning."

Finished clearing the containers away, he reached for the Ziploc holding several homemade chocolate chip cookies, obviously snatched from Mrs. Ryan's stash. Sarah did not take time away from working on new candle designs to bake cookies. Throw together a couple of sandwiches and pick up a bag of chips? Yes. Spend three hours feeding cookie sheets into an oven when she could be sketching designs, making molds, or creating the candles? Nope.

And the cookies were damn good, so they had to be from Mrs. Ryan. Plus, he'd been eating this recipe for years. This thought brought him back to Jess's topic.

"Not only Paula. I've had that discussion with every girl, every woman, I've dated." He thought back on numerous conversations. "Well, some, back in high school, I didn't even have to. It was just a given. Everybody, at least at Houghton High, knew Sarah and I had been friends forever."

Jess studied him, then took one of the cookies from the bag. When she took a bite, a look of appreciation shone across her face, confirming Reilly's conclusion that Sarah hadn't made the cookies.

"I know you had the conversations with the women you dated," Jess said after swallowing and taking a glance at how many cookies remained in the baggie. Reilly pushed the bag toward her. He had a hookup for those cookies that he could call on any time. She smiled and slid the bag closer to herself. "I'm guessing some of those women heard what you were saying, but figured they'd somehow move Sarah out, take her place in your life, or whatever."

Reilly snorted, thinking of anyone he'd ever dated taking Sarah's place. It was apples and oranges, a totally different dynamic.

But then he thought about the breakups he'd had. The little odd things that broke them up, seemingly inconsequential at the time.

He shrugged. "Yeah, I guess. Some have tried to steer me away from Sarah."

"But none have succeeded."

"Nope."

"Not even Paula."

"Paula hasn't tried. She gets it."

Jess ducked her head and broke off a piece of the cookie she held, but didn't put it in her mouth. Her red hair, which had been in a ponytail most of the day while they worked, fell in front of her face, obscuring her expression.

"Jess?" he said. He'd known her for over a year. They'd worked together at the National Park Service. And though most of the time their shifts as rangers were solo, they'd become friends.

Friends who had morphed into business partners, though for now, the financial risk was on Jess.

Paula had freaked when Reilly said he was thinking about investing his savings into the business. She'd been right, though, when she explained her fears to him. So for now, Jess was supplying the funds for their first house, he was supplying the bulk of the labor, and they'd split any profit they made.

Profit he was planning on putting right back into the next house.

He hadn't told Paula that part yet.

He watched Jess as she handled her cookie, knowing she wanted to say something but wasn't.

"Jess?" he repeated.

Her head shook, the red curtain shimmering. She looked up and shrugged. "Nothing. I guess I'm just glad that Sarah was the trailblazer of you having close female friends. So it won't be an issue for us working so closely together."

Oh, it was an issue. A big one. One that had put him on the couch for three nights instead of in his own bed next to Paula—at her request.

But he hadn't budged. Usually, Paula wore him down or talked at him enough that he came around to her point of view. Okay, caved. But not this time. Flipping houses with Jess—or at least attempting it—was something he was very interested in. And no sex for three nights while his girlfriend slept down the hallway, though unpleasant, was worth it.

On the fourth night, Paula had cuddled up to him and told him she missed him. Then they'd had mind-blowing (and other blowing) make-up sex.

She'd tried one more time in the morning to get him to back out of his deal with Jess, but even with a worn-out cock, he was able to say no.

He told none of this to Jess, of course, not wanting her to have a bad impression of Paula.

He did tell Sarah, who only hooted with laughter and punched him on the arm.

"It goes both ways, though," he said, realizing something. "When we started planning this, you weren't serious with Zeke. Now you're moving in together. Is he going to be cool with us working together?"

She waved a hand. "Oh, he pretends to be all territorial and alpha. But at the end of the day, he completely trusts me. Knows I'm crazy in love with him and would not mess that up."

Reilly nodded. That was good. He didn't need a former Navy fighter pilot glaring at him every time he and Jess needed to work. Like Paula did every time he left her to come to the tiny house in Dollar Bay that Jess had purchased.

Good thing Paula liked sex so much, or he might be permanently sleeping on the couch.

He gathered up the discarded baggies and napkins and put them in a pile. Jess was studying him again as she ate the last cookie.

"What?" he said.

She took a breath, cocking her head to the side, looking at him like he did when he stumbled upon some new-to-him vegetation on Isle Royale. Then she shook her head. "Nothing."

"What?" When she still didn't answer, he asked again. "What, Jess? We're going to be spending a lot of time in this stamp-sized house. Spit it out."

"I guess I'm just wondering... Not having grown up with you guys. And I know full well that men and women can have great friendships."

Ah, the question. The one he was asked by everyone who got to know him as an adult. Even by those he'd grown up with but hadn't seen in a while, when they found out Sarah was still his best friend.

"Why did we never get together?" he said. "Or *did* we ever get together?"

"I know you never got together," she said. "But yes, why didn't you?" She put her hand up. "You know what? It really is none of my business."

Reilly stood and took their trash to the large, empty cardboard box they were currently using for garbage. They had a dumpster outside, but used the box for small stuff, which they then took out to the dumpster. "No, it's okay. It's as simple as... it never came up."

He could feel Jess staring at his back. "Never came up?"

He returned to the table, suddenly wanting the conversation over and to return to his hammer. "Never came up. By the time we were interested in the opposite sex, we'd stopped thinking of each other as anything other than..." He searched for the words. He knew what Sarah was to him, but would Jess understand it? Could he even articulate it? "The other half of ourselves."

Jess blinked at him, saying nothing.

"She wasn't a girl to me, or me a boy to her. She was an extension of myself."

"Like another limb," Jess said.

"Yeah, exactly. I know it sounds dumb—"

"It sounds beautiful," she said.

Reilly thought about it. Yeah, it kind of was. "Whatever," he said, shrugging.

Jess snorted, knowing the truth of Reilly's feelings. She rose from the table, tossed her garbage in the box, and then ran her fingers through her hair a few times, scratching her scalp. She pulled the huge red mass back into a ponytail, securing it with a band that she'd had on her wrist while they ate.

He nodded at her, she nodded back, and they started moving into the living room to resume working.

And then a thought struck him. "Wait. How did you know we never got together?"

"Did you?" Jess asked, surprised.

"No. But how were you certain of that? Lots of people are friends after they hook up."

She walked past him to the corner where she was tearing up carpet. "I know. But there's something very, I don't know, *pure* about the two of you when you're together."

"Pure?"

She knelt on the floor and looked over her shoulder at him. "It must be like you said, you don't think of each other like that. In any sexual way. That comes through when you're together."

She turned back to the carpet and started putting on her work gloves. Reilly walked over to his ladder and grabbed his hammer. Yes, Jess was right. He and Sarah didn't think of each other as sexual beings, and that was obvious to those around them.

A vision of Sarah in a poufy peach dress flashed through his mind as he started to work. Her golden hair piled high on her head, her shoulders bare, a wavy neckline that showed the tiniest hint of cleavage.

The hammer slipped, smashing his thumbnail, and he yowled out in pain.

Four

Twelve years ago
Age seventeen

SARAH FELT A WARM ARM GO AROUND HER SHOULDERS. She should have been startled, but Reilly had made so much noise climbing the bleachers to get to her that he'd easily drowned out her tears.

"Hey, don't cry. It's okay."

"What are you doing here?" she said, dabbing at her snotty nose. Not so much surprised Reilly would know to find her there, but that he'd even know she'd left school early.

"I heard Travis telling a couple of guys from the football team," Reilly said. That news should have made Sarah cry harder, but it had the reverse effect. Her tears stopped, and anger overcame her.

"He was telling his teammates that he dumped me the day before prom? What an *asshole*!"

Before Reilly could answer with a completely justified "I told you so," she continued, "I mean, I knew that, but, you know, not to this degree."

Reilly's warm hand, even in the cool May air, felt heavy and comforting as he awkwardly patted her back. He hated tears, Sarah knew. Sniffling once more, and dabbing her eyes with a McDonald's napkin she'd—thankfully—found in the pocket of her jean jacket, she sat up straighter. "I'm okay," she said. It was true. Travis Harkonen was not worth her tears. Not in a million years.

"Atta girl," Reilly said, giving her one last pat on the back and then taking his hand away. Placing both hands on his knees, he sat beside her, looking out at the empty football field. All the snow was melted, but the grass was still dead. Keeping his eyes straight ahead, he said, "He wasn't good enough for you."

"Well, obviously," Sarah said, causing Reilly to snort. Which caused Sarah to smile. "I'm not even upset about Travis. I mean, I am, but I'm not, you know?" Reilly nodded right away. Even if he had no clue what Sarah meant, he always nodded in agreement.

"I just can't believe the timing. He must have known for a little while, right? Why wait until the day before the prom to do this? When he knew I was considering—" She slammed on the verbal brakes. Reilly was her best friend, and they shared everything, but she'd yet to tell him that she'd planned on sleeping with Travis for the first time after the prom.

She hadn't even told Travis her decision, even though he must've suspected. Maybe that was why he'd dumped her? He wasn't sure she would? Asshole.

"It's just my dress. It's so pretty."

She'd picked it out with her mother in Green Bay a month ago on a special shopping trip after Travis had asked her to the prom. They'd been dating only a week then, so she hadn't assumed he'd be taking her. But when he asked, she and her mother had taken a weekend for shopping in Green Bay, and Sarah found the perfect dress.

She usually faded away in lighter colors, but the peach of this dress made her blond hair seem like gold. Her mother hadn't even said a word about the tiny bit of plunging, scalloped neckline, or the large bit of plunging back.

And now it would be sitting in her closet tomorrow night, instead of on her body, where she could twirl and watch the tulle of the underskirt dance around her.

"I mean, this *dress*, Reilly," she whispered, willing herself not to start crying again. Travis certainly wasn't worth her tears, but that beautiful dress? Not getting a chance to wear it was worth a few. And she'd had to have the hem altered, so they couldn't even take it back. Not that her mother would be mad, but still.

"Want me to ask Steph if you can come with us? I'm sure she wouldn't mind," Reilly said, trying to convince himself.

Because Stephanie would most certainly mind Sarah tagging along on her prom date with her boyfriend of five months.

Stephanie had realized pretty early on that she'd need to allow Reilly his friendship with Sarah. Deal breaker. And Stephanie was a smart girl. But she didn't exactly embrace Sarah as an added bonus to her relationship with Reilly.

She might put up with Sarah joining them at the prom, but Reilly would pay for it later. All three of them would have a horrible night, not just Sarah.

Besides, was it even *legal* for a threesome to go to prom together? Kind of opening themselves up to a lot of three-way jokes. Which certainly weren't new to the both of them. A new round of jokes surfaced whenever one of them was dating someone.

"No, that's okay," she said. "I couldn't do that to Stephanie."

She heard Reilly exhale—a breath of relief, no doubt—and smiled. Such a good guy to take the heat from his girlfriend if it would help out Sarah.

If only Travis was more like Reilly.

If only any of the boys she dated were.

"Here," Reilly said, reaching into his jacket pocket and pulling out a package of tiger cookies.

She laughed and snatched the small package away from him. "Do you just carry a pack of these around with you? In case I have a trauma or something?"

He smiled and held out a hand for one as Sarah unwrapped the package, then placed a cookie on top of his palm. "Nah. I stopped and picked up a pack at the gas station. I wasn't really sure what I'd be walking in on."

"Tears. Sorry."

He shrugged and took a bite of his cookie. When he was done swallowing, he said, "Your tears don't scare me."

She laughed, taking a bite of her own cookie. The fudge stripes melted in her mouth and the sweetness of the shortbread eased her pain as she chewed. Ah, Keebler, such a sweet balm.

She knew that in the grand scheme of things, getting dumped the day before prom would not be the worst thing that happened to her. And losing Travis was really no loss at all. But in the back of her mind, she wondered if all her life's woes could be as easily cured as Reilly showing up, unafraid of what he might find, armed only with tiger cookies?

"GET YOUR DRESS ON. I'm picking you up in a half-hour," Reilly said to her on the phone the next day.

Prom day.

"You did not ask Stephanie if I could come with you," she said, even as she dashed across her room to the closet where her gorgeous, beaded peach dress hung.

"Nope. Even better. She's sick."

"She's sick?" Sarah held the flip phone to her ear with her shoulder as she pulled the hanger with the dress out of the closet and hung it over the slats of the closet door, checking for wrinkles or anything that would prohibit her from having the dress on and being out the door in half an hour.

"Yeah. Well, it's not *better*. Not for Stephanie."

"Of course. Poor Stephanie," she said, trying to muster up the appropriate tone of sympathy. She did feel it. Better than anyone, she knew the crushing blow of having a gorgeous dress hanging in your closet and no chance to wear it.

"Yeah, I guess she's barfing like a...whatever barfs a lot."

"You didn't see her?" Sarah smoothed a hand down the skirt of the dress, envisioning the movement around her legs.

"No, she didn't want me to catch it. She called this morning and said she wasn't feeling good, but was hoping it would pass. Just talked to her ten minutes ago, and she's still puking. Can't make it."

"And she's okay with you taking me instead?" There was no reason for jealousy on Stephanie's part, except for the fact that Sarah would be going to prom and not her.

"Um…"

She moved away from the dress and to her vanity. She'd cancelled her hair appointment this morning, but maybe her mom could put together some kind of updo. Something fast and easy.

Wait. "You did tell her you were going to call me, right?"

"Umm…"

She sat on the stool of her vanity, her shoulders slumped. "Reilly. You didn't tell her? Or *ask* her?"

"It's not like she can go," he said.

God. Boys.

"Reilly," she said again. She reached out her free hand and started pulling her makeup toward her. She typically didn't wear makeup, but she had bought some new stuff that day in Green Bay and had experimented with it a little bit in her room. She especially liked a couple of things she'd tried with the blush. She spun the small compact around with her thumb, her finger holding it firmly in place on the vanity. Not opening it. Not *quite* yet. "Probably not a good idea, Reilly. She's going to be pissed."

"Like I said, it's not as if she can go. And it's not like I'm *cheating* on her with you or anything."

Sarah snorted. "Yeah. As if."

There was a pause on the other end. She stopped spinning the blusher. Finally, Reilly cleared his throat. "You now have twenty-five minutes. Are you getting ready yet?"

"Are you sure, Reilly? Stephanie might be more than just pissed."

A long sigh. He knew it might be the end of Stephanie. And Sarah happened to know that Reilly was getting it regularly from

Stephanie. Not something a high school boy easily gave up.

She knew from Stephanie telling people and it getting back to Sarah, which Sarah figured had been Stephanie's plan.

It hadn't hurt Sarah, if that had been Stephanie's intention. Reilly had been having sex with girls since they were freshmen and a junior girl showed interest in him. His blond curls, blue eyes, and laid-back demeanor had him "getting it regular" ever since, even though he wasn't a jock.

She should be feeling a little satisfaction knowing that word would get back to Stephanie about Reilly taking Sarah to the prom. Probably minutes after they entered the high school gym that had been transformed into A Night to Remember.

But she didn't get any satisfaction from the thought. Only felt bad for poor Stephanie.

"Yeah, I'm sure. Now get your ass in gear," Reilly said.

She wanted to protest one last time, only because she knew how crappy Stephanie must be feeling at home in her sickbed. But Reilly stopped her before she could. "I'll deal with the fallout on Monday," he said.

Oh, and there would be fallout. But yes, Reilly could deal with that on Monday.

And she'd get to wear her fabulous dress.

"WHOA. SARAH, WHEN did you turn into such a babe?" Her cousin Petey had shown up just as Sarah was coming down the stairs, a grocery bag of what looked to be junk food in his big hand.

"What are you doing here?" Sarah asked, half stunned at his presence and half basking in his flattering words.

"Your mom told mine about that dipshit dumping you yesterday. Thought we could hang tonight and watch a movie or something." He pulled a DVD from the bag.

"No, what are you doing *here*? In the Copper Country."

He sighed and rolled his eyes. "Man, why can't my dad take a page from this household and not give a shit about the NHL?" At her confused look, he added, "We got knocked out of the playoffs Thursday. I drove up yesterday."

"Oh. Sorry," she said, not sure if she was apologizing for his loss or her lack of knowledge.

It was a big deal to have your cousin playing in the NHL, but Sarah relied on the guys in her class to let her know how her cousin's team was doing throughout the season.

If she hadn't ditched school yesterday after Travis had dumped her in first period, she'd probably know Petey was due back in town.

"But I guess you have other plans, after all," he said, dropping the DVD back into the bag.

"Yes. But you can leave whatever's in the bag," she said, causing her mammoth cousin to laugh.

She made her way down the stairs, sad that there was no moment of awe by a romantic admirer. Yes, Petey had noticed how pretty the dress was. And her mother had tears in her eyes as she watched Sarah come down, which she hid by fiddling with the camera in her hands. She could even go back up and come down again when Reilly arrived. He knew how geeked she was about the dress and would try to perform the appropriate niceties. But none of that was the same as a boy who *wanted* her watching her make an entrance.

Still, she was going to the prom in her peach dress. Not having Travis there, seeing the desire in his eyes…maybe it was just as well.

She reached the foyer as Reilly knocked once and opened the door, just like he always did.

"Young Turk," Petey boomed. "Heard you're gonna be the white knight."

Reilly nodded to Sarah's mother and said to Petey, "Sarah's actually doing me the favor. My date got sick at the last minute, and I didn't want to waste the tickets."

Petey studied him, then gave a good-natured punch to Reilly's shoulder. One that Sarah guessed Reilly would be feeling the next day. "Watch the tux, man," Reilly said, and Petey laughed.

"Our girl cleans up good, eh?" Petey said, motioning to Sarah.

Reilly took a glance at her and turned back to Petey with a nod. "Yeah, she does."

No, it wasn't the adoration of a guy who wanted to slowly strip the dress off her, but it was nice, and she'd take it. After getting dumped yesterday, she'd take anything nice thrown her way.

"You're beautiful, honey."

"Thanks, Mom," she said.

She could tell her mother wanted to say more but didn't. Sarah had been a witness to Mel having all the special moments a girl had without their father being present for any of them. She'd heard her mother crying in her room after Mel had left for her prom years ago.

She supposed with more time in between, the pain was less for her mother, and for that Sarah was glad. But she had her own twinges that her father wasn't there to see her grown and gowned.

"Okay, pictures," her mother said, and started putting her and Reilly in different poses.

"Can you email some of those to Tessa?" Reilly asked Sarah's mother. "I told her she couldn't come and take any herself."

"Dude, you gotta let them do shit like that," Petey said.

Reilly shrugged, pulled the corsage he held out of the box, and then set the box on the foyer table. He handed the flowers to Sarah. "Oh, I cancelled the boutonniere this morning," Sarah said. "I'm sorry."

He shrugged again. "I don't care." She knew he didn't. Couldn't care less about wearing a boutonniere on his lapel. At least one from Sarah. Except maybe so he could pull it apart tomorrow to study the petals or stamen or whatever it was that sweetheart roses had.

Her corsage was a pinned-on kind, not the kind you wore on your wrist. Sarah handed it back to Reilly. "I think you're going to have to help me with this."

"Oh, right," he said. He looked to Sarah's mom for assistance, but she was clicking away on the camera. He looked at Petey, who gave him a scowl and a "Dude."

So Reilly did his best to pin on the corsage to Sarah's beautiful dress. The straps weren't thick enough, so he had to gather up a bit of the material below, which was lying flat on her chest. The dress had an intricate scalloping along the neckline that Sarah had loved when she'd tried it on. She hadn't thought about how hard it would be for corsage pinning. She'd told Travis to get her a wrist corsage. Reilly's fingers grazed her skin, and Sarah swallowed down the gasp that tried to break free.

Weird, that's all it was. For Reilly to be touching her there. And it wasn't really even *there*.

She'd been touched *there* before. And from Travis just two nights ago. But she hadn't remembered those touches causing her to swallow a gasp, though they'd felt good. Sometimes really good.

It was because it was Reilly. Because it was just her friend and not anyone she thought of in *that* way. That was the reason. It had to be.

But damn, could the guy hurry it up and pin the flower on? Her skin became heated, and she tried not to look down as he struggled with the pin. Instead, she looked at his head ducked in concentration. His curls were so perfect, as if someone had taken a corkscrew to them and then gently, so gently, unwound the tool and pulled it loose, leaving perfect replicas in its wake.

Would he gasp if she ran her hand through those curls? Would he feel the way she did right now, with the back of Reilly's fingers pressing into her chest?

"There, all set," he said, stepping back. The effort, or maybe frustration with the pin, had made his face flushed. He was looking at her strangely, and she turned from him to the foyer mirror to see if he'd completely messed up the corsage. That, her mother could fix, but if he'd put a hole in her dress… But no, everything seemed to be fine, with the red roses of the corsage standing at attention. The red was to go with Stephanie's blue gown, Sarah knew. Knew this because she and Reilly had gone to the florist together to pick out Stephanie's corsage and Travis's boutonniere.

They didn't look as good on a peach gown, but Sarah didn't care. Much. At least she was getting to wear the dress, to go to the prom after all.

Let Travis hear from all his friends on Monday what he was missing.

Hell, this dress was such a departure for Sarah that his buds might not even wait until Monday to see Travis and instead have the phone lines burning up tomorrow.

There may even be a Sunday groveling session from Travis right here at Sarah's house.

She heard a crack behind her, like that of something hitting a human. "Ouch. That hurt."

She turned around to see Reilly rubbing his head and scowling at Petey, who was scowling right back at Reilly.

Sarah waited to see if she should intervene. She looked at her mother, who had been looking at the pictures on the camera and only shrugged.

"Dude!" Petey said to Reilly.

Reilly took his hand from his head—apparently the crack she'd heard—and took a deep breath, his head down. He tipped his head back quickly, causing the corkscrews to spring around his face and back into place. Reilly looked at Petey, struggle all over his face.

What in the hell had happened while she was looking in the mirror and thinking about Travis coming to beg for her forgiveness?

"I'm cool," Reilly said to Petey. Her cousin crossed his arms over his chest and raised an eyebrow at Reilly. "Seriously. I'm cool."

Petey leaned over and whispered something in her friend's ear, to which Reilly nodded.

"Okay," Petey said, clapping his hands once, like the whole

last minute hadn't happened. "How about I come over tomorrow afternoon, you tell me about the dance, and we'll make a dent in that bag of junk food."

"You don't have to," Sarah said. She knew he was just doing it out of pity. She had girlfriends and Reilly for that.

Petey scoffed. "I know I don't *have* to. I don't *have* to do anything until camp in three months. I'll be here around one."

He gave her mother a kiss on the cheek and one to Sarah. "That dipshit is going to shit a brick when he hears how you look in that dress," he whispered in her ear.

She smiled, his words confirming what she'd been thinking. "I know," she said, and they both laughed.

Petey left, her mother took her fill of pictures, and they finally made their way to the high school.

They were running late, which Sarah thought would help make a big entrance. One she wanted all of Travis's friends to see. But the utter silence that fell over the crowd as they entered the transformed gym was about more than just how good Sarah looked in her dress. And it was about more than just that she'd shown up with Reilly. Everybody by now knew he was only a friend to Sarah.

A *best* friend, yes, but only a friend.

Sarah saw what had silenced the group of classmates. Like the Red Sea, the mass of couples, decked out in their finest, parted, making a path for Reilly and Sarah.

A path that led directly to another couple standing at the end of the "sea." A couple with their arms around each other.

And guilty looks on their faces.

Travis and Stephanie. Together.

"Are you fucking kidding me?" Reilly said, starting to move to the other couple.

Sarah grabbed his hand, yanking him back to her. "No, don't," she said.

He turned to Sarah, surprise on his face.

Reilly didn't play games. If someone lied to him, he called

them out on it. But Sarah knew how stuff like this worked.

The surprise on Stephanie and Travis's faces confirmed that they didn't think—in a million years—Sarah and Reilly would attend the prom. But the surprise on Travis's face had quickly turned to gloating, and a sneer had crept up the same lips that Sarah had kissed two nights earlier.

"That's what they want," Sarah said. "Don't give them that." She pulled Reilly out of the opening and into the sea of their friends. Yes, it was hiding, but it was also buying time.

Music was playing, and the couples all got back into formation, slow dancing while their heads were all swiveling between the two couples.

Sarah wrapped her arms around Reilly's neck and stared at him until he finally put his hands at her waist and they began swaying to the music.

"Fuck," he said softly. "I did not see that coming."

"Me neither," she said. Poor Reilly. At least she knew Travis had dumped her. Reilly still thought—until a moment ago—that he and Stephanie were a couple. That yes, she'd be pissed that he'd taken Sarah to the prom—as friends—but that Stephanie was still very much his girlfriend.

Now he had to watch as Travis placed his hands on Stephanie's butt as they danced. Travis, who was watching Sarah as he kneaded the flesh of Stephanie's ass.

"Guess there's a little more fallout to deal with than I thought," Reilly said. He wasn't trying to be funny, but the words made Sarah giggle.

"This isn't funny," Reilly said. "You knew Travis was an asshole since yesterday. Time to process. I *just* learned my girlfriend is a total—"

"Don't say it. I hate that word."

"Jezebel? You hate the word jezebel? Because that's what I was gonna say."

Sarah was shocked Reilly even knew the word. Probably from watching old movies with his sister. But the word tumbling from his mouth, and that teasing smile, because that was *not* the word he'd planned on saying, all had Sarah bursting out in laughter.

"Stop, Ess. I need to project the scorned lover. Play the part."

"Jezebel? Scorned lover? Did you catch a Turner Classic marathon or something?"

"What? I can't know big words?" He looked down at her, trying not to laugh. The whole night was preposterous. All they could do was get through it and then get the hell out of there.

They danced the slow song, and then a medley of fast ones came on. Travis had hated fast dancing. Reilly didn't love it, but he did it.

For her. The whole night had been for her.

"You're the best, Reilly Turkonen," she said once they finally left the dance floor. Travis and Stephanie had left a half-hour earlier.

"Right back at ya," he said. "Want some punch, or you want to go home?"

"Punch," she said. "Let's close this thing down, yeah?"

He smiled at her. "Yeah, you betcha!"

Five

REILLY WALKED INTO HIS HOME AFTER A LONG DAY AT the Dollar Bay house with Jess. A cold beer and a hot shower were at the top of his list, and he didn't even care about the order.

Nearly tripping over two suitcases in the kitchen by the back door had him quickly realizing that the beer and shower were going to have to wait.

It wasn't the first time he'd walked in to see his girlfriend about to walk out—not even the first time with Paula—but something felt different this time. When Paula entered the room and Reilly saw the look on her face, he knew he was right. She meant business this time.

Fuck.

Things had been going pretty well with them too. Yeah, she got on him about the time he spent working on the house, but he figured she'd come around on that once they sold it and she saw that some profit came from his long hours.

A little extra money in his pocket always cheered Paula up.

Not that she was a gold digger. Hell, she wouldn't be with him if she were. But she kept an eye on his hours with the Park Service, letting him know when she felt he should pick up more shifts.

"How about I grab a quick shower and then we talk?" Reilly said. He moved into the kitchen, tossing his keys onto the counter and setting his empty thermos in the sink.

"It's too late for that," Paula said. She swung her long black hair over her shoulder in a dramatic fashion. He loved when she did that in bed as she rode him, staring down at him with a hint of smile on her face.

No smile now. Just the hair flick.

"It's never too late to talk it out," he said. He crossed the small room to the tiny Formica kitchen table and sat down. Motioning to the seat across from him, he said, "Please, Paula. Sit down and talk to me."

"Now you want to talk?" She walked over to the table and sat in the chair. Reilly started to think that maybe he'd overreacted and this time wasn't different from the others.

Maybe she'd let him know her frustrations, he'd promise to try harder, she'd pout but allow him to take her to bed, and they'd have fantastic almost-break-up sex. It was better than make-up sex, of which they'd had their fair share.

Yeah, maybe this was going to play out like the other times.

"It's different this time," Paula said, squashing his thoughts that had already jumped ahead to the fantastic sex part.

"Okay. Talk to me. What's going on?" His voice was calm, soft. He'd spent his life in the company of women. His mother, sister, best friend, most of his coworkers. He knew how to communicate.

"I can't believe you don't know," she said. Ah, this trap. The "I'm pissed because you don't know why I'm pissed" trap.

"I'm sorry. I probably should, Paula. But I don't know why you're unhappy. Or mad. Help me understand. Explain it to me." Her shoulders sagged, and he started to get nervous. "Is it the house? The hours I'm working on it? We talked about that."

"It's all of it, Reilly," she said, sadness in her voice. A sadness that had Reilly really nervous.

Shit, this was not going to be like the other times. He had a suspicion that this time those suitcases by the door were actually packed, not just there to get his attention.

"I'm happy you found something you like doing, Reilly. I

really am." He nodded and waited. "And it seems to fit the other side of you so well. The ranger side, the guy who wants to spend as much time outdoors as possible. The guy who likes to tramp around in the mud and look at bugs and flowers."

He started to smile, thinking of how she'd nailed him. The construction work was different, and so far on this job, all inside, but yeah, it fit him as well as his job as a ranger.

"See," she said, "you're really happy. So content with what you do. This new work just adds to it."

He thought he might be starting to get it. "And you're looking for that for yourself? Something that fulfills you? We can do that. Find that. There's no reason to break up to find what's going to make you happy."

"*You're* what makes me happy. Or, rather, I want to be happy making a home and a life with you."

"Well...but...that's what we're doing, right?"

She shrugged and looked away from him, sitting back in her chair. "Are we? I mean, I moved in, but it doesn't feel like my house. It's still your house. I want to have a nice dinner ready for you, but I'm never sure when you'll be done with work and come home."

That didn't quite ring true. Paula wasn't much of a cook—didn't seem to enjoy it. Reilly couldn't remember ever coming home to the aroma of a home-cooked dinner. Best not to call her on it, though. Maybe it was just a symptom of a bigger problem for her.

"So, if I had more regular hours? Or kept you better informed?"

"And I'm supposed to sit at home and wait for you to show up?"

He shook his head, trying to clear it. She always tied him up in knots. Most of the time, it was a turn-on. Now it was maddening. Still, he kept his voice mild, modulated. "I've never asked you to do that, Paula. I think it's great if you want to explore other interests."

He'd mentioned six or seven job opportunities to her since she'd moved in, but for whatever reason, she'd never followed up on any of them. He'd been content to let it go, not really caring.

Maybe he should have cared more.

He tried to reach across the table for her hand, but she was too far away. "What are you interested in? Let's start there."

"What if I said I was only interested in getting married and having your babies?"

He sat back. Sighed. Yeah, he should have figured it was about this. Marriage. Not so much babies, because he knew she wasn't dying for kids anytime soon, but she wanted that ring on her finger.

He liked Paula. A lot. Was probably a little in love with her. And there was that fantastic sex. That was no small thing.

But...

"I've never asked you to choose, Reilly," she said.

"Choose what?"

"I've never given you an ultimatum. Like, me or Sarah. I would never do that."

He narrowed his eyes at her. It sounded like maybe she *was* doing just that.

"Or now, with Jess. I've been really careful about the other women in your life."

He waved a hand. "They aren't women in my life. Jess is my business partner."

"And Sarah?"

His hand dropped back to the table. "My best friend."

"And I was cool with that."

Not really. Not always. But he let that slide. "So why bring them up now? Why pack your bags?"

"Because I've come to realize that I need something back for my sacrifices."

"What sacrifices?"

"I've made myself available to you, to this home, and I haven't once asked you to give up your friendship with Sarah. Or discouraged you from going into business with Jess. I just want something in return."

"In return?"

"A bigger commitment. I need to know that I matter in your life."

"Paula, you live here. We sleep together every night. I discussed all the Jess stuff with you first. You make most of our joint decisions. Of *course* you matter."

"Prove it."

"A ring."

"Yes."

Well, there it was.

"A ring is what you need to feel more secure in our relationship?"

"Yes."

"So secure that it won't bother you that I have a female best friend or business partner."

"Right."

"And yet you're not giving me an ultimatum."

She shrugged. "Call it what you will. It's what I need."

He'd gone along with girlfriends in the past, mainly because it was all stuff he didn't care about. It made them happy and his life simpler. And it would be easy to go along now. He could be happy with Paula. He *was* happy with her. They could have a good life, a couple of kids down the road.

Yeah, why the hell not? It'd be the simple way out. Then they could race each other up the stairs and fuck each other's brains out.

The corner of Paula's mouth started to quirk up, and he knew she'd read his mind. Knew he was just about to cave.

"No," he said.

She was mid-smile, but it died on her full lips. "What?"

"No ring. At least, not yet. If and when I propose, Paula, I want it to be because we're both ecstatic about the idea of spending the rest of our lives together. Not because I'm afraid you're going to walk out the door if I don't."

She looked at her suitcases by the door. It seemed to him that she was gauging whether she'd miscalculated. How far was she willing to take it? Finally, she took a deep breath and then let it out.

"I'm done, Reilly."

"Seriously?"

"Yes. I want a ring. I want to know you're committed."

"Or else."

"Yes. Or else."

"Living in my house, asking you to move in. Doesn't that say I'm committed?"

"It's not enough."

And that was when he knew. Nothing would ever be enough for Paula. Still, he tried.

"Let's give it a while. We've got something good here, Paula. Let's build on it. There's no reason to toss it away because it's not moving at the pace you would want."

She rose quickly, the chair skittering along the tile floor behind her but staying upright. "You're an asshole, Reilly Turkonen. You know that?"

He rose too, but didn't move toward her. "Because I want to stay together? Because I don't want to force something if it doesn't feel right?" he said softly. "That's in both of our best interests."

"It seems like everything is all about you. My interests never enter the picture."

Well, that was completely untrue. Paula ruled the roost, which was fine with Reilly. Most of the time. He didn't voice that thought. Some part of him was still hoping to salvage the relationship. He wasn't ready to put a ring on Paula's finger today, but he thought he might be someday. Maybe.

"Why don't we talk about this again, like in a few months. Take our temperature then?"

She moved around the table. "I'll tell you what. You take your own goddamn temperature in a few months. I know how I feel now!" She passed him and went to the door.

The gentleman in him wanted to rush over and help her with her bags. But that seemed wrong, somehow, to help her leave him.

So he sat back down at the kitchen table and watched as Paula left the home they shared.

Six

THE POUNDING AT THE FRONT DOOR OF HER CABIN startled Sarah. A quick look at the clock showed nearly ten at night. As she moved to the door, she glanced at her answering machine to see if she'd missed a message while she'd been in the shower. No. The light wasn't blinking. The cell reception was spotty enough in the Harbor, particularly the wooded area where her tiny cabin was, that she kept a landline and answering machine in case her mother needed to get in touch.

But that was definitely not her mother pounding on the door. A thought that was confirmed when she opened the door to see Reilly leaning against the jamb, sliding into the room as the door swung open, mostly due to the weight of his body.

"What's going on? Is everything okay?" she said. She closed the door behind him and followed him into the one-room cabin she called home most of the summer months.

"No. Everything is definitely not okay," he said. Slurred, actually.

"Are you drunk?" she asked. The look he gave her over his shoulder as he made his way to her couch proved the uselessness of her question. Definitely drunk. And from his apparel, he'd come from working on the house.

Fury rose in Sarah. "You drove up here? Like that? Are you insane?" She stomped to the couch and stood over him. "How could—"

"Slow down. I didn't drive. Relax."

She did an about-face and walked back to the door, opening it and checking that indeed her little Subaru was the only vehicle in the driveway.

When she turned back to him, he said softly, "I would never do that, Sarah. You know that."

She did. Or thought she did. After losing her father to a drunk driver, Reilly knew that was something she could never forgive.

So, he hadn't been driving, but he had the drunk part down. He lifted a bottle of Jim Beam that she hadn't seen to his mouth.

So much for heading to bed early with a good book. Moving into the kitchenette, she started a pot of coffee and stood with a hip against the counter, studying the back of Reilly's head as he sat on the couch.

It wasn't unheard of for one of them to turn up on the other's doorstep late at night. She'd crashed on his couch—and vice versa—too many times to count. But she hadn't been to his place for a late-night visit since Paula had moved in. And it'd been that long since he'd shown up at her place—either here at the Harbor or the basement apartment at her mother's.

Paula. That had to be it.

"So, wanna talk about it? Or do you just want to tell your buddy Jim Beam?"

He grunted and took another swig from the bottle, his curls falling back, then forward with the motion.

"I'm guessing Paula?"

Another grunt. Another swig. "She dumped me. Left me."

Sarah tamped down her first reaction, which was to fist-pump and yell out "Yaaaasss!" Instead, she turned around in case Reilly looked behind him. Sarah had been in this position before, but not with Paula. There were times Paula had threatened to leave, but she'd never followed through. Those other times, Sarah had only found out much later, after Reilly felt the situation was well under control and told her.

Paula was perfectly fine, but she wasn't right for Reilly. Sarah had known it from the beginning, but she and Reilly had both learned not to comment on the other's choices in significant others. It was one of the reasons they'd been able to maintain their friendship.

Okay, so what to say now? There was a good chance—a very good chance—that Paula would come back to him in a few days, and Sarah knew Reilly would probably take her back. So, she couldn't tell Reilly how she really felt—that Reilly was much better off with Paula out of his life.

She made two mugs of coffee, adding cream and sugar to hers, leaving his black, and came around the couch. After putting the cups down on the coffee table in front of Reilly, she sat on the big chair that faced the couch.

The cabin was small, with the kitchenette, two-seater round café table, couch, and chair in the main area, and a queen bed tucked into the small nook that was basically her bedroom.

Small, yes, but also cozy, with a big fireplace that took up most of one wall.

When she first bought the little building that became her candle shop, she thought she'd turn the back room of that into somewhere she could sleep when she wanted to stay in the Harbor. But it became obvious that the smell of paraffin and essential oils would follow her, and she'd need to sleep in a different space.

When she started getting custom orders—and the ability to charge exorbitant rates for them—she purchased the tiny cabin and, with Reilly's help, had fixed it up enough to live in during the summer months.

For her, it was just perfect. For her and a drunken Reilly, it would work. For her, Reilly, and Paula's looming ghost? Not so much.

"So, what happened?" she asked.

"That's just it," he said, "I have no idea. I mean, not a clue."

"Did you talk to her? Or was there just, like, a note on the table or something?"

"No. She was there."

Of course she was. There was no way Paula would miss a dramatic exit opportunity.

"And?"

"I mean, I know why. I just don't know why *now*?"

"You want to start with the why?" But Sarah knew. She knew Paula wanted more from Reilly, had from the beginning. Sarah didn't blame her, not really. They were all in their late twenties. If you wanted marriage, kids, the whole nine yards, it was probably getting time to start nailing it down. Paula thought she was nailing it down with Reilly.

Reilly, like many guys, was clueless about what his woman was really thinking.

Partly on Reilly, but partly on Paula too. Sarah had sworn she would never do that in a relationship. Never assume the guy knew what she needed, then be pissed when he didn't deliver it.

Maybe it was from having a close male friend for her whole life, but she knew guys needed a lot more help in knowing what women wanted.

"Did she say exactly what she needed?" Sarah asked.

"A ring. Now."

Well, she couldn't fault Paula for putting her cards on the table. In a way, Sarah admired that.

"With her bags packed in the hallway. How's a guy supposed to respond to that?"

Any admiration, small as it was, went out the window. Yeah, no. You didn't make demands with one foot out the door. Not with your packed bags.

She tucked a leg up under her and nodded toward Reilly's untouched cup of coffee as he shook his head and instead drew from the bottle of Jim Beam.

"Do you… I mean, if she wasn't threatening… Do you *want* to give her a ring?" Sarah always knew Reilly would marry first of the two of them. She wasn't sure how she knew it, but she did. Probably because he was easily led by the women in his life, and

Sarah assumed when one finally put the hammer down, Reilly would say yes.

Apparently, he hadn't.

"I don't know," Reilly said, swinging his arm in an exaggerated motion. Thankfully, the bottle of Beam was empty enough that none sloshed over. Though she was sure Reilly wouldn't be thankful in the morning when he had one unbelievable hangover.

"Maybe. Who knows? Probably, even. But we'll never know now, will we?"

Sarah assumed that if Reilly called Paula tomorrow and said he'd been an idiot and he'd go ring shopping that day, she'd take him back in a second.

She didn't say those words. Kept that little bit of feminine intuition to herself.

He shook his head, curls flopping in disarray. "Christ, Sarah." He looked up at her, those blue eyes full of sadness. "I might have really fucked up this time." His voice was a whisper. Sarah realized that it wasn't so much sadness as fear radiating from him.

Her heart leapt, as did she, moving quickly from her chair to sit beside Reilly on the small couch. She wrapped an arm around his shoulder as she'd done so many times before.

As he had done so many times to her.

"Hey, Reilly, you didn't fuck up. You can never fuck up when you tell the truth. You know that."

A long, shuddering breath came from Reilly, and she pulled him closer. "It sucks that you hurt Paula, someone you…care about. But the truth is always the best way."

"Polishy," he said, his voice muffled by his chin smooshed into his chest. Or maybe it was just slurred.

"What?"

"Polishy. Honeshty is the best polishy."

"That's right, it is. And you did the best thing being honest with Paula now." He started to lift the bottle again, but Sarah slid her hand down his arm and carefully disengaged the booze from his fingers, then set it on the other side of the couch.

Maybe it was time to tell a little truth of her own, even if it would be a mistake in the long run if Reilly and Paula got back together.

"It's okay, buddy. She wasn't the one."

She felt him stiffen slightly, but she held tight. She'd never said anything like that to him when he'd had a breakup, though he'd told her plenty of times that the guy who'd broken her heart was a loser/asshole/fuckwad.

He was always right.

And Sarah knew she was right now. It was a limb that was new to her, but she tromped out on it, willing to hang out over the rushing water.

"She wasn't the one for you, Riles. You know it too, or you'd be celebrating your engagement tonight instead of being here on my couch, half in the bag."

He shrugged petulantly, like he was trying to shed her arm from his shoulders. She only hung on tighter.

"You know I'm right," she said softly.

"Doesn't make it any easier," he said. He slumped back in the couch, taking her arm with him, causing Sarah to lean back as well. Reilly put his hands to his face, scrubbing them up and down.

"Jesus, we could be having make-up sex right now." His hands dropped, one landing on Sarah's thigh. The heat from him seeped through the light cotton of her pajama bottoms. Bottoms her sister Mel had gotten her for her birthday last year. They had Lumiere from *Beauty and the Beast* all over them.

"Cute. Candles. I get it," Reilly said, his gaze on his hand resting on her thigh.

"They're from Mel," Sarah said, hoping maybe this turn of subject would be enough to pull him—

"Make-up sex, Sarah. Do you know how good make-up sex with Paula is?"

"Can't say that I do," she said, trying to hide a shudder.

"It's fucking fantastic, that's what it is."

"Like poetry," she said.

"Wha?"

"Nothing. I'm sure it's great. And yeah, you're going to miss her. That's only normal. But that's still no reason to do something you're not ready for."

He leaned forward and swung a knee up onto the couch, facing her. "But that's just it. *Why* aren't I ready? I mean, I *am* ready. I think. I could be."

"Reilly, if you have to talk yourself into it, then you're not ready."

"I think that works differently for guys."

She snorted, then rose from the couch. "Yeah, I think it probably does. Doesn't mean I'm wrong, though."

She went to the linen closet next to the bathroom and pulled out a sheet set, blanket, and pillow. After plopping them on the couch beside Reilly, she moved to the chest of drawers by the foot of her bed and grabbed a pair of sweats that were baggy on her and an old tee of Reilly's that had ended up in her wardrobe somehow.

"Besides, Paula wasn't going to have make-up sex with you tonight even if you had put a ring on it," she said, dropping the sweats and tee on top of the bedding pile.

"Wha? Why?" Reilly said, looking up at her. The blue of his eyes was unfocused and glassy, and Sarah wasn't sure if it was from unshed tears or the booze.

Maybe a little of both.

She moved down closer to him and tousled his curls, just like the old-timers that hung at the bar at the Seafarer used to do when Reilly was a kid. "Because. You stink to high heaven."

He looked down at himself, seemingly amazed that not only was he on Sarah's couch but he was still dressed from working on the house.

"Take a shower. Crash on the couch. Sleep it off. It'll all look a little better in the morning."

"Promise?" He looked up at her with such hope that it broke

her heart to have to be honest with him.

"No. It'll still suck. It will for a while. But you did the right thing."

He nodded, returning his gaze to the floor.

"Night," she said quietly.

"Night," he said.

She turned the bathroom light on and left the door open a crack. Then turned the others off and crawled into bed.

She heard the glass bottle slide from the floor and Reilly take another loud swig. Should she get back up, dump the bottle out, and tuck him in herself, filthy as he was? She watched a few minutes tick off her alarm clock. Finally, just as she was about to get up, she heard him heave himself from the couch and shuffle to the bathroom.

She should probably listen to make sure he didn't fall or something, but it had been a long day for her making candles, and she was exhausted, her body sore and stiff. But maybe just to make sure he made it back to the couch okay?

That was her last thought before she fell into a deep sleep.

Seven

"Move over," Sarah heard in her ear just as she felt gentle pressure on her hip.

"What?" she said, trying to pull herself out of her sleep but not quite able to.

"You need to— There. 'S good." Reilly wound the sheet around him, snuggling in next to her.

Reilly was in bed with her. The thought should have alarmed her, had her jumping up and banishing him to the couch, but it didn't. For one, it wasn't the first time she and Reilly had shared a bed. For another, she was too lethargic to do more than roll enough for Reilly to pull some of the sheet out from under her.

They lay there, the fresh smell of her soap coming from him, wrapping around her. Soon their breathing was in sync, and she was back to sleep.

Or maybe she wasn't.

Or maybe time had passed and the feel of Reilly's hand on her hip woke her again. Her mind was hazy, dreamlike, and she wasn't sure if she heard him really say, "It was fantastic with Paula, but it would be better with us. Wouldn't it?"

She smiled, loving the dream where Reilly knew she'd be better in bed than Paula. It was a dream, right? "Wouldn't it?" he whispered, his body close now, his breath skittering across the back of her neck.

"You're drunk," she said, burrowing into the sheet, her

movement causing Reilly's hand to slide from her hip down and to the front.

"I am," he said, his voice even closer now, like a ghost weaving around her in the darkness. "But I think I'm right." The words were said from lips that pressed against her nape. A hand swept her hair from her shoulder, baring her neck while his other hand toyed with the hem of her camisole at her stomach. "Am I right, Sarah?"

One elbow in his gut would do it. A "get out of here, Reilly" would do it as well. But the image of Reilly having fantastic sex with Paula burned against Sarah's closed eyes. A tingling zipped through her body, lodging at the back of her neck, right where Reilly's lips lightly kissed.

No elbows jabbed. No harsh words were said to pull him out of his drunken haze.

"Yes," she whispered. The word was barely out of her mouth before Reilly's strong hand scooped under her and turned her body to his.

"Reilly…"

"Shhh…let me…"

"But…"

"God, Sarah, you feel so good. So different."

The words should have jarred her out of the dream she'd convinced herself she was having. He was not only comparing their what-if sex to his and Paula's but also their bodies. Paula was long and lean, a body that Sarah, with her curves, envied. Oh, she liked her curves, loved her body—most of the time. But she was well aware that the woman Reilly had thought he'd be in bed with that night was completely different.

"Fuck," he whispered as his hand skimmed up to cup her breast over her thin cotton camisole.

Ah, there she definitely had more than Paula.

Wait. What was she doing? Potentially having sex with her best friend? Possibly forever ruining the best relationship she'd ever had? Because she wanted Reilly to know she could put Paula to shame between the sheets?

And also because she hadn't gotten any in so long that she was starting to wonder if her body was going into permanent hibernation.

"Reilly, this is insane," she said, the last word on a gasp as his finger circled her nipple, causing it to pebble and snag on the cotton.

"Seems like it's all finally making sense," he said. She felt the yank of material as he pulled down the camisole, and then the warm heat of his mouth on her breast. Squirming underneath him, she moved her body closer, even as her mind was desperately trying to catch up.

No. Don't catch up. Don't ruin this. This could be...everything.

"Christ," Reilly said against her skin, his tongue circling her nipple, his hand scooping up the fullness of her breast from underneath.

"Yeah," she said, her body loosening even as her mind tried to sharpen. But it wouldn't. And somewhere deep inside—deeper than any competition she may have felt with Paula—she didn't want it to. Didn't want to sharpen to the point where she'd call a halt to what Reilly was doing to her.

Because it felt so damn amazing.

Wrong, of course. Because surely in the morning, Reilly would feel like an ass and regret that he'd crawled into bed with her. And wrong because he was drunk and she wasn't.

But it also felt right. Like a wavy, heavy velvet curtain was rising from the bottom of a stage and a spotlight was shining down on them.

"Light," Reilly murmured as he switched to her other breast, pulling the camisole down her shoulders.

"What?" she said, wondering if he was able to see into her mind. If he shared the visuals she was having as he did delicious things with his mouth. They shared everything. Would it be such a leap that he could see into her mind?

"Light. I need to see you."

That would do it. Surely lights would jolt him back to reality. And if not him, her. She would no longer be able to tell herself that it was a dream, a phantom in the night.

"It's...it's good like this."

His tongue swept up her chest, and he planted a warm kiss on her neck.

It was very good like this.

He pulled away, and she heard rustling as he did something on the bedside table. She waited for the blinding light of her lamp, but it didn't come.

His body shifted, and she saw a lit candle on his bedside table at the same moment she picked up the scent.

Cinnamon. Creativity.

Reilly had it together enough to wake up and light a candle. Was he not as drunk as she thought? And what did that mean, exactly? Did that make it better or worse that she seemed to be participating in this very, very bad idea of his?

"Don't think," he whispered around her nipple, as if he had crawled right out of her head. He moved to her other breast, pulling down the camisole for better access, rolling Sarah so she was more on her back than side.

She lightly rested her hand on his head at her breast. Gently, as if she didn't want to wake him from whatever fever dream he was in.

Seriously? She *hoped* she wouldn't startle sense into him?

Yes. That was exactly what she hoped. God help her.

She tentatively played with his curls, no longer damp. So, she *had* been asleep awhile. That was why she was so slow to react.

Yeah, right.

Her fingers moved deeper, and she fessed up. At least to herself.

Not in a million years would she have thought she and Reilly would sleep together. But now that he was doing delicious things to her? Now that his hand had joined his mouth, plumping her breast up so he could lick her nipple into a hard, tight nub?

Not in a million years was she going to stop him.

It was stupid. It could cost her the best friend she'd ever had.

But it had been a long time for her, maybe forever, since she'd felt this way. The tug of Reilly's mouth pulled a desire from her that had been dormant longer than the Copper Country winter.

She sighed with her acceptance as Reilly squeezed her breast.

She left one hand lodged in his curls, weaving through them, and moved her other lower, wrapping around his shoulder.

Reilly shifted, moving over her more, his weight like a heavy blanket protecting and warming her.

"'S nice," he said. Was that a slur? Should she stop and determine just how drunk he was? Was there an issue of consent here that was murky?

"Christ, I love your tits," he murmured. He gently pulled a nipple into his mouth and raised his head, causing a tight sensation that bordered on pain but was most definitely pleasure.

Thoughts of how drunk Reilly was or wasn't fled her brain, and she wrapped both arms around his shoulders, keeping him close.

He wiggled his hips so he was on top of her, and it felt like the most natural thing in the world for her to open her legs and let him settle between them.

God. It had been way too long since she'd felt the weight of a man's body on hers. In some ways, she wanted to block out that the man between her legs was Reilly. It made it more than it had to be.

Couldn't it just be two people needing a little physical release? Helping each other out?

Wasn't that what friends were for?

A hysterical laugh bubbled up inside her, but came out as a gasp of pleasure instead when Reilly bit down on her nipple.

"So good," he murmured, and she silently agreed.

He pulled away from her and sat up on his knees, looking down at her. His eyes were on her bared breasts, and she almost moved to cover them up, reality seeping its way into her fog.

Anticipating her move, he took both of her hands in his, holding them at the sides of her body and pushing them into the bed, as if commanding her to keep them there.

She did.

Her skin tingled as he brushed his fingers up her arms and over her collarbone, bringing them together at the little indentation in the front. He tucked his thumb into the notch while flattening his hands at the top of her breasts.

She felt the hard outline of his erection on top of her. His boxer briefs and her cotton pajama bottoms were the only barriers between them. He rose on his knees, grinding his hard cock into her, making her gasp at the shards of electricity that burst through her. Not even skin on skin.

It *had* been a really long time for her.

He ground for a couple more strokes, once completely off target, then sat back on his haunches, his ass resting on the top of her thighs.

His warm, rough hands skimmed across the top of her chest to her arms, taking the useless straps of her camisole down so that she slipped her hands free from it, putting them back on the bed afterward.

The camisole was already below her breasts, but Reilly pushed the fabric even lower, in effect making a belt out of it. He reached up, and she held her breath, wanting back the aching sensation he'd just created in her.

Instead of settling on her breasts, he moved his hands further up again to the collarbone. One finger traced along the edges, not really following the line of her collarbone, but in a pattern that seemed to make sense to Reilly, since he repeated it several times while she lay under him and took in the sight of his body.

The cinnamon candle on her bedside table was a small one, not throwing much light. She kept it there to do morning meditation when she was trying to think of new candle designs, hoping the creative power of cinnamon would help get the juices flowing.

Now the candlelight danced across Reilly's hard, smooth chest, toned by both ranger duties and construction work. Tanned from being outside and shirtless whenever he could be, his skin radiated gold when the light flickered across his beautiful chest.

She'd appreciated his body, of course, over the years when they'd be at the beach, in the sauna, or whenever Reilly would strip down for whatever task.

She could appreciate the tight, hard, compact body of her friend without feeling even a twinge of attraction.

But the twinge she was feeling now as his fingers continued in his phantom pattern and his eyes stared down at her was completely different.

Beyond a twinge. Beyond curiosity. Beyond knowing they were taking a risk with their friendship that she'd never—ever—take.

"Always wondered," he whispered, his eyes, glassy and unfocused in the candlelight, moving from her face to watch his hands glide along her.

Every second or third time through his pattern, a finger would skim lower and graze her breast, making her wiggle beneath him.

"Peach. So soft. The peach against your skin."

She looked down at her belt/camisole, pretty sure that—yep—the one she wore to bed that night was baby blue. Hard to see in just the small flicker of candle, but also hard to mistake for peach.

She was just starting to think that it was time to stop this madness and sober Reilly up when his hands stilled.

"Fucking peach. Was hard all night."

Did he think she was Paula? Did they do kinky things with a peach? Did she wear peach camisoles to bed?

A bubbling heat stole through her. She didn't want to be compared to Paula while at the same time wanting to best her.

At what?

"Reilly," she said softly, not really sure what she wanted to say. *Stop? More? Please?* "Fuck me," were the words that came past her lips, shocking her and seeming to pull Reilly from his mysterious tracings on her chest.

"Always wondered, Ess," he whispered, using her first initial like he had years ago when they were kids. "Always wondered. Taste." He ran a finger over her nipple, still glistening from the wetness of his mouth. "Feel." His finger again traced the same line of dips and scallops against her chest. "Smell." He bent forward, coming down fast and clumsily, and Sarah lifted a hand to steady his shoulder as he buried his face in her neck, taking a deep inhale.

She breathed him in as well, the distinct essence of man overtaking her shampoo and soap. Just a hint of the lavender came through, but it was all Reilly.

"Awesome," came from his mouth buried in her neck.

He sprang back up, and she felt his erection again right where she needed it. Well, not *exactly* where she needed it, but pretty close.

"Right," Reilly said, as if remembering the task at hand.

"Condom," Sarah said as Reilly stared down at her. He blinked several times, and her desire started to waver. Then he smiled. A smile she'd seen a gazillion times. No smirk, no grin, just a big, almost dopey smile. This smile seemed different, and her temperature ratcheted back up as her legs moved below his ass.

"Hurry," she said, and the smile broadened. His white teeth and big smile with those golden curls surrounding his tan face?

Gorgeous.

"Where?" he asked.

She motioned with her head to the bedside table on her side, and he leaned over her to reach inside, pulling out a condom.

He tore at the package twice, his fingers slipping from it, until she took it from his hands and ripped it open, then tossed the wrapper to the floor.

He moved his free hands to the waistband of his boxer briefs, pulling them down. She thought he'd get off the bed and take them off, but instead he just pulled out his hard cock, pushing the material out of the way. She started to put the condom on him, itching to wrap her hand around his impressive girth. A pleasant surprise to her, not that she'd given thought to the size of Reilly's dick over the years.

Not much, anyway.

As her hand got near, he took the condom from her and swatted her hands away. "Won't last if you touch me," he said. "Gonna be close as it is."

Not exactly the words a woman wanted to hear right before a man entered her body, but whatever. She slid her hands up his hard thighs as he fumbled with the condom, his aim off.

Again, not exactly what you wanted to know just before. Aim was pretty important.

Finally, the condom was on, and Reilly shifted on the bed, lifting and spreading her legs as he did.

She started to shimmy out of her pajama shorts, but Reilly just took one of the loose-fitting legs and moved it out of the way, easing his hand inside.

"Knew it. Knew it would be good," he said as he encountered her wetness.

His aim with his fingers was a little off, and Sarah was just about to guide him to where she needed him when he moved the cotton further aside and started putting his cock inside her.

He filled her, and she dropped her hands, content to let the slow build consume her.

"Christ, Ess," he said. She smiled, knowing that the feelings swirling through her were going through Reilly too. Complicated, sure. But maybe it was as simple as taking things to the obvious next level?

Four hours earlier, there would have been nothing obvious about this step to either of them. But maybe the breakup with Paula had shown them both something they'd never seen before?

Helped generously in Reilly's case by a boatload of booze.

"Mmm," she said, liking the glide Reilly was working. "Yeah," she added.

"Fuck yeah," he said, and started speeding up.

She liked the slow build better, but his quick strokes were nice too. She lifted her arms, wanting to pull him closer, wanting to *be* closer. Her hands didn't even get to his chest before he grunted once more and drove deep inside her, coming.

Coming? He came? Already?

"Fuck," he said, and she mentally rolled her eyes in agreement. Soon would come the apologies that it was so fast, and a promise to help her get hers. "That was awesome," he said, rolling off her and away.

"Umm," she said, then stopped while Reilly disposed of the condom in the trash can on the other side of the nightstand. He stumbled a little as he leaned over, making Sarah realize it was a good thing he hadn't gotten up and gone to the bathroom to get rid of it.

He slid under the covers, and she did too, waiting for him to come back to her. To help her finish.

"Reilly?" she said when he didn't turn back her way. Oh crap, was he regretting it already?

Maybe he was, but by the large snore that came from him, it wasn't going to be something he lost sleep over.

She rolled over, away from him, and debated finishing herself off. Deciding not to, she willed herself to go back to sleep, knowing there would be a hard discussion to come in the morning.

Another snore from Reilly had Sarah bunching up the covers and pulling them all to her side of the bed.

Eight

REILLY'S HEAD WAS ON FIRE. LIGHT STREAMED IN through the window and scorched his eyes. He shifted and felt something at his back. A couch. He was crashed on a couch, not in his bed.

"I know you're awake," he heard Sarah say. From somewhere close. He knew her voice, didn't need to even open his eyes for that.

He shifted on the couch, slowly opening his eyes, realizing he was at Sarah's cabin in Copper Harbor, crashed on her couch.

Memories of the night before came screaming through his brain as sharply as the sun shattered his frontal lobe.

"God, I think I'm going to die," he said, ducking his head and holding it in his hands. He swung his legs to the floor, but didn't try to rise. Not even the aroma of fresh coffee was enough for him to take the chance of tumbling to the floor if his legs wouldn't hold him.

"You're not going to die," Sarah said, coming around the couch from the kitchen holding two steaming mugs, one of which she—blessedly—handed to him.

He pulled the sheet higher to give her a place to sit and to cover himself, since he was in his underwear. Wearing the sheet like a half kilt/half toga, he took a shallow sip of coffee, waiting to see if it caused a revolt. When it didn't, he cautiously took another sip.

More memories came back to him. God, what a horrible night. How could he even look at Sarah this morning?

"Better?" she said, nodding toward his mug, which he was hanging on to with both hands like he'd fight anyone who tried to take it from him. Yeah, he would indeed.

"Yeah, thanks," he said. She nodded and continued to stare at him.

He sighed. So, there was no way they were going to pretend last night hadn't happened. Not with Sarah. She'd want to talk it out, make sure he was okay. Offer her opinion.

Which normally would be great. Normally, he'd want to hear everything she said and would weigh her words with great importance.

But not today. Not about this.

It was still too fresh, too raw.

Too goddamned confusing.

"I can't talk about this with you," he said. "Right now, I'm really embarrassed about it, and I think maybe I need to sit with it for a while. Like, on my own, you know?"

"I guess." She wasn't convinced.

"I'll be okay. It's just…I really don't want to think about it right now," he said.

She nodded. "Well, we certainly don't have to dissect it all, if that's what you think I want to do."

"No. Not…all of it."

"Besides, it wouldn't take that long," she said, laughter in her voice. Reilly looked at her, confused. And then she burst out laughing.

Laughing!

"I'm sorry. I couldn't resist," she said.

She was laughing at him! He'd been his most vulnerable, had made a fool of himself, and she was laughing? What the fuck?

"It's not funny, Sarah," he said. "I'm sorry, okay?"

She sobered, but there was a smile on her face. "I'm sorry too. I should have known better. I was the sober one."

"Yeah, so?"

"I should have stopped it," she said.

Wow. She didn't want any of it? It had been messy, sure, what he could remember of it. But for Sarah to say she should have shut it down? Well, he had to admit, it stung a little. Okay, more than a little.

She was dressed for a day at the candle store in her gauzy skirt and loose blouse. Her still-damp golden hair tumbled around her shoulders, the waves starting to form as it dried.

She would be in the shop today instead of Maya. When Maya was manning the shop and Sarah was candle making, she wore different clothes. Nothing so blousy and flowy, usually close-to-her-skin yoga pants and tank tops.

"You probably have to get to the shop," he said, wanting the discussion to end and not having any idea what time it was. Thankfully, he didn't have a ranger shift for the next few days and would just be working at the Dollar Bay house.

First, he'd have to find a ride back to Houghton. Maybe he'd just borrow Tessa's car for the day.

"I've got time," she said. "And I get that you don't want to talk about it. But I don't want to leave until I make sure we're okay."

"I'm okay," he said, and took another drink of coffee.

"Not you. I mean, obviously I care that you're okay. But *us*."

"Us?"

"Yes," she said. "Are we okay?"

What was up with her? He'd unloaded to her before after a breakup. And Lord knew she'd cried on his shoulder plenty of times. Why would now, this time, be different?

His memory of the end of the night was hazy. Had he tried to call Paula and Sarah had stopped him? Had he burst into tears? Gone on a rampage?

A quick look around her cabin confirmed that he hadn't gone rock star on the place. She kept a tidy space, which was good, since it was small.

She'd already made the bed she'd slept in last night. And Reilly knew he'd find towels placed out in the bathroom for him, like any other time he'd crashed on her couch.

Except this time it was different.

"Did I lose it over Paula?" he asked softly. The memories of his fight with Paula played back.

"What?" Sarah asked, clearly confused.

Which confused Reilly. "Last night. The way I was. Did I... like, cry or throw a fit or something? Is that why you're worried about *us*?"

She sat back on the couch, into the corner opposite him. "What do you remember from last night?"

Oh, shit. Had he said something to Sarah about Paula? Did she have to rip a phone out of his hands or something?

"I remember bumming a ride with one of Tessa's bartenders up here. Drinking on the way. Then telling you about Paula dumping me."

"And then?"

He shook his head. "Nothing. I mean, I helped you make up the couch. I remember that. Then I crashed."

There was a look of hurt on her face. Oh, shit, had she given him some great piece of advice that he couldn't remember?

"What happened after that?" he asked gently.

"Umm...nothing," she said. Unconvincingly.

"Sarah, did I say something? About Paula?"

She stared at him, then shook her head. "No. It was nothing."

"Did you hear me sobbing in my sleep or something?" he asked.

"*Were* you sobbing in your sleep?"

He shrugged and set the mug on the coffee table. "I have no idea. But I don't think so."

"You weren't sobbing in your sleep."

"So, why do you think we wouldn't be okay?"

"Umm, well, you see—"

Then it hit him. "Oh, I see."

"You do?"

He sat back in his corner, pulling his sheet kilt with him. "It's okay. If you trashed Paula, I don't remember it."

"Trashed Paula?"

He waved a hand. "I know how you feel about her. You've been a good friend to keep it to yourself, but if it all spilled out last night, it's cool."

"It's cool?"

Why did she keep repeating his words back to him as a question?

"Stuff that's said in the heat of the moment like that isn't held against you. Even if Paula and I get back together."

She froze at that, her tanned skin actually paling. "You're thinking of getting back together with her?"

Ah, so that *was* it. Sarah had let her feelings about Paula be known. Probably a good thing Reilly couldn't remember it. It would be awkward if he did get back together with Paula.

Assuming she'd take him back.

Assuming he wanted that.

"Who knows? It was pretty brutal. And if I did, I'm guessing I'd need to have a ring in my pocket if I approached her."

"A ring." Not a question this time, just a soft whisper.

Sarah looked around her little cabin, seemingly trying to find words. Reilly wasn't sure about anything that pertained to Paula, so he jumped in before Sarah found whatever she wanted to say.

"Look. Last night was bad, a blur. But it's over. And whatever I said last night, whatever you said, it's a new day, right?"

She nodded, but eyed him suspiciously.

"I don't know about Paula and me. That's going to take some thinking on my part. Or maybe not. She seemed pretty done last night."

Sarah opened her mouth to speak, but he held up a finger to stop her.

"But one thing I do know is no matter what was said last night, we—you and I—are okay. I would never hold anything you said in an effort to help me, or in my defense, against you. You know that, right?"

"But you don't even remember all of last night," she said.

"Doesn't matter. We're solid. We'll always be solid, yeah?"

She didn't say a word, and for a second, he thought that maybe she'd said something last night that was really over the line. Best that he didn't remember it, then. There was no way he could lose his best friend on the day after he lost his girlfriend.

One he could survive, but not the other. He didn't let his mind go to which would be the more devastating—he already knew.

"Yeah, we're solid, Reilly," Sarah said.

Reilly exhaled a breath he hadn't realized he'd been holding. He nodded and then stood, taking the sheet with him, making sure his head was steady before he took his first steps.

"Right. Good. So let's just forget last night ever happened, okay?"

"Okay," she said, and didn't meet his eyes, instead taking a drink from her coffee mug. She rose too, her movements more graceful and surer than his. "Okay, then. I'm off to the shop. You know where everything is. Do you need my car to get back to Houghton?"

"When do you need it next?"

"I'm supposed to have dinner at my mom's tonight."

"Then I'll find another way. Somebody will be heading down I can hitch a ride with. If not, I'll borrow Tessa's car."

She nodded and made her way to the kitchen, where she poured her coffee out, rinsed her mug, and gathered her purse and keys from the counter.

At the door, she paused and looked back at him. There was something more she wanted to say. He could read her that well. But apparently not well enough to actually read her mind, though there had been times when he'd swear he could.

But not today.

"Okay. Well, if you want to talk, I'm in Houghton tonight.

I'll probably stay at Mom's."

"Okay. Thanks. I'll be fine."

She started to say something, but stopped and nodded once at him.

After she left, Reilly took his time showering and dressing, making sure he tidied up after himself. He had a vague memory while he was in the bathroom of stumbling in there the night before. Had he puked? Was that what Sarah had been uncomfortable about?

It had been a while since he'd gotten puke-inducing drunk, but Sarah had seen him like that before. Not a lot, but some.

The thought of what she hadn't said bothered him most of the drive back to Houghton. He'd gone to borrow Tessa's car but saw Sawyer Beck driving into town at that exact moment and flagged him down.

He and his fiancée—and their dog—had been on their way back from their place beyond the Harbor and had given Reilly a ride to Houghton.

When they dropped him at his place, thoughts of Sarah and the night before left Reilly as he entered his empty house. Paula had indeed left him. All her stuff was gone.

He sat at the kitchen table with a cup of coffee, thinking about his next steps.

After a half-hour and no clear answer, he changed into work clothes and headed to the Dollar Bay house.

Maybe a long day of banging shit around would bang some answers into his head.

Probably not, but he could hope.

Nine

Ten years ago
Age nineteen

"Where are we going? I really need to be studying tonight, I told you that."

"You did. Several times," Reilly answered Sarah. That was all he'd give her, which, of course, pissed her off. She sighed loudly and clenched her hands in her lap.

Oh, man, she really needed this. Reilly knew Sarah needed to blow off some steam. Tech was a tough school, and halfway through their sophomore year, things were only getting tougher. Plus, she was dating some hockey player who, in Reilly's opinion, was only adding to her stress level. So he'd set up a study date for just the two of them. A sure sign things were getting out of hand—they had to make an *appointment* to see each other.

When he picked her up, he'd thrown her weighted-down backpack in the rear seat of his ancient Blazer. Instead of driving to campus, he had headed north to Calumet.

She'd badgered him the whole way about where they were going, how she couldn't afford a night away from studying, how Brett would surely be calling her soon.

"If we really were studying, you wouldn't answer anyway."

"I'd answer his texts."

"He texts, not calls?" Reilly didn't text. He didn't have one of the new smart phones. Just a flip phone that technically could text, but it took him too damn long to punch it all out, so he seldom used it. Seldom used the phone at all. Hated the thing, but he kept it on him in case Tessa was trying to get a hold of him. Especially now that her husband Elden was so sick.

"He texts *and* calls," Sarah said, bringing Reilly's mind off his sister's dying husband and back to Sarah's boyfriend.

"And he doesn't know you're with me tonight?" Reilly said. They were at their destination, and he pulled to the curb, having his choice of parking spots right outside the building. He cut the engine but waited for Sarah to answer before leaving the car. Was she not telling Brett about the time she spent with Reilly?

Granted, it wasn't all that much lately with classes, his job at Tessa's place in the Harbor, her time with Brett, his time with… whoever. Partying here and there when they could find the time, like all students at Tech. Like all college students everywhere, he assumed. Tech students just did it with more snow and harder class loads. But whatever—or *whomever*—they were doing, Reilly and Sarah tried to find some time for each other. It was a stress relief in itself. But they'd always been upfront about it with the people they were seeing, if either of them happened to be dating someone. That Sarah wouldn't tell Brett that she was with Reilly tonight should be a red flag to her that Brett wasn't going to last long.

He knew there would be *some* man that Sarah would spend the rest of her life with. That man would get all of Sarah, the parts that only Reilly knew.

But Brett was not that man.

It might take Sarah a little longer to figure that out, but Reilly had a busy term anyway. He could wait out that relationship to get his friend back completely.

"I told him I was studying tonight," Sarah said, looking out the window to where he'd brought her, confusion on her face. "Because that's what I *thought* I was doing."

"But did you tell him who you were studying with?"

She ignored his question, which was answer enough. "What is going on in there?"

"Let's go find out," Reilly said, opening his door and getting out of the Blazer.

When he came around the front, Sarah was already out of her side. She always did that, never allowing Reilly to open the door for her. Gentleman shit that Tessa had drummed into his head.

The first time he tried to open Sarah's car door, way back when they were sixteen, she'd rolled her eyes and laughed at him. From then on, he'd tried, but she'd always been quicker on the draw.

He did get to the front of the store before her, though, opening that door for her. But only because she was staring through the large window into the makeshift workshop.

"Is this some kind of class or something?" she said softly, because it was a small storefront. Even at the door, the inhabitants were close enough to hear them.

If you could call three people inhabitants.

"Welcome. We're so glad you could join us. Please come in and find a workstation. You must be Reilly and Sarah."

Sarah turned around and glared at him. She now knew that whatever this was, he'd planned it. Planned on not studying. It wasn't just some lark he'd driven her to. He had the receipt of pre-registration in his pocket that proved just that.

"Thanks," he said. He pushed Sarah's back until she moved deeper into the room. It was a small, old store in Laurium that apparently was rented out for various things. He knew there was a tai chi class there on certain nights because Tessa had attended before Elden had gotten sick. He also knew that there were pop-up craft sales and that kind of shit in the building. No permanent dwellers. The room itself had been redone with sleek hardwood floors and neutral paint. Even the tin ceiling had been uncovered and refinished, showing off its intricate scrollwork design.

For tonight's gathering, there were tarps down covering most of the floor. It looked like a murder was about to take place.

From the look Sarah was giving him, he knew she was hoping for one—his.

"That's right, those two tables there at the end. I'm Maya. And this is Esther and Naomi. We're so glad you could join us. It's nice to have some young people show interest in candle making."

"Candle making? What the fuck?" Sarah said under her breath so only Reilly could hear as they made their way to the two work areas Maya had indicated. Sarah might be pissed at Reilly, but she still had her manners. "Thank you. This is completely new to me," she said to Maya. She nodded to Naomi and Esther.

Reilly followed her lead, nodding to the other two participants in the class. They nodded back, smiling and seemingly delighted to have a young couple in their class.

He'd met Maya last week when he'd dropped off the payment for the class at her home a few blocks away from the store where they now were. It was one of the tiny homes from the mining days and was well taken care of, but it was obvious Maya wasn't getting rich from her candle-making classes. Especially if four attendees were the norm.

She was dressed like what Reilly imagined in a candle maker. Flowy skirt, peasant blouse, heavy wool socks, and Birkenstocks. Her long hair was loose and starting to turn gray, though some of the white-blond hair was still visible. She was a towhead like himself, like half the population in the Copper Country with its Finnish heritage.

Not a golden blond like Sarah, whose hair was sliding free as she took off her knit hat and then her jacket. She tucked both onto a chair along the wall behind them. Reilly added his own jacket and gloves to the pile, then returned to his table.

"Okay, let's begin. Sarah, Reilly, this is new to you, you said?" They both nodded. "Well, we're going to make this easy on you. Esther and Naomi are old hats at this, so if you need assistance, they can also help you out," Maya said. Reilly was bad with ages, but he guessed her to be mid-to-late fifties. "First, you'll want to choose a mold. This will be the finished shape of your candle. We have several to choose from here." She slowly waved a hand across a bunch of things at the front table like she was a ta-da girl on a game show.

Sarah and he made their way across the small storefront to the table where Maya stood. "Pillars are usually a good way to start. But, of course, there are the traditional tapers and—"

"What's this one?" Sarah asked, holding up a metal half orb.

"A round candle mold. The other half is here." Maya moved around Sarah's side, handing her the other half of the globe-like mold.

"Is this harder? Should I not try it for my first time?" Sarah asked. Reilly hated the uncertainty in her voice. He'd been hearing it more and more lately and had tried to talk to her about it. They never seemed to have enough time together anymore, and they certainly did not have enough time for him to break down whatever walls she was trying to build around herself. Was it because of Brett? Was he treating her badly? Or was it just the pressures of a Tech curriculum? Sarah was a business major, not in engineering. The majority of Tech students were engineering majors, including Reilly. But the business program was still demanding.

"I think you'll do just fine with a round candle, dear," Maya said to Sarah, causing her to break out in a smile that he hadn't seen nearly enough lately.

Sarah nodded and took both halves of the mold back to her worktable. Reilly took a pillar mold back to his, noticing that Esther and Naomi were both working on tapers.

"Okay, let's begin," Maya said. Reilly heard Sarah's deep sigh. But this sigh wasn't the kind she'd made in the car, the kind she made when she was exasperated with him. This one was what she sounded like when Tessa made them burgers, fries, and hot fudge sundaes.

Yes, he knew the difference in Sarah's sighs.

And if he wasn't sure enough, Sarah leaned over and

whispered, "Thank you, Reilly," just before all her attention for the next three hours was focused on candle making.

"I DON'T WANT TO RUN the insurance agency," Sarah said three and a half hours later as they were driving back to Houghton. The smell of warm wax permeated the air, their candles on newspaper on the floor in the back seat. "And I haven't been able to tell my mom," she added.

So *that* was what had been bothering her lately. He was glad, of course, that her boyfriend wasn't treating her poorly, but Reilly might have been hoping that Brett was the cause of the change in Sarah. Enough for her to wake up and body-check hockey boy into the boards.

"What do you *want* to do?" he asked. A feeling deep inside started bubbling to the surface, making itself known.

"I'm not sure. But I don't want to run the agency. I know my mom is planning on it. Carla is happy in California with Billy and the kids. Mel is never leaving New York."

"That doesn't mean you have to run it. Not if you don't want to." He said the words to her, but they bounced around his mind, pinging like little pistons trying to fire.

"I know," Sarah said, and then sighed deeply. "I tried to fake it, kind of talk myself into it. I'd be sitting in class thinking about how what the prof was talking about would apply to the agency, and I'd just get so sad, you know?"

The little pistons were really jumping around in his brain now. "Yeah, I know," he said. He didn't elaborate, waiting for Sarah to do that. It seemed she had a better handle on how they were both feeling.

"The thing is, I really like the classes. I like the business program. I just hate thinking that I'm going to end up applying everything I'm learning to the agency."

Yes, that was him too. He liked the math and science that was the basis of the engineering degree he was pursuing. He just couldn't picture himself actually…engineering anything.

He'd kept waiting for the passion for it to kick in, for it all to *click*, but it hadn't. He did fine in the coursework and enjoyed the classes—for the most part—but, like Sarah, it wasn't what he wanted to *do*.

"And you have no idea what you really want to do?" he asked, more for himself than her.

"I don't know. Well, maybe. I'd like to run a small business, just not insurance."

Small business was good. That could potentially keep Sarah in the Copper Country after graduation. The area was full of small businesses. Maybe one of them would need a manager when they graduated.

Reilly knew he'd never live anywhere other than the Copper Country. The place, the outdoors, spoke to his soul in a way he knew no other place ever could.

He didn't know if Sarah felt the same way. She seemed to like it here well enough, and she got along well with her mother. It had been assumed for years that Sarah would take over the insurance agency when her mother retired. Mrs. Ryan was past retirement age now and was presumably just waiting for Sarah to get her degree.

When Sarah told her mom she didn't want the agency, would that cause a rift so deep that Sarah wouldn't want to live here anymore?

The thought of her moving away added to the weight in his chest caused from their current conversation.

"I guess all I can do is tell her," Sarah said.

Reilly had found over the years with Sarah—and with every one of the girls he'd dated—that women found their way to their own answer all on their own. All you had to do was just listen and give advice—without straight-up telling them what to do—and they invariably decided on their course of action.

He knew some guys laughed at him. Said he let the chick "wear the pants." (What a stupid fucking expression.) But Reilly was a keen observer of nature, and an offshoot of that was human nature. He knew that letting a woman talk something out and come to her own conclusion yielded the best results.

"Yep," he said.

"It's not like she's going to throw me out or anything," Sarah said.

Reilly snorted at the preposterous mental image of Yvonne Ryan tossing Sarah's clothes out her bedroom window and onto the snow-covered lawn. "Of course not."

"She'll be hurt, though."

"Probably."

"She might even cry," Sarah said.

Reilly had never seen Yvonne Ryan cry, so that was a little harder to imagine.

"Not so I'd see it, of course. But later, when she's alone."

Had that been a thing? It would be natural for a widow to do a little crying over the years. And Yvonne was the type of woman to try to hide it from her girls, so as not to upset them. "She might," he said.

He could feel Sarah mulling it over beside him as he drove into Houghton. He stayed silent. He took the turnoff to her neighborhood, the two rights that got them to her street, and then pulled into the driveway of the large home Sarah had lived in since birth.

Mrs. Ryan had never even considered downsizing after Carla left, Mr. Ryan died, and then Mel left.

He put the Blazer in park, but kept the engine running.

"Right. Okay," Sarah said. She turned to him. "Thank you for tonight. It was just what I needed. Whoever could have guessed that?"

It hadn't been guesswork. He only nodded. She got out and went to the back to pull out her backpack and candle. Standing straight, she put her shoulders back. Reilly put an arm over the front seat so he could turn to watch her better.

"I'm going to tell her tonight," she said. Firm, defiant. The strands of her golden hair that were not caught in her knit cap were blowing in the January wind.

"Good luck," he said.

She put her chin in the air. "You too," she said.

"What do I need luck for?" he asked. But he knew. He was just surprised Sarah did.

Or maybe not surprised at all.

"For when you tell Tessa you don't want to be an engineer." She shut the Blazer door and walked up the driveway to the door by the side of the garage.

He waited—as he always did—until she was in the garage and flicked the light twice so he knew she was at the inside door to the kitchen, then left the Ryans' neighborhood full of large, beautiful homes.

He drove to the small, old neighborhood where he'd grown up with Tessa. She now split her time between Houghton and the Harbor, having married the owner of the Seafarer. Her car in the driveway said that tonight she was in Houghton, which Reilly took as a sign.

He parked the Blazer, took his lopsided, sorry-ass candle into the house, and proceeded to tell his sister—the woman who'd sacrificed everything for him—that he wasn't going to be an engineer.

He was going to be a forestry major instead.

Ten

"THIS IS SO COOL," SARAH HEARD SOMEONE SAY FROM behind her in her workshop. Carefully around the candle she was working on, she turned on her swivel stool to see her cousin Petey's wife Alison in the doorway.

"I'm sorry to bother you," Alison said quickly when she saw Sarah holding the small, scalpel-like tool that she used for carving. The pillar candle swung on its wick behind her. "Maya sent me back, but I can see you're busy."

"No, no. It's fine. Come on in," Sarah said. She set the pillar down from its wick and onto an empty space at her worktable. After putting the scalpel in a glass with alcohol in it, she rose and pushed the rolling stool out of the way. Her studio was tiny and full of all her candle-making supplies, so there was barely room for her and her little stool.

"I've caught you right in the middle of something, though," Alison said. "I really just wanted to say hi, since I was in your shop."

Sarah rolled her shoulders, feeling the deep ache she got when she lost herself in one of her designs. "Actually, this is good. I needed to stretch. I lost track of how long I was working."

"Lost in the art?" Alison asked.

Sarah smiled. She didn't really think of herself as an artist, but she supposed that's what she was. Or that was how others saw her.

"In fact, let's step out. I need some fresh air," Sarah said.

Alison nodded, taking another look around Sarah's workshop, then preceded her out the door.

"You were in the store?" Sarah said, leading Alison to the two cushioned Adirondack chairs she had placed behind her workshop, facing the harbor.

Her little store was on the highway just outside of Copper Harbor. Behind it were her even smaller workshop and the cabin she stayed in during the summer when her store was open. It had a small, pebble-strewn path down to the harbor. It was technically waterfront property, but only a little patch had been cleared. So while you couldn't see the water from the store or the cabin, you could from the back of her workshop.

"This is beautiful. I didn't know this was back here," Alison said.

"I know. It's kind of my own private paradise. Tiny, but enough for a couple of chairs. A place to relax after the store closes."

"I met Maya. She seems really nice."

Sarah nodded as she and Alison settled into the chairs. "She is. She's the one who taught me candle making. She's retired now—she was a school teacher—but she watches the store a few days a week during the summer so I can work uninterrupted."

"Until I interrupted you," Alison teased.

Sarah waved her objections away, then kept her hand in the air, bringing her other up to join it and doing a deep stretch. She let out a soft groan as she felt the muscles release after being hunched over with her candle work for the past—she looked at her watch—three hours. She tilted to the side, stretching out her hips.

"She actually encouraged me to come back," Alison said. "Said you never took enough breaks."

Sarah smiled, thinking of the conversation Maya probably had with Alison. "She's right. But I get caught up in something and lose track of time, you know?"

Alison started to nod, then stopped. "Actually, no. My days are spent in strict fifty-minute intervals. There is a lot of clock watching, though I certainly get lost in what I'm doing."

Alison was a therapist. Sarah didn't know Alison well, since she and Petey had only been married since Christmas. But they'd been together at plenty of Sunday dinners with Aunt Ellen and Uncle Dan, and Sarah had come to like Alison a lot. Anyone who could give as good as she got with the intimidating Petey was someone not to be underestimated.

"Are you up here alone, or is Petey with you?" Sarah asked.

"Alone. I only had one appointment this afternoon. They cancelled, so I decided to take a drive, since it was such a nice day. Once I got on the canal, I decided to drive all the way up here. And then I thought about your shop. My friend Katie Luna just had her baby a couple of days ago, and I wanted to get her something different. I thought maybe one of your candles."

"Oh, that's a nice idea."

Alison nodded. "Her oldest, Peaches, is not even two, so she had most of the baby stuff covered. I thought maybe some kind of commemorative candle. You were talking about a new mold or something a few weeks ago at your mom's place. I don't know. Really, I just wanted an excuse for the drive up here."

"It's a beautiful time in Copper Harbor. I don't blame you." Sarah's mind turned back to her current inventory. "I haven't done much with this particular mold yet, but it could be kind of cool. It's a silhouette of the Upper Peninsula. Thick, with three wicks. Nothing really intricate, though."

"She's away a lot because of her husband on the golf tour. They have a house in Florida too. She'd probably love to have a piece of home down there."

Sarah thought on it. She could dye one of the U.P. bricks she had. Maybe even carve in the baby's birth date on the bottom.

"Did she have a boy or girl?" she asked.

"A boy. Which is nice, since they have a girl. Michael Luna. I think it's in honor of his father, with whom he recently reunited.

But they're calling the baby Mick."

"Oh, that's nice. Okay. I'll have you write down the date and everything before you leave. Unless you wanted to take something with you today."

Alison shook her head. "Not necessarily, no. Since this was kind of an impulse anyway. Take as much time as you need."

"A week or so ought to do it," Sarah said, her mind already turning to design ideas of perhaps a companion candle of some sort. Isle Royale? Lake Superior? The Lower Peninsula? Something golf related? She let her mind wander, Alison seemingly doing the same as they sat in their chairs, letting the late afternoon sun ease into their souls.

They were having a lovely summer in the Copper Country, which Sarah had enjoyed until three days ago, when Reilly had crashed at her place.

And then not remembered it the next morning. She stretched again, letting out a deep moan that was probably more about that night than it was about her sore muscles.

"Everything okay?" Alison asked in a soft, smooth voice. Sarah imagined it was her therapist voice. She could see how people would open up to the small woman with the sharp wit but kind face.

"Umm, yeah," Sarah said, not putting any conviction behind her words.

She hadn't slept well since that night, replaying the bad sex over and over. When she wasn't trying to forget it completely.

But what played on an even more continuous loop in her head was the morning after. Reilly knowing that she was keeping something from him but assuming it was her feelings about his breakup with Paula.

Paula. God. Were they back together? She hadn't heard from Reilly since that morning. Which wasn't unusual. They often went a few days without speaking. More if he was on the island.

"I know we haven't known each other—closely—for long," Alison said, pulling Sarah from her thoughts. "But Petey thinks of you as a little sister, so if you ever want to talk about anything. And not with my shrink hat on or—"

"I slept with Reilly three nights ago," Sarah said, the words bursting out of her like the smelt ran through Cole's Creek in May. Fast. Hard. And not looking back.

"Oh," Alison said, the surprise evident on her face, even though she quickly hid it. Years of practice, Sarah guessed. "I assumed you and Reilly were just good friends. I think Petey told me that."

"We are. That's just it…" God, were they still friends? Did that one night ruin everything? That thought had run through Sarah's mind when Reilly had put his hand on her hip for the first time, but she let other thoughts—other feelings, other sensations—push it away.

And all for just so-so sex. Hell, she could have gotten that from a night trolling at the Cat's Meow and not wrecked a friendship over it.

"Oh," Alison said again, sitting back in her chair, therapist firmly in place now. "And this is the first time that something like this has happened?"

Sarah nodded, wishing the Adirondacks were a couch and she could truly unburden herself of that night.

"I'm happy to listen. As a friend. As a professional. As a cousin-in-law. Whatever you need."

Sarah didn't have many female friends. Reilly had been her best—though not only—friend for so long. She'd hung with other girls in high school and at Tech, but most of them had either moved away or were married with small children and didn't have much time for girlfriends. There was Maya, whom Sarah thought of as a friend, even though she was nearly the age of a grandmother. Sarah was also close to her mother and her sisters, but she could never tell them—any of them—about her night with Reilly.

But she could tell Alison. Who knew her, knew Reilly, listened, and gave advice as a career.

And so Sarah did, relaying every detail of that night. Well, not every detail, but enough that Alison was nodding sympathetically by the time Sarah was done.

Maybe she did the sympathy thing automatically. Whatever. It felt good to have it off her chest and be able to voice the main concern that had been bothering her since that night.

Beyond the fact that she'd slept with her best friend.

"The thing is… Well…there are a lot of things, actually," Sarah said.

"I imagine there are."

Sarah sighed and stretched again. Getting through the story was almost as much a grind on her shoulders as a morning spent in her studio. "But the biggest thing I've been worrying about… I mean…"

"Yes?" Alison gently asked.

"Are there, like, consent issues here? If the situation were reversed and he were the woman, would we be outraged? He didn't remember in the morning. Which means he couldn't properly give consent, right?"

Alison looked at her, thoughtful. "I'm going to ask you to give me more details on how the physical contact started. How it went on."

So Sarah filled in any of the blanks that she'd left out the first time through. The more she talked, the more confused she became.

"So, he was the initiator, and the…coaxer, for lack of better term," Alison said.

"Yes, but if he wasn't competent?"

Alison thought on it for a minute, making Sarah take a deep breath, both glad she had Alison to talk with it about and dreading what might come out of the therapist's mouth.

"Honestly, I don't know what legal ramifications there would be to something like this, since he was the aggressor and the initiator. I'm guessing there's no fault here. And there only would be if Reilly were to feel he'd been taken advantage of in his inebriated state."

"And to know that, he'd have to remember it," Sarah said.

"Right."

She let that sink in. She hadn't *really* been worried that she'd be charged with a crime for giving in to Reilly's seduction. But ever since realizing he had no recollection of their night together, Sarah had felt a deep sense of…scuzziness.

"Okay, so maybe not legally. But morally?" she said.

Alison leaned forward, scooching her chair so she was more face to face with Sarah. The legs stuck in the grass and would only rotate a few degrees, so Alison stood, moved the chair, and sat back down.

Sarah braced herself for what would come next.

"I'm not going to bring morality into it," Alison said. "That's not for me to say."

Sarah relaxed, slumping back in her seat. Until Alison added, "I will say, however, that I think this is a burden on you and will drive a wedge into your relationship with your best friend."

"You think I should tell him." It wasn't a question.

Alison nodded.

"But what if…" Sarah didn't finish. She wasn't sure what the finish of that sentence was. What would be her worst fear?

Losing Reilly as her friend.

As if Sarah had spoken aloud, Alison said, "You'll lose him anyway if you *don't* tell him. It won't be the same for you with it between you, and you'll start acting differently. Then he will. And the dynamic will have changed anyway."

"So why not rip the Band-Aid off and change the dynamic now?"

Alison leaned forward and put a hand on Sarah's knee. "The dynamic changed the minute Reilly climbed into your bed. Right now, you're the only one that knows it."

Sarah nodded, knowing Alison was right. But also knowing she had a very tough conversation with Reilly ahead of her. And she was not sure what the outcome would be.

"Would you like me to be with you when you tell him? Maybe help with any fallout?"

God, that would be nice. Let a professional handle it. Maybe even do it in Alison's office so it had an almost clinical feel to the whole thing.

So, Reilly, you fucked me—selfishly, by the way—while you were drunk and pining over your ex-girlfriend. And I just thought I'd let you know so we could go back to normal, 'cause it's been really bothering me. 'Kay? Great. Thanks. I think our time is up. Wanna grab a burger?

She almost giggled at the thought. "Thanks, but this is probably best done with just the two of us," Sarah said. "And yeah, I have to do it. Mainly because I know he'd never keep something like that from me."

Alison squeezed her knee, sat back in her chair, and tipped her head up to the sun, closing her eyes. "Let me know if you want to talk afterward. I'm always happy to talk over beers at the Commodore. Cheaper rates."

Sarah laughed, feeling the tension that had been flowing through her body ease just a tiny bit.

They stayed like that for another ten minutes—Alison face up to the sun, Sarah strategizing when and where to tell Reilly.

"Sarah, honey, a call for you," Maya said from behind them. She was walking from the shop with the cordless landline phone in her hand. Maya took most of calls for the shop while she was working, handing off only the calls that were about custom jobs or something she couldn't answer.

There was a strange look on Maya's face that made Sarah realize the call wasn't just a question about candles. Maya handed the phone to Sarah, then stood behind Alison's chair, her hands resting on top of the Adirondack, a sympathetic look on her face. A look that worried Sarah.

Had Reilly remembered? Had he called to yell at Sarah and somehow Maya had sensed it in his voice? Maya had a sensitivity about those kinds of things.

"Hello?" Sarah said into the phone.

"Hey. It's Petey. Maya said Alison is still with you?"

"Yeah, here—"

"Don't give her the phone!" he said quickly, and Sarah kept the phone at her ear. "Would you be able to drive Alison in her car down here?"

"When?" Sarah asked, confused.

"Now. After I talk to her. Are you available? Maya can stay in the shop?"

"Yes. I was just working in the studio. But yeah, I can leave."

"Great. Thanks. I'll figure out a way to get you back up there to your car for when you need to be back."

"Not until tomorrow afternoon. And I know lots of people I can catch a ride with in the morning. But—"

"Okay. Here's the thing. Alison's dad just died. I want you to give her the phone so I can tell her, but I don't want her driving back by herself. So if you'd drive her, I'd appreciate it."

Sarah was trying to hold her face together and just nodded. She realized Petey couldn't see her, so she said, "Sure. Of course. No problem."

"Okay, thanks. You can hand the phone to Al now."

"Okay," Sarah said. "It's for you, Petey," she said, handing the phone to Alison.

If Sarah hadn't realized it by now, seeing how quickly Alison put things together—the look on Sarah's face, the hovering Maya, the fact that Petey had spoken to Sarah first—confirmed that Alison was one sharp woman.

Alison held the phone in her lap and looked out to the lake. She took a deep breath, let it out, then put the phone to her ear. "My mom or my dad?" she said.

Sarah and Maya exchanged glances, and watched as Alison received the horrible news from her husband.

The circumstances were different than when Sarah lost her own father. Alison was grown, and her father was quite elderly. He'd been in an assisted living situation, and from what Sarah understood, he'd had Alzheimer's for some years.

But watching Alison still brought back memories of Sarah's father dying so many years ago. And of Reilly being right there to hold her hand at the funeral.

Yes, she had to tell him about the other night, even if he did hate her for it.

That was what best friends did.

Eleven

REILLY BROUGHT THE LAST OF THE DISHES INTO THE kitchen, handing them over to Alison. "That's it."

"Thanks so much, Reilly," Alison said.

"Why don't you let me finish this up? Sarah can help. You go sit down or something."

"Yeah, babe. Let Young Turk handle this," Petey said, coming into the kitchen of his home and slinging a huge arm around his wife's shoulder. "You've been on your feet all day."

"I sat at the church," Alison said. She turned back to the sink, but her gaze was out the window toward the lake.

"Your sisters will be back soon from settling your mom at the Ridges. Let's relax until then."

Alison kept facing the water. "Poor Mom. I think she knew what was happening for the most part. She knew Sherry and Janis. I don't know, maybe it's better that she doesn't know what's going on. The pain of losing Dad is probably less."

Petey moved from beside his wife to behind her, wrapping both arms around her front and pulling her little body into his towering one. "That's what I want for us, babe. To be so nuts at the end that we don't even know we lost each other."

Alison chuckled, and Reilly took a step back, trying to busy himself at the kitchen table, which was brimming with leftovers from the after-funeral gathering that Petey and Alison had hosted.

"I thought you wanted us to die simultaneously from heart

failure while having mind-blowing sex at the age of ninety-eight. Wasn't that your plan?" Alison said.

Reilly heard Petey's deep rumble of laughter and smiled to himself while stacking dirty plates.

"Yeah. I forgot. That's plan A. Let's go with the nutso thing as plan B."

"Deal," Alison said.

Reilly wanted to stay and help, but he figured it would be more helpful long-term to let the couple have a quiet moment together.

"Hey, Young Turk, Sarah's down at the lake looking like she needs a friend."

"On it," Reilly said, confirming that time in her husband's arms was what Alison needed more than help loading the dishwasher.

"Reilly?" Alison said, causing him to stop in the doorway and turn back to her. She had her hands on top of Petey's forearms and a look of calm on her face as she let her husband comfort her. "Sarah's great, you know?"

Reilly nodded, confused. Of course he knew Sarah was great. She'd been *his* best friend since forever, while Alison had only really gotten to know Sarah since she'd married Petey and joined the family.

"And you know, sometimes we all mess up. Friends weather that kind of stuff. Real friends do, anyway."

"Babe, what are you talking about?" Petey said, the same thing Reilly was thinking.

Alison shook her head, leaned it back into her husband's chest, and looked up at him. "Nothing. Nothing. Never mind." Looking back to Reilly, she said, "Thanks for helping, Reilly. Consider yourself officially off duty."

He nodded and then hesitated in case she wanted to say some more cryptic shit. When she didn't, he chalked it up to a woman who had lost her aging, ailing father and was feeling philosophical.

Sarah was indeed down at the dock, and Reilly rolled up the sleeves on his dress shirt as he approached her. He'd shed his suit coat and tie the minute guests started leaving. The stiff cotton of the shirt he hardly ever wore was a reminder how great his life was that he didn't have to don a coat and tie every day. Yeah, he had to wear the ranger uniform when he had a shift, but that was different. That was a symbol of being outside and not behind a desk, so even though it was a uniform, it was one he gladly wore.

Sarah was the same way and had already lost the heels she'd worn to the church, standing barefoot in her sundress. The little jacket thing that she had worn over the dress was gone too, and she stood at the end of the dock letting the soft wind swirl around the skirt of the dress and lift her hair slightly off her back.

It was early evening on a Wednesday, a week after Paula had dumped him. Today was the first time he'd even seen Sarah since, though she'd called him to let him know about Alison's father and the funeral arrangements if he wanted to attend. Which he did, since it was extended family for Sarah. That was what friends did.

Was that what Alison meant in the kitchen?

"Hey," he said as he approached Sarah. She didn't jump or anything, so she must have heard him coming. Or knew he would follow her.

She turned and leaned against the tall piling at one side of the dock's end, putting her hands behind her back and resting her butt on them. "Hey," she said.

He took up a similar position directly across the dock from her, leaning on the end piling, hands around the rough wood.

"Everybody's gone. Just Petey and Alison in the kitchen."

"I should go help," she said, but made no motion to leave the dock.

"I think they want some alone time," Reilly said. "That's why I came to find you."

She nodded and looked out at the lake, giving Reilly her profile. "Alison has two older sisters like I do. Much older, like me."

"Yeah, I met them. They seem nice."

"I thought so too," Sarah said.

Something was off with her, but he couldn't place it. Which was weird. He could usually read her moods pretty accurately. Not that she was moody. Sarah was pretty even-keeled. And compared to Paula? Sarah wouldn't even know how to be a drama queen if she wanted to.

Which all made Reilly jump to attention when Sarah turned back to him with tears in her eyes. He started to move to her, but she put a hand up like she was scared of him or something.

What that hell was happening?

"What's going on? Is it the funeral? Did it remind you of your dad's?"

"Yes, a little. But that's not why I— Reilly, I need to tell you something, and I need you to listen to me and not freak out."

Freak out? If Sarah was even-keeled, then Reilly was near dead when it came to being overemotional. It just didn't happen. Which might have been one of the reasons Paula had dumped him. Maybe. He had fuzzy memories of their last argument. Of that whole night.

"Okay," he said.

She nodded that she heard him but didn't speak right away. Instead, she stared out at the lake again, taking a deep breath and straightening her shoulders. Like she was facing a fucking firing squad.

"Sarah, it's okay. You can tell me anything. I won't freak out."

Could she be pregnant? She wasn't seeing anybody that Reilly knew of, but that didn't mean she hadn't slept with someone at some point recently.

He couldn't think of anything else that would have her so hesitant to tell him.

"That night that you and Paula fought."

"Yes?" Shit. Had Paula done something—said something—to Sarah? Had she wrongly believed Sarah had something to do with Reilly's hesitancy about marriage? He certainly wouldn't put it past Paula to confront Sarah about any slight she felt. But Sarah could hold her own. And would probably relish the chance to tell Paula exactly how she felt about her now that she wasn't with him anymore.

"When you crashed at my place."

"Yes?" he said again, more cautiously now. If the fight with Paula was hazy, the night on Sarah's couch was in blackout territory. Had he said something hurtful to Sarah? He couldn't imagine that, even if he'd been totally shit-faced.

"Well, we talked, do you remember that?"

"Vaguely. And then I crashed on the couch, right?"

She nodded, steeling her shoulders again. Christ, what the hell was it?

"Yes. But later, you got up to go to the bathroom."

Had he broken something while stumbling around her cabin? Something that was irreplaceable? He nodded and waited.

"And you crawled into my bed instead of going back to the couch."

A chill slowly crawled up his back. And oddly, heat rushed to his cock.

No. No way. No fucking way.

But Sarah's face. Tears slid from her eyes, and she quickly brushed them away.

Oh Christ, what had he done? He couldn't believe he'd ever hurt a woman, even blackout drunk. Any woman, let alone Sarah.

"Sarah, did I... Did I hurt you?"

She brushed the last tear away and sniffled, looking at him with confusion. "Hurt me? No. Of course not."

The chill subsided but still hovered.

"So...we *didn't* sleep together."

"Yeah, we slept together."

Fuck. Wait. Slept together. They did that from time to time, not completely unusual. Still, the chill made him need to clarify. "I mean *slept* together. We didn't do that, right?"

"Yeah, Reilly, we did."

Jesus Christ. He'd climbed into Sarah's bed wasted and taken advantage of her.

"Oh, Sarah. I'm sorry. So sorry. I... Jesus Christ, did I force you?"

She barked a noise that was part laugh and part sob. "No." The horror he felt must have shown on his face, because she started shaking her head. "Oh, Reilly, no. You would never do that."

His shoulders sagged with relief. The chill was gone. And yet his head was filled with questions.

"So I—"

"If anything, I took advantage of you. You were drunk. I didn't realize how drunk until the next morning when you couldn't remember."

"So, I crawled into your bed after taking a piss, and you jumped me?" That did not sound right. But shit, none of this sounded right. It wasn't *them*. There had never been those hidden glances, those thoughts of what if, between the two of them.

Right?

"No. But I should have stopped it. If I'd said the word, or given you a shove, you would have just rolled over and gone back to sleep." She looked down at her bare feet, her shoes likely back in Alison's house somewhere. Her dress skimmed the top of her knees and swayed gently in the soft breeze. "I'm so sorry, Reilly. I mean, there are issues of consent here. And if you want to talk to, I don't know, someone legal or something, I would totally—"

"Wait. What?" He took the three steps across the dock to stand in front of her. "Look at me, Sarah." Her head came up, and he saw new tears forming in her eyes. "I made the first move?" She nodded and started to speak, but he placed a finger on her lips.

Lips that apparently he'd kissed. Lips that may have been on his body. Had they wrapped around his hard cock? Jesus, he couldn't believe this was happening. But before he could rack his brain for some details, he had to put Sarah's mind at ease. "There is no issue of consent, Sarah. Please stop worrying about that."

"But if the situation was reversed, and I was the drunk one..."

"Listen. It wasn't like I was too drunk to give consent. Obviously I was the…aggressor." God, he hated that. That he'd put Sarah in that position.

"But I—"

"No."

"I'm just so sorry that—"

"Christ, Sarah, you have nothing to apologize for. Or feel bad about. I need to apologize to you. I can't believe I put you in that position. I'm so sorry."

She waved a hand halfheartedly. "You were drunk. And hurt. And—"

"Don't make excuses for me. Maybe we should talk about consent, though. If I pressured *you* in any way at all."

A flush came up her neck, but Reilly couldn't decipher what it meant.

"You didn't."

"Are you sure?"

She nodded.

"Okay, then as far as I'm concerned, there is no consent issue. Nothing like that. Just drunken sex between friends."

But it was much more than that, and they both knew it. Because nothing like that had ever happened before. And Sarah had been sober.

He wanted to ask so much more. Why *hadn't* she kicked him out of bed? Did they do it more than once? Surely they'd used a condom. Yeah, she'd probably be freaking out a little more if they hadn't.

And most importantly—how good had it been?

But the relief on her face that he wasn't pissed stopped him from asking anything further.

"Okay. Yeah. Like you said. Just a weird night. We'll just forget it ever happened, right?"

There was hope on her face, so he stomped the unasked questions down deep. "Right. Yeah. I'll just say I'm sorry, and we'll move on. Like you said, forget it ever happened."

Another weird bark of sob/laughter from her. "Not hard for you. You've already forgotten it."

Yeah, and wasn't that just a pisser?

Had he run his hands through her mass of honey waves?

Whoa. Where had that come from?

He didn't think of Sarah in terms of her hair. Or those whiskey-brown eyes. Or the lips that he'd just touched.

Fuck. Now he couldn't stop thinking about her like that.

So weird.

She wiped her face again, took a deep sniffle, and nodded. "I'm so glad I told you. I didn't want to, but I think it's good, right?"

Was it? Was it only going to lead to him wondering about what sex with Sarah had been like?

"Right," he said. He'd been the horny drunk who'd brought this all on. Whatever made Sarah comfortable about it from now on was how he was going to play it.

She squeezed his arm and brushed past him. He could smell her scent. Oranges. And a trace of paraffin that never really escaped her.

"Okay. Good. We'll just forget it and move on. I'm going to go help Alison. Catch ya later."

Catch ya later.

Words they said to each other all the time. Almost daily.

And yet now they had a sting to them for Reilly. He felt like his life had been altered in some soul-deep way, and Sarah was all "catch ya later."

"Yeah. Catch ya later," he said, watching her walk back to the house.

She looked over her shoulder at him, and there was a sadness in her eyes that made him rethink his earlier thought. About breaking something in her cabin while drunkenly walking around.

Something irreplaceable.

Maybe he had.

Twelve

"Wow," Jess said to Reilly as they took a lunch break at the Dollar Bay house. They sat outside in two soccer chairs getting some fresh air while they ate their sandwiches.

"Yeah," Reilly said. Jess had been hounding him for the past couple of days to unload whatever was bothering him. He'd held out as long as he could, but after putting a cabinet door on upside down that morning, Jess had insisted that they take a break.

And then the floodgates opened, and Reilly confided in Jess about the night he'd slept with Sarah.

The night he couldn't remember.

The odd part was he wanted to talk about it, to tell someone. But the person he most wanted to share it with—his best friend—was the one person he couldn't talk to about it.

"And so you're both just going on like nothing happened?"

He nodded and took a bite of his bologna sandwich. He couldn't taste a thing. It was like all of his senses had been messed up since the day at Alison's place.

"Do you wish she'd never told you?" Jess asked. It was the question that had been swimming around his head for the past few days.

"I don't know. Kind of. But it was obviously eating her up, so I'm glad she did."

A compassionate look crossed Jess's face. "You're a good guy, Reilly Turkonen."

"Yeah? Do good guys take advantage of their best friend like that?"

"From what you told me, Sarah said she could have pushed you away or said no and that you would have stopped."

"I think so, yeah. I have to believe that or I'd go crazy, you know?"

Jess nodded and took a sip from her can of Diet Coke. "You would have. I know it. And Sarah knows it too."

He didn't answer, just took another bite of the tasteless sandwich.

"I guess I'm wondering…"

"What?" he asked.

She shook her head. "Nothing. It's none of my business."

"I made it your business. What were you wondering?"

"I guess I'm wondering why didn't she? Push you away. Say no. Kick you out of her bed."

He scrubbed a hand across his face, then ran it through his hair. "Shit, Jess. You don't think that's been running through my mind since the second she told me?"

"You didn't ask her?"

"No."

"Why?"

He sat back in the chair, feeling his ass dip a little lower in the netting. "I don't know. It didn't feel right. Like it would be victim blaming or something."

Jess rolled her eyes at him. "She was not a victim. She said as much to you. She's an adult, and when you made a pass, she accepted. Don't put her in a box she doesn't want to be in."

He closed his eyes and tipped his head up to the sun. On the days he worked in the house, he missed the fresh air and sunlight. He had a couple of ranger shifts coming up on the island, so he'd be able to recharge, but even the lunch hour outside helped.

"So you didn't ask her why she joined in, but you're wondering," Jess said.

"I'm not wondering about just that," he said, still keeping his eyes closed, not wanting Jess to read his thoughts. Like wondering what Sarah's skin felt like. In the places he'd never touched her before.

"Yeah, I can imagine," Jess said. There was teasing in her voice, and Reilly knew she'd read his thoughts after all.

He groaned, and Jess laughed. "It's not funny," he said halfheartedly.

"Not to you, no. But to anyone else, it's kind of hilarious. All this time, you never sleep together. Never even kiss?" Reilly nodded. "And you finally do, and you can't remember a thing."

"Fuck, this sucks," he said, and Jess laughed again.

They finished their lunches in silence and started to clean up, refolding the chairs and putting them on the porch.

"You know," Jess said as they made their way back into the house, "there's another question to ask."

"What?"

"Why was Sarah so adamant that you put it behind you and not talk about it?"

He held up his hand, ticking off reasons with his fingers. "Umm, she's embarrassed. She was horrified that I had no recollection. She realizes that it could wreck our friendship. She—" He stopped at Jess's skeptical expression. "What?"

"Nothing," she said.

"What?"

She shrugged and grabbed a screwdriver, heading to the cabinet that he'd fucked up. "Maybe there's another explanation."

"Like those reasons aren't good enough?"

"They absolutely are," she said. She started undoing his mess, and he jammed his hands in his pockets, tamping down the urge to rip the screwdriver out of her hand.

"But? What's the other explanation?" he said. He put his hip on the counter, watching Jess.

Another shrug from her. She finished unscrewing the hinges and handed him the door of the cabinet. Then she looked at him and dropped a bomb that hadn't crossed his muddled mind in all the time he had been thinking about that night.

"Maybe it was bad."

He just stood there while Jess took the door back from him, turned it right side up, and reinstalled it. She smiled as she did it.

Fuck.

Thirteen

SARAH PLOPPED DOWN AT A BARSTOOL AT THE Seafarer wondering if maybe she should—for the first time in her life—have a drink.

Well, not the first time, but the first *real* time.

Before she could make that decision, Tessa placed a Diet Coke in front of her. "Lunch, honey?" she asked.

"Mmm, please. A BLT, I think. And Maya wants me to bring her a salad."

"Got it. Eating here or pack it all to go?"

Sarah took a sip of her pop and leaned back in the barstool. "I'll have mine here. I need a break."

Tessa nodded and headed to the kitchen to put in Sarah's order.

"I think I have you to thank for the great cookies I had with my coffee this morning." Sarah turned to see Jim Peterson on a stool two down from hers. She'd been so deep in her head that she hadn't even noticed him when she came in.

She took in his words, then made sense of them. "Oh, Jess gave you some, eh? Glad they weren't wasted. And actually, my mom made them."

"Then pass on my compliments to her," he said, and Sarah nodded.

"Did Jess bring them to you here, or have you been to the house in Dollar Bay?" Sarah asked. She'd stopped by the house yesterday morning on her way to the Harbor, but Reilly wasn't there. Jess had told Sarah he was on the island.

Something Sarah probably would have known if there weren't this weirdness between them. Which she was trying to bridge by bringing Reilly and Jess cookies like she'd done before.

Nothing's different here, folks. Same delivery of homemade cookies. What could possibly be wrong?

"I went by the house late yesterday to have dinner with Jess and Zeke. And to take a peek at how it's coming."

"How is it coming?" Sarah asked. At Jim's questioning look, she continued, "I haven't gone past the kitchen when dropping off food. Not in a while, anyway."

"It's coming together. I was really impressed with what they're doing with it. And Jess seems to love it."

"So does Reilly," Sarah said. She could speak to that point confidently, seeing the subtle changes in Reilly since he'd become partners with Jess.

"Speak of the devil," Jim said, and Sarah turned to see Jess and Reilly walk into the Seafarer, both wearing their ranger uniforms. Jess's boyfriend Zeke Hampton was with them, wearing what charter pilots wore. In this case, it was khaki cargo pants and a dark green shirt with his company's logo on the chest.

"Am I the devil?" Jess said. She gave her father a kiss on the cheek, then took the stool next to him. "Hi, Sarah."

"Hey, Jess. Zeke. Reilly."

Zeke took the stool on the other side of Jim, shaking the man's hand. Reilly took the stool left open between Jess and Sarah.

"I'm glad you're here. I was going to try the shop next, but Zeke was meeting Jess here, so I had to come here first."

"Why?" She studied him. He seemed agitated, nervous. Not at all like he usually did after a stint on the island. Typically, he came back to the Copper Country blissed out on nature after spending a day or two on Isle Royale.

"Did something happen? On the island?" she asked.

"What? No. I mean, yeah, kind of."

Tessa came back from the kitchen and seemed as surprised to see Reilly as Sarah had been.

"I thought you were on the island until Friday," Tessa said to her brother.

"I was supposed to be, but when I saw Zeke was flying back this morning, I got another ranger to cover my shifts."

"What's wrong?" Tessa asked.

Reilly looked around and saw that their little party was all staring at him, waiting for his answer. It wasn't just Sarah that thought it was weird that Reilly would cut short his time on the island.

"Nothing. I just... Nothing's wrong."

Tessa studied him for a second and nodded, but the look said she didn't quite believe him. She took Jess and Zeke's orders, but Reilly didn't want anything. That alone had both Tessa and Sarah looking more closely at him.

"I'm not hungry, that's all."

Tessa went back to the kitchen, and Jess swiveled in her barstool to talk to Zeke over Jim, which gave Sarah and Reilly a little privacy. Reilly swiveled in her direction, making them even more private.

"Can we go for a walk? I need to talk to you about something."

At that moment, Tessa brought out Sarah's BLT and a bag with Maya's salad. Reilly sat back in his seat and sighed.

"It's just a sandwich. It'll take me ten minutes to eat it," Sarah said, then grabbed a fry and popped it into her mouth.

Tessa had put a Coke down in front of Reilly even though he hadn't asked for one. He took a sip of it, then snatched a fry from Sarah's plate.

She maneuvered the plate around to be more in the middle of them and edged half of the huge sandwich to the side of the plate near Reilly. He took a few more fries, sighed again, and took up the other half of the sandwich, digging in.

Sarah ate slowly, like an inmate having their last dinner. That was how she felt, because she knew what Reilly wanted to talk about. He was going to get back together with Paula, and he wanted to make sure Sarah didn't mention their one drunken night together.

Drunken on Reilly's part, at least. Which was easier to explain. She'd been stone-cold sober.

That had to be it. Sarah couldn't imagine what else Reilly would have hurried back from the island for. They had already talked about their night together. Had settled it. Put it behind them.

Apparently, Reilly was moving on and wanted to make sure it was dead and buried.

They ate lunch—Reilly scarfing it down, Sarah nibbling slowly. Zeke and Jess's food came, and they all chatted while enjoying their meals. Except Reilly, who never said a word, just kept eating from Sarah's plate.

Once he'd popped the last fry in his mouth and there was nothing but a corner of crust left on her plate, he rose from the stool, reaching for his wallet.

"I've got it," Sarah said.

"I ate most of it," Reilly said as he pulled out a twenty and put it on the bar. "Let's go."

"But Maya's salad was on there too."

He put another ten on the bar. "Let's go," he said, then walked toward the door, saying goodbye to Jess and Jim and thanking Zeke for letting him tag along on his flight.

Sarah grabbed the bag with Maya's salad and followed Reilly out, telling the others goodbye and to thank Tessa for her.

When she reached the parking lot, she saw Reilly rounding the corner of the building. He headed to the front side, which faced the harbor.

When she got to the front, he was already heading down to the dock. Sarah was reminded of their talk on the dock in front of Petey and Alison's house when she told him about their night together.

That had been bad. Awful. So why did she feel like this—

hearing from Reilly that he was getting back together with Paula—would be so much worse?

But really, would it be worse? It'd just put them right back where they'd been two weeks ago. Reilly with Paula and close friends with Sarah. It would be nice to get back to the way things had been between them.

Wouldn't it?

The uneasiness she felt about the real answer to that question had her barking out to Reilly once she'd caught up with him on the dock.

"Okay, okay, what do you want, Reilly?"

"A do-over," he said, turning to face her.

The harbor glittered behind him, almost causing a halo around his angelic white ringlets. Sarah shook her head, trying both to dislodge the image and to understand his words.

"What?"

"You asked what I wanted. That's it. A do-over."

"A do-over?"

"Yep." He put his hands on his hips, almost challenging her to ask. She wouldn't. She knew.

"You're crazy," she said, and turned to head back to the parking lot. Back to her car. Then to her shop. Give Maya her salad. Head to her studio and work on the custom candle for Alison.

Forget Reilly and this nonsense.

She was almost to the grass when she heard Reilly call, "Bwooock."

She stopped dead in her tracks, then looked over her shoulder at him. Sure enough, he had his fists in his armpits, flapping his elbows to give it the full effect.

"Bwooock," he repeated. He dropped his hands, and she didn't even have to hear the word he spoke next. She could read it on his lips.

"Chicken."

Fourteen

Thirteen years ago
Age sixteen

"SARAH RYAN IS WANTED IN THE OFFICE," CAME AN announcement from the student office aide who poked his head into her biology classroom. Office aide Reilly Turkonen.

It was a perk he was careful about abusing, seldom pulling his friends out of class if they were not actually needed in the office.

Sarah gathered her book, nodded to Miss Kukkonen on her way out of the classroom, and joined Reilly in the hallway.

"What's up?" she asked as they walked toward their lockers.

"We're ditching," he said.

"We are?"

"Yep," he said.

He could tell she was about to argue, so he quickly walked ahead of her, hearing her footsteps behind him. She wouldn't dare call out to him, fearful they'd be heard by a teacher or someone else who would bust them. They'd never ditched class before. And given that Reilly's office aide period was early in the day, this wasn't just cutting out a little early.

"Where are we going?" Sarah asked once they'd driven out of the school parking lot. It was cute how she'd slouched down in her seat, hoping no one would see her. If any teacher happened to look out the window and see them driving away, they were both busted.

One, because of Reilly's instantly recognizable piece-of-shit Blazer that he had been driving since getting his license. Two, because if Reilly was up to something—anything—Sarah Ryan was sure to be in on it.

"I'm not sure," he answered. "I just needed to get out of there."

He could feel Sarah's eyes on him, knew she wanted to push. And knew the exact second she decided not to, sitting back in her seat, looking out the window.

"Okay," she said.

They could go for a drive along the canal, see some sights. But Reilly knew he wanted to be stationary, needed to be able to talk without having to pay attention to the road.

He took a right up the hill and then a left.

"The football field?" Sarah asked.

He shrugged and drove another half-mile down a long road that led to the school's field. Nowhere near the school, it sat alone at the top of the city. From the bleachers, you could see all of Houghton and Hancock below.

And Reilly knew a way in.

He parked, and they got out. It was early October, and a chill was in the air. They hadn't stopped at their lockers, had just gotten the hell out. Reilly went to his trunk, where he knew he had some blankets.

And beer, he realized when he lifted the lid of the Styrofoam cooler that was always in the trunk.

He spent a lot of time going between Houghton and Copper Harbor, where his sister had gotten him a part-time summer job busing tables at the restaurant where she worked. It made sense to keep clothes, food, and essentials in his car.

And essentials included beer that his brother Jed had purchased for him a week ago. It was cold enough outside that he hadn't even needed ice in the cooler to keep it cold for a week. In fact, Reilly had forgotten it was even back there.

And a hoodie. Excellent. He grabbed it and handed it to Sarah, who put it on. After snatching a couple of beers out of the cooler, he snagged a couple of blankets and slammed the trunk shut.

"There's a place on the visitors' side fence where you can slip through," he said, heading that way. Sarah followed, saying nothing.

They found the break in the chain-link fence and scrabbled their way inside, which was easier for the smaller Sarah than for him.

They laid their blankets on the cold metal bleachers and sat, then wrapped the edges of the blankets around their legs. Reilly had worn an old sweater of Jed's that was too big on him. He was glad now, needing the warmth.

He handed one of the beers to Sarah. "Cheers."

Sarah looked at the offered bottle like it was going to bite her. "No, thanks."

"Come on. One beer."

She shook her head.

"Bwock," he said.

She started laughing. "Dude. That is not going to work on me. I don't respond to—"

"BWOCK!" He added the wing-flapping motion this time. She took the bottle from his hand. They both twisted off the tops, but she only held hers in her hand.

He knew she'd never drunk before. Reilly hadn't much, either. An occasional beer when he was hanging out with his guy friends. And this past summer, his father let him join in when he and his brothers would have a cold one at the end of a long day working construction outside.

He'd felt like he'd finally arrived when his father handed him that first beer after Reilly had worked on a roof all day.

And now, it was all going south.

Literally.

"My dad, Jed, and Cam are leaving today," he said.

Sarah looked up at the sky, at the leaves that were turning a brilliant orange, and nodded. "Yeah, it's about that time of year, isn't it?"

"They're not coming back this time."

She hadn't touched her beer, but now she took a long drink. Her face smooshed up, but like a true Yooper Girl, she took another swig. Less squish this time, but Reilly didn't have to worry about Sarah drinking up his beer stash.

A stash that wouldn't be replenished now that Jed was leaving.

Had left. For surely they'd be gone by the time he got home from school.

"Do they know that for sure?" she asked, setting the beer bottle on the bleacher and wrapping the edge of the blanket around her hands.

"Yep. They told me last night. Sat me down at the kitchen table. My dad and Tessa."

"Were Jed and Cameron there too?"

He shook his head. "No, they were out. They each came into my room when they got home to say goodbye."

"Wow," she said.

Yeah, that was how he'd felt. Only to the nth degree and with more colorful language.

"There's more," he said.

Sarah looked at him, her expression a mixture of dread and empathy.

"Tessa is getting married."

"Married? To whom?"

Reilly hung his head, braced his feet on the bleacher below them, and dropped his elbows to knees. Letting out a long breath, he ran a hand through his hair before letting it dangle between his legs. "That's just it. She's marrying the guy who owns the Seafarer. Elden Mahoney."

"Her boss?" she asked. He nodded. "But isn't he, like, really old?"

"Yep."

"And kind of sickly?"

Reilly nodded again. From the corner of his eye, he saw Sarah reach for her beer, take another drink—a small sip this time—and put it back.

He took another drink himself, longer than Sarah's. The taste reminded him of summer, of working on houses with his dad and brothers.

Shit, beyond losing his family, he'd lost next summer's main income too.

"She's doing it for me," he said softly. More of a whisper, really, because he was just coming to the realization himself. He'd been too much in shock last night when they'd talked to him to put it all together.

But now, in the bright sun of the Copper Country, the cold, crisp October air, and with his best friend by his side, things were clearer.

Things were always clearer when he talked them over with Sarah.

"What do you mean?" she said. Her voice was quiet too, as if she knew that Reilly was just figuring it all out himself.

"I don't know. I mean, I don't know *all* of it, but somehow Tessa marrying Elden is because of me. *For* me."

"So she'll live in the Harbor? With him? Like, for good?"

There was trace of panic in her voice. The same panic he'd felt last night.

His father and brothers went to Florida for construction work every fall, returning in late spring. In the two years since Reilly's mother had died, they'd left a little earlier and returned later. Somewhere in the back of his mind, Reilly knew the day would come when they would just stay down there.

"She said it wouldn't be much different from now, the amount of time she'd be up there."

"But how will—"

"They're keeping the house until I'm done with high school. Tessa will come down every couple of days and spend the night, help with whatever I need to do around the house." He shrugged. "So yeah, not that different from how it is now."

"It's different. It is. Let me ask my mom if you can—"

"No," he said. Firmly. But Sarah was about to barrel on, as he knew she would when he told her. "No, Sarah. I'm not moving in with you. If they're willing to keep the house for two more years, then I'm going to stay there."

She huffed. "Well, that's the least they could do."

He knew she wanted to say more. Knew what Sarah thought of his family, of how his dad and brothers treated Reilly. Sarah's family was different. Yes, they had both lost a parent, but Sarah's father had been to a drunk driver, whereas Reilly's mother had drunk herself to death.

Different.

And their remaining parents' attention to their child was like night and day.

Reilly loved his father and brothers, and he would miss them. But the Tessa thing really bothered him.

"I'm just not sure why she's marrying him."

"Did you ask her?"

He took a drink of his beer, then held the neck of the bottle with a thumb and finger, dangling it between his knees. "Yeah, of course. She said it made sense, that she was very fond of him, that—"

"Fond of him? *Fond* of him?"

He looked at Sarah, at the incredulous look on her face. "Yeah?"

She gave him an eye roll. "How old is Tessa? Thirty?"

He nodded.

"You don't—a *girl* doesn't—marry someone at thirty because they're *fond* of them. That's what you do when you're eighty and your spouse has been dead for fifteen years."

"Umm, that seems oddly specific," he said.

Another eye roll. "Whatever. You're right—there's more to it than that."

"Yeah, me."

"But how? Why?"

"I don't know. Every time I tried to get her to talk about it, she shut me down. My dad was getting irritated about it, so I let it go."

"So weird," she said.

"Yeah."

They sat in silence, Reilly sipping occasionally from his beer, Sarah not touching hers.

"Reilly, let me just talk to my mom. I'm sure—"

"No, Ess. That's not happening. I feel like a charity case enough. I'm not going to make it worse."

"You're not a charity case," she said. But there was no conviction behind her words.

No judgment, either. Sarah had never judged him for his trashy family. Reilly was pretty sure it wouldn't even occur to her that she could.

He finished his beer then set the empty bottle on the footrest of the bleachers.

"Here," she said, handing him her bottle, which was three-quarters full. "I'm not going to finish it."

He took it from her and took a long swig.

"Ugh. I don't know how you can drink that shit. Tastes awful."

Reilly knew it was more than just the bitter taste of beer that kept Sarah from drinking. Whether it was at parties or with small groups of their friends, she always declined when the drinks were shared.

Her father. Killed by a drunk driver.

Reilly had been a shitty friend to "chicken" her into even taking a few sips now. Selfish. But he was feeling selfish today.

"And I'm driving us when we leave," she said. Reilly nodded. "Hey, what are… How old are these?" she said. Reilly looked over to see she'd pulled a package of cookies out of the pocket of his hoodie.

"No idea," he said.

"Doesn't matter," she said as she tore open the package. They were Keebler striped shortbread cookies. Sarah pulled one out and offered the package to Reilly, who declined. Chocolate and beer did not mix. She gave him a "your loss" shrug and put the package back in the hoodie pocket. Like they did when they were kids, she placed the circle of the cookie over her finger and took bites off it like it was an edible ring.

"I haven't had one of these in years. Mmm, I love tiger cookies," she said.

"What?"

She twirled the ring on her finger, showing off the stripes. "Always reminded me of a tiger."

"Whatever," he said, but he smiled right along with her, watching as she enjoyed the probably stale-as-hell cookie.

There were always homemade cookies in the Ryan household—something Reilly counted on and regularly took advantage of. He doubted Yvonne Ryan had ever bought a pack of Keebler cookies.

Sarah gobbled them up like forbidden fruit.

He drank, she ate the entire four-pack of tiger cookies, and they sat until Reilly started to make sense of his life as he now knew it.

Yeah, it wouldn't be much different. Tessa was at the Harbor most of the time now anyway. And his father and brothers being gone through the winter would be nothing new.

And yet…

"They didn't even ask if I wanted to go with them."

"They probably knew you'd say no. That you'd want to stay and finish high school in Houghton," Sarah said.

"They still could have asked," he whispered, his voice cracking and uneven. He moved forward, hanging his head. Shit, were those tears? Was he fucking crying? In front of Sarah?

Actually, that was the least of it—doing anything he was embarrassed of in front of Sarah. He knew she'd never call him on it.

Never bring it up in a weak moment or rub his face in it.

He felt her arm go around his shoulder and her body move into his side.

She didn't offer empty words, didn't tell him it'd all be okay. She didn't know that it would. Neither did he.

But he did know that whatever the next few years brought, he'd have Sarah at his side.

Fifteen

THE CHICKEN CALLING GOT HER, AS REILLY KNEW IT WOULD.

"Did you just call me a chicken?" she asked, turning to face him. He didn't say a word, just raised a brow. A challenge.

That got her walking back down the dock to the end where he stood.

"This isn't grade school, you know," she said. "I'm not going to try the highest slide just because you call me chicken."

"What if I double dog dare ya?" he said.

A small trace of smile edged up the corner of her mouth, but she quickly hid it. "That won't work either."

"Okay, how about we just talk about it, then?"

"Talk about a do-over?"

"Yes," Reilly said.

"Fine. This should take about ten seconds." She folded her arms against her chest—universal body language for "no way is this going to go the way you want."

First, he had to get her to relax, so she would hear him out. "Come on, let's get our feet in the water." He turned to the edge of the dock, kicked off his shoes and socks, rolled up his pant legs, and sat down. He dangled his feet down into the water, waiting for her to join him.

Which she did, but not before letting out a huff of impatience. But her flip-flops were kicked off and placed next to his shoes. Then her butt was next to his, and her long, tan legs were over the side of the dock, the water coming up to mid-calf on her. Her yoga pants were just above the water line, and she pulled them up so they rode over her knees.

She twirled her foot in the water. Her nails were painted a light pink that caught the sun and put out a shimmering effect through the small wave she created.

Did she always wear nail polish on her toes? Had she that night?

Why was he thinking about her toes? God, his head was so fucked up.

"So?" she said.

Yeah, this was his deal. His case to make. And it should be easy. He'd been thinking of nothing else the last couple of days on the island. No, before that. Since Jess had put the idea in his head that the sex with Sarah had been bad.

Before that, really. Ever since Sarah had told him about his drunken pass.

And Sarah's acceptance.

That. That was the part that had him up the past few nights. All of it did.

"Reilly?"

Right. "Yeah, a do-over."

She tilted her head back as if looking to the heavens for help. Her mass of hair fell down her back. Had he grabbed handfuls of it that night? Because if he got a chance at what he was proposing, he'd definitely do that.

"I feel like I'm in a *Seinfeld* episode or something," she said. "Like I should start walking back to my place yelling, 'You've got ten minutes, Reilly.'"

He snorted a laugh. They were definitely entering Bizzaro World, that was for sure.

"Well, okay, let's start there. If I recall correctly, Elaine gave Jerry a do-over because it came to light that during their relationship that she never…"

"Right."

They had watched *Seinfeld* reruns nearly every day after school at Sarah's house. During the winter, when Reilly couldn't spend the hours outside messing around.

"So, what I'm getting at is…"

"Did I come?"

They'd talked about everything, the two of them. Even sex with their respective partners at the time. But not this. Not nuts and bolts. More in general terms. And never, obviously, with respect to each other.

"Yes," he said.

"No," she answered.

Well, yeah, he should have figured that. But still, he picked at the scab. "Was it…was it really bad?"

"It wasn't good," she said.

Shit.

From the corner of his eye, he saw Sarah's shoulders shaking. Shit, was she crying again? Had talking about it at all brought back the waterworks? The fear that she'd done something wrong?

"God, I can't believe we're talking about this!" she said through her laughter.

Laughter! Not tears.

Relief poured through him, and he started chuckling. Then gut-busting laughter rolled out of him, like a valve releasing all the pressure he'd pent up.

The sound of them laughing together felt good, so good. He hadn't thought of it in such specific terms, but a part of him had wondered if they'd be able to get back to that. Apparently, they could.

So should he just leave it there? Where his ridiculous request was just something that got them laughing together again? Yeah, he probably should.

"So, this do-over," she said. "Are you thinking, what? A friends-with-benefits situation?"

He pushed away the thoughts of letting it drop. Fast.

"I mean—"

"Because I don't think I'd be down for that. That could really mess us up. And that would be unbearable to me."

"Right," he said.

"Besides, if we were going to fall into that type of thing, we would have by now, right?"

"Uh, yeah, I guess."

"And if, you know, you wanted to get back with Paula—"

"I'm not thinking about that right now," he said. Curious that he'd put the "right now" qualifier on it. Something he'd stow away and think about later.

"Or I wanted to date someone…"

Sarah dated all the time. Though it had been a while since her last real boyfriend. So why did the idea of her dating someone all of a sudden have Reilly's eye twitching?

"Are you planning on dating someone?" he asked.

"No. But it becomes less likely that I would be out there looking if I was sleeping with you a few nights a week."

A few nights a week. Blood rushed through his head, and now it was something other than his eye that felt like twitching. But wait, she was saying that wasn't what she wanted. Didn't think it'd be good for them. Right. Right.

"So, just one time. The do-over?" he asked.

"Right. But why, again?"

"You mean righting the wrong I did to my manly pride isn't enough of a reason?"

She shrugged, her shoulder brushing his as she did. "Not much in it for me, is there?"

"An earth-shattering night of orgasms isn't enough of an incentive for you?"

She half snorted. "Thinking mighty high of yourself, eh?"

He laughed. "So you think that was it? That's as good as I've got to give?"

"I wouldn't really know, would I? Maybe you're a horrible lover and the reason women keep wanting you to settle down with them is because of your…cooking skills?"

They both knew Reilly couldn't cook for shit.

"Nobody is staying with me for my cooking skills."

Her foot stilled.

"So, just so I understand. We have one night of sex. You get to prove to me—or probably more importantly, to *you*—that you're a stud in bed. I get to have a couple of—"

"Maybe more," he said.

She did an eye roll but continued, "I get to have at least two orgasms, and we never speak of it again. We go back to the way we were three weeks ago. You're free to go back to Paula, and I can start hitting on guys who come into the shop."

"Yeah, like so many single guys come into a candle shop."

"I know. But a girl can dream."

They both laughed, and it felt so good to Reilly. Maybe that was all they needed—to talk about the absurd situation they were in with some humor. Maybe the do-over was just an abstract idea that got them back to this place. Laughing side by side on a dock while dangling their feet in the water.

"Yeah, okay. I'm in," Sarah said.

Relief rushed through Reilly.

"But Reilly, I really don't want to mess us up, you know?"

"It won't, Ess. I messed us up by crawling into your bed that night. Now I'd just like to…close the circle, I guess."

She took a deep breath and let it out slowly. He'd get to hear that sound with her naked in his arms. A sigh, a moan, other sounds.

Sarah, naked in his arms, making noises as he made her come.

"When?" he asked.

She shrugged, her shoulder again brushing his. But this time, the connection held. Whether he'd moved slightly to keep it or she had, he wasn't sure. But he knew that no matter what happened during their night together, their connection would hold.

It had to. He couldn't fathom the idea of not having Sarah in his life. That she would just be a woman he'd slept with.

No. Never that. Not with her.

"Soon," she said, and again, the relief rushed through him.
"Soon," he agreed.

Sixteen

"Do you want a drink? There's probably some beer in the fridge that you've left here," Sarah said.

"No," he said quickly. "Nothing to drink."

"Right. Because that's why the sex was so bad that night," she said.

She was teasing him, he knew. And yet it still stung. But that was why he was here, right? To wipe the smirk that was forming on her face right off. Not physically, of course. With mind-blowing sex.

"That's exactly right," he said. She laughed.

"Whatever. No beer," he said.

"Fine." She walked to the couch and sat down. "So, how do we go about this? Just…go at it?"

Go at it? With Sarah?

This was all so weird. What had he been thinking about when he'd suggested a do-over? And it wasn't even some monumental case of performance anxiety, although he supposed that was mixed up in there too.

Sure, there was no pressure on her end.

And then he saw it. Sarah put her glass of water down on her coffee table and did that thing with her hair.

She had lots of moves she did with her hair, and Reilly knew them all.

When her shoulders ached from carving an intricate candle,

she'd gather her mass of hair, pile it on top of her head, roll her shoulders, and then pull strands out of the messy bun with one hand until it was all tumbling down again.

And when she was fired up about something, trying to find the words, she'd dig her hand into the crown of her scalp, whipping her hair back and to the side, like a warrior going into battle.

When being gentle, as if sharing bad news, she'd tuck strands behind her ears with both hands at the same time, in a synchronized movement.

But this move, the one she was doing now? Reilly relaxed, the nerves that had been with him the whole drive to the Harbor easing from his body. He made his way around the couch and joined her.

She continued to twirl a strand of hair from the nape of her neck around a finger, bunching it in her fist when it was completely wound.

Let it go. Started again with another strand.

He slouched into the couch and then leaned over to take off his work boots. He propped his feet up on the coffee table and leaned back, his hands folded over his stomach.

And watched as she twirled her hair like she only did when she was nervous about something. From the way she was going at her hair, she was even more so than he was.

"So, what now?" she said as she disengaged her fingers from the honey-gold strands.

Reilly was about to let her off the hook. Tell her that it was a stupid idea. That if they were both so nervous about it, then it was bound to backfire on them.

But then she reached for another strand, her fingers sliding down the long length, and all he could think about were those fingers sliding down his chest. And when she twirled and the hair starting winding, he imagined her wrist twirling as she held his cock.

Ah, so he *could* sport wood for Sarah. And not when he was

stinking drunk and probably had thoughts of Paula entwined with the warm body next to him.

He'd seriously wondered if he'd be able to go through with it. If there'd be enough attraction. If the old "kissing your sister" adage would come into play.

He wasn't blind. He knew Sarah was attractive. He'd been the first one to notice when she'd started to develop, since it was over the summer and they spent every day together.

But ever since he'd proposed this idea—the do-over—he'd wondered about the actual physicality of it.

His cock twitched again as she sprang her fingers free from her hair, smoothing it down.

So okay, at least getting it up wouldn't be a problem.

Just don't let him mess it up.

"Maybe we start with last time," he said.

Her hand stilled, and one perfectly arched eyebrow rose. "Really? 'Cause I'm thinking we don't want any repeat performances."

He shook his head, as if shaking free the bad memories. Memories he didn't have, dammit.

Although maybe that was a good thing.

"Right," he said. He quickly rose from the couch and took her hand, feeling the silken strands she'd been clutching fall away.

He yanked, and she rose. Taking her hand more firmly in his, he led them to the bed and motioned for her to sit down, which she did.

She was wearing a loose, gauzy skirt and a white cotton tee with a deep vee. What she'd normally wear when she worked in her store.

Somehow, it looked different on her tonight. Was the vee of her shirt always so deep? Did that hint of cleavage always appear? Was her skin always glistening with the combination of her summer tan and body heat?

He cleared his throat, which had suddenly become tight.

Shit, everything was becoming tight.

"You're going to have to help me out here," he said.

She leaned back, her hands resting on the bed behind her, elbows locked. "This is your party, cowboy."

He nodded while he scrubbed a hand over the back of his neck. "Yeah, I know. I just mean I have no memory of that night. You say it was bad, and I want to make it good. But…"

"You don't know exactly what you sucked at?"

"Right."

"I can tell you what you didn't suck at," she said. She'd tried to sound sexy, provocative. And had those words come from someone else—hell, *anyone* else—he'd be pulling down her skirt and commencing with all kinds of sucking. And licking. And everything else he could do to her with his mouth.

But those words, dirty talk directed at him, when coming from Sarah, were just…

She cracked first, a soft giggle coming from her.

Then the dam broke, and he was chuckling too.

He flopped down onto the bed, lying on his back, covering his face with his forearm.

"Seriously?"

"I know," she said. "Sorry. But I…"

"Yeah, I know." He waved a hand in the air, as if encompassing the absurdity of the situation. The hand flopped down on the bed, between their bodies.

Sarah let her hands slide down so she was also lying. She scooched up so she was next to him, turned on her side.

He turned to face her, their feet dangling off the side of the bed.

The cotton of her tee fell to the side and bared a little more of her cleavage. Only the lamp beside the couch had been on when he'd arrived. It was enough of a glow to see her skin, her face, her hair. But with his back to it, the light was mostly blocked, allowing them to have some cloak around them.

Someplace to hide, to forget that they'd never done anything like this with each other before.

Except they had. That was why they were doing a repeat. Because Reilly had fucked it up.

He propped his head up in his hand, elbow sinking into the bed. With his other hand, he reached out and traced a finger along the neckline of her shirt. Not dipping in, or not much, but just gliding along the edge of the cotton. Half on the shirt, half on her warm skin.

"You did that the first time," she said.

"Did I?" he asked. It wasn't a patented move with him. Not that he had *moves* at all.

Sex had always been easy with him. Nice, smooth, whatever felt good to him. Whatever felt good to her.

But this was not smooth, not easy.

Her skin was, though—smooth. Warm. Soft.

"Yeah," she said, her voice quieter now. She leaned a tiny bit, and her body got closer to his touch.

"What else did I do?" he asked.

She looked up at him, her head still tilted down. Shit, that was hot as hell.

"Do you really want a play-by-play of a night we don't want to repeat?"

"I suppose not."

Except...

"Were the lights on?"

She shook her head, hair falling down the front of her shoulder, tangling with his fingers. "No, it was completely dark." She did a thing with her eyebrows that she did when there was more she wasn't saying.

"What?"

A shrug, more hair falling to the front. "It *was* dark. You lit a candle."

He looked past her and saw a candle on her bedside table. A couple of them. Three on the other side's nightstand.

"Did we... Do you want to..."

"What? Light one? Yeah, we could."

Before he could clarify, she was off the bed. He watched as she grabbed matches and lit one of the candles. She moved to the other side of the bed and lit one there. Then she went back to the living room part of the one-room cabin and turned off the lamp.

The glow from the candles gave her a ghostlike aura as she came back to the bed. As she was about to climb back on, he held up a hand, stopping her.

He lifted his chin to her, to her shirt, then reached behind his head and grabbed the neck of his own shirt and yanked it up. He peeled it off and threw it over the foot of the bed.

He moved up the bed, righting his angle, moving pillows out of the way and easing his back against the upholstered headboard.

He patted his lap and again nodded to her tee.

Her hand rose, and for a second, he thought that she was going to nervously twirl her hair again. But her fingers just brushed through her hair and dropped to the hem of her shirt. Her other hand joined in, and up, up, rose the hem, showing first the waistband of her flowery skirt, then her smooth stomach with just a hint of tan on it, and then—oh dear God, yes—a light pink bra.

She tossed her shirt in the general direction of his and climbed onto the bed. She hesitated when she reached him, but he patted his lap once again. He saw the movement in her throat as she swallowed. Reilly knew exactly how she felt. Part challenge, part desire, part "what the fuck is even happening right now?" bafflement.

Either the desire, or the challenge—or both—won out, and she slid a leg over him, gently easing down onto his lap, straddling his hips.

"So weird," she whispered. Reilly assumed the thought was to herself, but he nodded in agreement.

She took a deep breath, her chest rising. Reilly reached out and placed both hands lightly on her hips. He breathed deep too, the scent from the candles enveloping him.

"Hmm, what is that?" he asked.

She took another breath, closing her eyes as she did. "Cinnamon. Creativity." Her eyes opened, looking down at him furtively.

"What?"

She shook her head. "Nothing. It's just…"

It was something with the candles.

"Did we play? With the candles? That night?"

Her forehead squinched up. "What?"

"You know, play with the candles? That night. Do a little tease with the wax? A little burn play?"

She sat back on him, making him "oof," but in a very good way.

"What? No. Do you *want* to do that?"

He shrugged. Not especially. Pain with his pleasure was fine, but hot wax on nipples had never been his thing. Unless… "Do you?"

"Dude, I spend a good half-hour at the end of every day getting all that stuff off me. I find traces of it on me all the time. No way do I find that sexy."

He laughed, and she smiled. The tension eased, and he squeezed her hips, causing her to roll forward.

Onto his dick. His very hard dick.

Her brown eyes widened.

"Did we kiss?" he asked. "That night?" Like she would wonder when he was talking about. Dumbass.

"No."

He felt relief. Relief that he hadn't missed their first kiss. His dick went harder. Christ, really? He'd never thought of kissing Sarah before and the thought that he might have missed the memory of it got him hard as a rock?

Sarah didn't seem to question whatever goofy thoughts were making him hard. She started to rock against his cock, through his briefs and jeans, her skirt and panties. It was too many layers away and yet felt so raw and sensitive.

He moved his hands from her hips to her thighs, pulling the

fabric of her skirt from beneath them. It billowed out, forming a tent over the lower half of their bodies.

One layer gone. The skirt was a film of nothing, and yet it felt like a steel barrier had been removed.

Too many barriers still in place.

He eased his hands under the gauzy skirt and over her thighs. She did yoga, and her legs were lean and strong. Muscles tightened as he smoothed his hands up, thumbs spreading along the tender inside.

She leaned forward, bracing her hands on his bare chest. He regretted that he hadn't taken her bra off, but he wasn't about to take his hands out of her skirt now. Nor did he direct her to take it off herself. He liked the feel of her hands on him too much. Hands that were exploring his chest as his hands moved to the leg of her panties.

She eased up enough for his fingers to slide into her panties.

Thank God, she was wet. He probably would have put a stop to this whole crazy idea if she hadn't been at least a little turned on.

Him? Yeah, his cock could pound nails about now. But he was a guy, and shit, sometimes a whiff of a woman's perfume would do that to him.

He moved a finger through her folds, testing the wetness, gauging. Slick, not drenched, but the way she started moving her hips over his hand told him they were on the right track.

He looked into her eyes, but she was looking down at his chest, watching her hands as they moved across his pecs. A hiss passed his lips as her nails scraped his nipples.

Her eyes quickly moved to his face, but before he could lock on her gaze, it returned to his body.

Okay, so not big on eye contact during sex, his Sarah.

At least not with me.

His thumb joined his fingers, and he spread her, moving up toward her clit. A soft grunt escaped from her, and her thighs tightened against his wrist.

Well, if she wouldn't look at him, at least he'd be able to get her off this time, if the way she was rolling her hips was any indication.

He stroked softly, teasing circles around her. A tightening. More circles.

Moving his free hand, he slid it into the back of her panties, grabbing her ass to pull her closer.

Slicker now, his thumb gliding, then catching on her clit.

That's right, come on out and play. I'll make you glad you did.

Her hands moved up from his pecs and gripped his shoulders. Gripped hard. Damn, but he liked that.

She ground into him, and he maneuvered his hand deeper on one of her upswings. He continued the circles with his thumb, but sped up. Sliding his middle finger inside of her, he knew she was close.

And shit, he still hadn't kissed her. Starting to lean forward to right that wrong, Sarah dropped her head back and closed her eyes. Instead of the lips he was now dying to taste, he went to her neck, bared and available.

He licked her skin, tasting her. The scent of oranges swept over him. And…heat. He didn't know how someone could smell like heat, but Sarah did.

"Yeah, like that," she said, then let out another grunt. Reilly wasn't sure if the direction was for his mouth or his fingers, but he kept up with both.

He decided it was definitely his thumb, because he felt her clit tighten and grow, and he made his wide circles more targeted.

"Reilly, there," she said.

Reilly had always been good at taking direction from his woman, and now was no exception.

Not that Sarah was his woman.

Her arms wrapped around his shoulders, pulling him closer. He nuzzled her neck, finding his spot. Tasting, licking. There, right at the crease where neck met shoulder.

He stopped circling his thumb and went right at her clit,

while curled up his finger inside her and rubbed. And his mouth…
He gently nipped at that warm, smooth skin.

"Fuck, Reilly," she said through a moan.

For a second, he wondered if the bite had been too much. But then she started spasming around his finger, and she was deep into her orgasm.

He kept it up, feeling her pulse around him while he sucked on her neck, feeling the same pulse at a different spot.

Every spot. I want to feel her heartbeat through every spot on her body.

"Go, Ess, get it," he whispered between nips and sucks on her tender skin.

"Yes," she gasped. Her hips rocked as she rode it out. Fingers dug into the back of his shoulders, and he reveled in the deepening feel of it.

Her tits were crushed against his chest, and he cursed the fact that she still had her bra on. But no way in hell was he moving his hands now. Shit, he could keep his hands in her pussy all day the way she felt around him. His other hand was full of her ass, the muscles contracting as she came.

Slowly, she came down, a few aftershocks sending jolts through his fingers, arms, and right to his cock.

He bucked his hips, thinking about when he could get inside her. He knew her pussy would milk his cock like she'd just done to his fingers.

As if reading his mind, she untangled her arms from around him and shimmied down off his lap and onto the tops of his thighs, almost to his knees.

Strong hands slid down his chest. Hands that created, molded, carved. Hands that made art. Hands that undid his fly, eased down his zipper and reached inside.

Her hair was down and sexy as fuck, but it fell in front of her face, so he couldn't see her pull out his cock, though he sure as hell felt it.

And he couldn't exactly see when her lips would come into

contact, but the shiver that went through his body let him know.

"Christ, Sarah, that feels good," he said. He leaned back against the headboard, wanting to throw back his head and close his eyes to the sensation of it all. But watching her head move as she angled herself to take him deeper into her mouth was too good of a show to miss.

He moved his hands to sift through her hair, pulling some of it up and back so he could see her face. But she was too far away and moved down a little more so that he had to let go of her hair.

The mass of honey waves pooled around his jeans and down to the comforter. He spread his legs, and she shifted so that she was on her haunches between them. And then she went right back to sucking on his dick.

Her hand wrapped around him and stroked, coming right to the head as she sucked.

She was good at it but wasn't into it. Reilly could tell the difference. Knew when a woman's heart wasn't into a blow job. When she was only in reciprocation mode.

Shit. He didn't want her doing something because she felt she had to.

"Sarah, it's okay. You don't have to," he said.

Her head came up, and she was looking in his direction, but again at his damn chest and not his eyes.

"You good to just…"

"Fuck?" he said.

She nodded and started to dip her head again. Like it was a goddam chore.

"Yeah, I'm good to go, Ess. Let me get a condom from my bag."

She moved off him, and he got off the bed and grabbed the duffel that he'd thrown on the floor when he arrived.

They'd agreed he'd spend the night when they made their arrangements.

Not so much that they expected to go all night long (though that was fine with Reilly), but it was practical, since they both needed to be in the Harbor the next day.

He could hear her doing something with the bedding as he grabbed a box of condoms from the bag and took one out.

He imagined her taking off her clothes and he'd turn to find her lying on the sheets with all that hair pooled on the pillows, her tan legs spread wide, arms open to him, and he'd finally see those tits.

But when he turned back to the bed, the sight was quite different.

She'd pulled down the bedding, yes. And she was on the sheets, true. But she still had on her skirt and bra. She'd discarded the panties, though, as Reilly could easily tell, because she was on her hands and knees with her skirt flipped up to reveal her bare ass.

Reilly wasn't fool enough to think she wanted him to take her ass, but she was definitely down with doggie.

Her ass was perfect. Heart shaped, with tan lines, but also enough color that Reilly wondered if she had somewhere around here where she lay out naked.

That thought, and the sight of her ready to take him, had him ripping the condom wrapper open and rolling the damn thing on faster than he ever had. He didn't even bother taking off his jeans and briefs, pulled them down enough to feel her skin against his as he moved up behind her.

"You sure, Sarah?" he asked just before he put a hand on her. "We can just call it a night, if you want."

Please, don't say you want.

"You promised me a two-orgasm night," she said, and wiggled her hips.

Well, shit, the woman was challenging him now.

"You got that right," he said. Her bed was the exact right height for it. Smoothing his hands down her hips and thighs, he moved closer, putting his cock head right at her entrance.

A furnace. She was heat and liquid, and any other kind of earthly element, all rolled into one.

He eased in, and they both sighed. Sarah went down to her elbows, her hair sliding down her back and off her shoulders.

The strap of her pink bra taunted him, but also became a focal point as he began to move inside her. It edged a tiny bit up her back as he thrust, then would ease back when he pulled out.

Almost out. Not completely out. He couldn't bear that thought.

The pink strap edged back and forth as his speed picked up. So did their breathing and sighs.

He wanted to make it last, go forever, and focusing on the pink strap against her skin helped. But then her skin became slick and his grip on her hips tightened.

"Mmmm," she said, and dropped her elbows so her face was in the bed, turned sideways, barely visible through the curtain of her hair. It looked like some kind of yoga pose. An erotic yoga pose.

Thoughts of making it last left him as he thrust into her tight body. The slap of him against her ass made a delicious sound.

He felt a spasm come from her, soft, subtle. Reaching around, he moved her skirt out of the way and made his way to her slick curls, finding her clit again.

Hard and throbbing this time, ready for him. No time for slow circles, she was ready as she pushed her ass back against him.

She clenched her inner muscles, and it was all he could do to keep pumping. But he did. Fast and strong, making that pink strap move, making her clench more.

"Reilly, I..."

"Yeah, I know."

"I need to..."

"I got you, Ess." He did. Had her coming apart under his fingers as he fucked her from behind. Surreal did not even begin to describe it.

Fucking great did.

He pumped again, and again, and on the third grind, he exploded. Groaning as he did, he made sure that she was also getting hers, rubbing her clit even as her pussy pulsed around him.

"God," she yelled the same time he said, "Fuck."

They both meant the same thing.

He stilled inside her, then pulled out after she came back down. He smoothed his hands down her thighs, snagged the material of her skirt, and brought it back down, covering her.

Moving to the bathroom, he got rid of the condom and cleaned himself up. He wet a washcloth with warm water, wrung it out, and brought it back to the bed. He'd worn a condom, so there wouldn't be much of a mess, but he'd still soothe Sarah with the cloth.

They still had a lot of night left ahead of them.

Except Sarah apparently thought differently. She'd taken off her skirt, but pulled her tee back on.

As he watched, she reached into her tee, did some arm-twisty movements, and came out with the pink bra through the sleeve. She dropped it to the area rug beside the bed. Climbing under the covers, she saw the washcloth in Reilly's hand and reached for it.

He'd planned to place the cloth on her pussy himself. Ease, stroke, get ready for round two.

But she took the cloth and moved it over her face and the back of her neck. Finally, she wiped her hands on it. (Her hands!) Then she placed it on the floor next to the bed. "Thanks," she said.

He only nodded, dumbfounded. She turned on her side and pulled the sheets up around her. Looking over her shoulder at him, she said, "Well, you delivered. Two orgasms, as promised."

He seemed to remember an "at least" in that conversation. Like, as an appetizer.

"And they were lovely," she added.

Lovely? Lovely? Puppies are fucking lovely.

"So, you were right. The do-over was a success. Everybody's happy," she said, then blew out the candle on her side of the bed and burrowed into the sheets.

The comforter was down around her ankles. She was

obviously too heated to want it now. Yeah, he knew how she felt.

At a loss, he looked around her little cabin. Yeah, they'd both come—her twice. Yeah, he'd been sober for it all.

So yeah, he guessed she was right—the do-over was a success.

So why did he feel like shit?

Shucking his jeans, he wondered if he should sleep on the couch like he normally did when he spent the night. What was the postcoital etiquette when you'd just fucked your best friend?

Her hand shot out, and she turned down the sheets on his side of the bed. Inviting him in, while still keeping to her side, keeping her back to him. He kept his boxer briefs on and slid into the bed. He blew out the candle on his side. Cinnamon. He turned on his side toward Sarah, wondering if he should spoon her, reach out, something?

They'd just had sex. She'd come twice under his fingertips. And now he wondered if he should touch her.

He shifted, but before he could reach out, she said, "Night, Reilly."

"Night, Sarah," he replied, staying on his side of the bed.

The do-over was supposed to make this whole situation a little less fucked up.

Reilly realized the outcome was more confusing to him than waking up with no memories.

And probably worse.

Seventeen

SARAH SET THE SCALPEL BACK INTO A CUP OF RUBBING alcohol on the shelf and rolled her shoulders, letting the candle she was working on swing from its long wick.

She surveyed her work. Not bad. But not up to her usual standards. This one would be donated.

She had several places that got her rejects—old folks' homes, community centers, those kinds of places. She kept a list, even shipping them at her own expense when areas in the Copper Country were full of her candle mishaps.

They didn't happen a lot anymore. She'd mastered the candles she made regularly. Could do them in her sleep. It was the custom molds, custom paints, or specialty carves that would produce a few throwaways.

But the one she was working on now wasn't custom. It was just a pillar with its edges carved back, revealing the layers of different colors inside.

Easy-peasy, and yet its edging was uneven and sloppy. Maybe not to anyone else, but Sarah knew this one wasn't going to be a seller.

Stupid sex, rattling her concentration.
Stupid Reilly.
Stupid orgasms that had kept her body buzzing all night.
Stupid Sarah, not wanting it to be awkward about kissing so opting for doggie style.

And now it was over. The do-over, over.

And yes, she'd been able to run her hands all over Reilly's strong chest, wider than she would have thought, even though she'd seen him shirtless countless times.

And yes, she'd tasted his cock. Had him in her mouth.

And yes, she had climaxed the promised two times.

And yet…not so good.

It hadn't been as bad as the drunken night. But even though they'd both gotten off, she wouldn't necessarily call it a night of great sex.

And certainly not one of passion. But that had never really been an option with Reilly. They knew each other too well for that. They were the personification of Friend Zone. And it showed.

"Hey," she heard from behind her.

Turning, she tried to wipe any emotion from her face. Reilly had done his part. There was no sense showing her disappointment. Besides, it was over now, and the next few minutes would be pivotal for keeping their friendship as it was.

Before.

"Hey," she said. She smiled. Not a big, beaming, "holy wah, look at the size of that fish" smile, but a smile.

He was wearing his jeans and a light blue tee. The same clothes he'd arrived in last night. Feet bare, but that was Reilly. Always wanting his feet next to—and in—the ground.

His curls were tousled and a little wet around his face, like he'd thrown some water in his eyes.

He'd obviously done what she'd done—thrown on the clothes on the floor and gotten the hell out of her cabin.

She'd exiled herself to her studio.

And he could have just gone home, but he hadn't.

"So…" he said. He took her in, obviously noting that she was in the skirt and tee from last night. Did he notice that she wasn't wearing a bra? She'd thought she'd snagged it and her panties when she grabbed her skirt and dashed to the bathroom, but they were still on the floor by the bed. She was so worried about waking him up that she'd bypassed them and come to the studio commando.

He was awake now.

"So," she replied.

They were on the edge, and they both knew it. Whatever was said, or done, next would blaze the path for years to come.

Sarah instinctively knew it was for her to set the tone. Because, mainly, Reilly was a guy.

And Reilly was *very* guy in those instances.

"Well, you were right. A do-over was the key. And now it's behind us, and it's just *us* again." She smiled again, a little bigger this time.

"See," he said. "I told you it'd get the weird stuff out of the way."

Oh, *that* weird stuff was out of the way. Sarah wasn't worried anymore about taking advantage of a very drunk Reilly. Or Reilly having no memories of their night together. Or any of the other stupid reasons that made her agree to last night.

Mainly being called a chicken.

But now, they had *this* weird stuff to deal with.

"And you were right, like I said," she said.

He nodded, his curls jostling. His eyes darted around her studio, looking at things that he'd seen a million times. Anywhere but at Sarah.

Shit, she was really going to have to walk him through this. Okay, reassure him and then get him the hell out of there. Give her time to get her thoughts more together.

"How about I stop by the Dollar Bay house tomorrow with some lunch? I'm going to be in Houghton all day."

His face snapped back to hers, his head already nodding. "Yeah, that'd be good."

"Jess be there too?"

He shook his head, jamming his hands in his front pockets. It made his shirt bunch a bit, and she saw the smooth, tan skin she'd liked putting her hands on so much last night. And also saw that he hadn't done the button on his fly.

"No, she's on the island tomorrow. Just me."

She swallowed hard, thinking about the fine blond hair that got coarser down his treasure trail.

"Okay, lunch for just two, then. Tomorrow."

"Right. Tomorrow."

He should leave—it looked like he wanted to. But he also looked a little lost. Like he had when they were kids and he'd tell her that one of the creatures he'd found escaped. Or died. That was even worse.

Oh, shit. She couldn't let them die. It was the best part of her life.

She moved across the studio—which only took about five steps—and wrapped her arms around his shoulders.

Instantly, his arms were around her, and his head was buried in her shoulder.

Yep, *just* like when they were kids.

"It's okay, Riles. Like you said, we were just closing the circle. We're going to be fine."

"Yeah?" he asked, burying his head in her hair.

"Yeah," she said. In years past, she'd tell him that whatever insect/animal he'd lost would be better off in the next world and that she'd help him bury it.

But she couldn't say that now. Because she wasn't sure they would be better off in their next life.

The life after last night.

And she sure as hell didn't want to help him bury them.

"Sarah, I was such an idiot, thinking that…"

She wasn't sure which incident he was referring to, but she wrapped her arms tighter. "Shh, it's fine. We're good. We're solid." She pulled back to look at him. "Right?" she asked when he met her eye.

He nodded. "Right," he said.

No tears. Not sadness, even. But the emotion on his face hit her in the gut. She knew it, though she couldn't name it. Knew it because it was roiling through her too.

He opened his mouth as if to say something but remained quiet. His mouth.

The one she never even kissed. The one that carried the scent of her toothpaste. The one with quite a beautiful bottom lip.

Had she ever noticed that before? How plump his bottom lip was?

Well, it looked plump and juicy, but it couldn't be *plump and juicy*, could it?

Could it?

"Sarah?" he said softly as she leaned into him, moving her face so it aligned with his mouth.

"Yeah?" she said just before she touched her lips to his.

Oh yes, plump and juicy indeed.

But also firm. And…engaged.

Reilly was kissing her. Okay, technically kissing her *back*.

And it didn't seem all that weird.

It seemed *hot*.

He closed his hands around her waist, pulling her closer. She wound her hands around his neck, plunging her fingers into his curls.

Another thing she'd missed both of their nights together—playing with that mop of white-blond ringlets.

Holy wah, it was so soft. But the arms that clamped her to him were anything but. Hard vises of muscle that she felt across her back, one hand high between her shoulder blades, the other inching lower to her ass.

And all while they kissed. They *kissed*. *They* kissed!

She needed more of it, to taste more of him. Sliding her tongue into his mouth, she was rewarded with his playing with hers. Dancing, finding a rhythm.

He moaned softly. Grabbed her ass. Not softly.

"Sarah," he said as he pulled back from her mouth.

"Yes," she whispered, the word swallowed by Reilly's mouth back on hers. She wasn't sure if she asked a question or made a declaration. Both, probably.

"Reilly," she whispered. His name, which she'd said a million times, suddenly felt different on her lips. On his lips.

That could have been all it was. A kiss. Because they hadn't experienced one last night.

But then she thought about that little hint of skin at his waistband, and she knew she needed to feel it. Taste it.

She broke from the kiss and dropped to her knees.

"Sarah, you don't have to—"

"Shh," she said, already pulling his fly open. She pulled out his erect cock, surrounded by blond hair. Stroked it, then placed it in her mouth.

Reilly's hands were in her hair, pulling her closer. With one hand, he wound her hair around his wrist until he had a fistful of her. He tugged, and she felt the zing go right to her core.

She began to suck him, alternating with long licks up his shaft, while she cupped his balls.

"Christ, Ess, you're going to kill me," he said after a long groan. He didn't let go of her hair, though, only tugged her face closer.

She sucked more, taking him deeper. The weirdness of it being Reilly she was kissing, Reilly who had been in her body, Reilly with a fistful of her hair. That weirdness now turning into something else.

Not weird. Beyond hot.

Passionate.

She felt passionately about wanting Reilly Turkonen. As in, *needed* Reilly Turkonen in that moment more than she'd ever needed anything.

He released her hair and stepped back, his cock springing from her mouth. He reached under her arms and pulled her up. Not to standing, beyond that. Up in the air, and a few steps behind her to her worktable. Sitting her down, Reilly stepped between her legs after spreading them with his strong hands. He moved her skirt up so it was bunched at the top of her thighs.

Pulling at the hem, he had her T-shirt up and over her head, tossed to the floor behind him.

It was early morning, but the sun was up and the studio had several windows. It was far enough from the store and highway, with the cabin in between, that it was unlikely anybody could sneak up on them.

And right then, Sarah didn't care. The way Reilly was looking at her body, the heat in his eyes, the gentleness of his touch as he raised a finger and traced down her neck, collarbone, and to the tip of her breast, made Sarah muddled of any thoughts of being discovered.

"So beautiful, Ess," he said, then bent forward to take her hardened nipple into his mouth.

She wrapped an arm around him, anchoring him to her, and planted her other hand in his hair. It wasn't long enough to wind around her wrist, but so soft and so white next to her tanned, work-roughened hands.

His mouth was warm on her, sucking gently, then not so gently. He played with her other breast, teasing the nipple, plucking, pinching.

She rocked on the table, needing the friction.

"I know." He left her breasts and wrapped a strong arm around her waist, lifting her butt off the table. With his other hand, he whisked the skirt off her, then placed it on the table beneath her before lowering her back down.

"Not one sliver in that beautiful ass of yours," he said.

He smiled at her when he said it. The smile she knew so well, better than anyone's. But different now. They'd had secrets between them before, but this was their biggest.

The secret that they desperately wanted each other.

Reilly whipped his shirt off, shoved his jeans down, and stepped out of them. He'd gone commando, like she had. Sarah held a hand up, covering a breast. It was more of an "Oh, my Lord, look at that man" move than one out of modesty.

"God, you're like Botticelli's Venus," he said.

Her hair was a mass of waves hanging down her body, some in front, some in back. But that was as far as Sarah figured she resembled a work of art. One she knew Reilly was familiar with because they'd taken the same art appreciation class at Tech their freshman year.

But Reilly. He could have walked Olympus with the other gods, his body was so tan and golden. Not big or bulky like a jock but toned from construction, tanned from being outside as much as possible, and very aroused.

"I didn't bring a condom down here," he said.

"I'm on the pill," she said.

He nodded. He'd probably known that, she'd probably told him at some point.

They held secrets, but not many from each other.

He stepped back into her spread legs, and she scooted to the edge of the table. Leaning back on her arms, she bit her lip as Reilly positioned himself.

They both moaned their delight when he slid into her, the table the right height for him. For them.

"Oh, that feels good," she said. She leaned forward, took her hands from the table, and wrapped them around Reilly's shoulders. Wanting the connection this time. Not hiding behind sexual positions.

Skin on skin.

Pulse on pulse.

Reilly inside her.

"Sarah," he said, then kissed up her neck to her mouth.

She kissed him back when he got to her, sucking on his tongue, playing with him.

He started to pick up his pace, moving inside her. She timed it so she clamped down on him with her inner muscles, loving how her body clung to him.

"Fuck, that's good," he said, then devoured her again with his mouth.

He quickened his thrusts, and she lost thought of any kind

of timing. And just felt.

The tension was building in her, and Reilly could feel it. He nodded, not saying a word. His mouth left hers, traveled down her neck, and latched on to a nipple. A soft nip was all it took to throw her over.

"Reilly," she said, her voice ragged, breathless. Her body was as warm as the wax on the burners behind her and just as liquid.

Melting.

He held her close as she kept coming down, placing softer kisses on her breasts, first one then the other. When her breathing came back to normal, he grabbed her ass and pulled her almost off the edge of the table, rocking faster into her.

She stretched her arms down over his back, scraping, loving the shifting of his muscles as he drove into her.

"God, Sarah, you feel so good," he said just before he let go.

She wrapped him in her arms, feeling his shudders, the harsh exhales of his breath blowing back the hair by her ears.

Slowly, they came down, their arms still entwined with each other's bodies, reluctant to let go.

Reilly kissed her shoulder several times, then pulled away from her—out of her—to where he'd dropped his jeans. He pulled them on as he handed Sarah her shirt. She pulled it over her head, pulling her hair out the back.

Reilly watched the troublesome mass as it fell around her. Sarah watched him as he put on his shirt, covering up that beautiful chest.

What a shame.

He held a hand for her as she hopped from the table, skirt in her hand, then quickly slipped it on.

"Well, that was…"

"Unexpected?"

"I was going to say a bonus, but yeah, that too."

They both laughed. "Well, we didn't put a time limit on the do-over, so we can just say that that was a part of it."

"You did say there could possibly be more than two orgasms,"

Sarah said.

"That's right. We're still in the same twenty-four-hour span, so it's all perfectly legal."

"Exactly."

They laughed again and left her studio.

The do-over now officially over.

Eighteen

"REILLY? YOU HERE?"

Reilly put his screwdriver down on the bathroom vanity. "Up here," he yelled to Sarah. He took a step back to make sure the light fixture over the vanity was straight. Satisfied, he turned to find Sarah in the doorway of the bathroom.

"I was coming down," he said.

She nodded, her eyes roaming through the room. The newly completed, much larger bathroom. "I wanted to see. You said this room was almost done."

He swung so his ass was against the vanity and he could see his and Jess's handiwork through Sarah's eyes.

The bath being larger and "like a spa" had been important to Jess. Reilly was cool with the size being expanded, but was afraid the cost of the fixtures would eat into their profits.

And he might be right, but as he saw Sarah's face as she took in the bathroom, he knew Jess had been right also.

This room would probably sell the house.

"Holy wah," Sarah said. "I can't believe you got all this in here."

"Well, it's now a two-bedroom house instead of three, but—"

"So worth it," she said.

They'd taken the space from the tiny third bedroom and put it all in a walk-in closet and this bath.

It had a freestanding claw-foot tub and a walk-in shower with frameless glass doors. The tile on the floor was white with black diamonds that complemented the subway tile along the vanity. He and Jess had installed the above-counter dual sinks a few days ago. The light fixture Reilly had just finished completed the room.

If the rest of the place came off half as nice as the master bath, they were sure to find a buyer, even though the house was in little Dollar Bay and not Houghton or Hancock.

Sarah walked into the room, her fingers gliding over the granite vanity. She slipped off her flip-flops and got into the tub.

"Nice," she said.

"It came with the house. Basically the only thing we kept. It cleaned up nicely."

Sitting down in it, she leaned her head back on the high rim, like she was neck-deep in bubbles.

Her hair cascaded over the back of the tub, and a piece of her skirt came out over the side.

She was wearing her basic work outfit of flowy skirt and a T-shirt. A few silver necklaces hung long down her chest, nestling in her cleavage as she leaned back into the tub.

"Oh, man, somebody is going to love this," she said.

He did. He loved it right now. Watching Sarah relax into a nonexistent bath of steaming water, soaking her skin, washing all those lovely bits and pieces.

Bits and pieces he had now seen up close. Tasted. Touched.

But that was yesterday. And the do-over was over.

Except his cock didn't seem to know that the finish line had already been crossed.

And Sarah might not have been aware of it either, the way her gaze was now on him. Like his bare, sweaty chest was one of the bath's main fixtures.

He crossed his arms over his chest, giving a subtle flex as he did so. Crossing an ankle over the other helped press his cock a little so he didn't sport full-on wood in front of her.

Not that she hadn't seen it.

Tasted. Touched.

Shit. He shifted again and felt a trickle of sweat drip off his forearm onto his stomach, then race down to his waistband. A waistband that was hanging very low due to the weight of his tool belt.

He looked at Sarah and watched her eyes as they followed the droplet of sweat slide down his body.

Did she just lick her lips?

"Jesus, Reilly, you're like a porn version of a carpenter or something."

He looked over his shoulder at the dual framed-out mirrors that he'd hung earlier that morning.

"What do you mean?" he asked, looking at himself. He looked the same as he always did. Working alone today, he'd stripped off his shirt early, since it was hot and there wasn't much breeze coming through the bathroom window.

"Nothing," she said, shaking her head. "It doesn't matter."

He put his hands behind him, grasping the edge of the vanity, looking down at himself, wondering if his growing hard-on was hidden by his jeans.

Sort of.

He heard Sarah make some kind of sound, sort of a sigh, sort of a gurgle in her throat.

"You okay?" he asked.

She nodded, then looked flustered. Her eyes darted everywhere in the small (but still bigger than it had been!) room except at him.

"Yeah, um, so lunch is downstairs. I have time to stay and eat with you. If you want. But if you want to keep working, I—"

"Stay," he said. If she hadn't shown up, he would have kept on working. The bath was now done, but there was still a shit-ton of work to be done. And he had some ranger shifts coming up, so he wouldn't be available to work on the house.

"Stay," he said again. He wanted her to stay and eat with him. Hell, he wanted to feed her while she stayed in the bathtub. That could be messy, though. Supposed she spilled down her white tee? Better for her to just be naked in the bath while he fed her.

Jesus.

He pushed off from the vanity behind him, trying to bring back some sense of sanity.

He'd gotten his do-over, she'd bent over backward to grant him that.

Bent over backward on her studio table.

He coughed and walked over to the shower, opening the door. "Rainfall showerhead," he said proudly.

"Ooh, I love those," she said. She scrambled out of the tub, her leg hitching over the side, then dropping to the tile floor. Her skirt billowed as her other leg lifted and came over the tub.

Reilly reached for the handle on the shower and turned it on. Cold. He took off his tool belt and put it out in the hall.

"I think I'm going to grab a quick one. Feel pretty gross. I'll meet you in the kitchen in a few minutes, and we'll eat." He leaned over, took his work boots off, slid his socks down, and threw them on top of the boots.

His gym bag was in the corner of the room. He'd brought it up this morning. He'd fully intended to use the shower at the end of the day and had a change of clothes and a couple of towels with him. Even had a bar of soap and some shampoo.

But a cold shower in the middle of the day was what he needed right now.

Especially with Sarah standing there staring at him, her brown eyes trailing up and down his chest. Like she was going to watch while he showered.

Or better yet, join him.

But no. She'd agreed to the do-over. He wasn't going to push his luck. It seemed they were able to still be friends, so he wasn't going to fuck that up.

Friends who looked at you like they wanted to have *you* for lunch and not whatever was waiting downstairs.

He moved back to the shower and placed his hands on his hips, watching Sarah. Not daring her, but certainly not giving a "get the heck out of here so I can shower" look, either.

She took a step toward him. Holy shit. But then stopped. Aw, damn.

"No neighbors on this side, eh?" she said as she looked out the window behind the tub.

"Nope. That's why Jess said a floating tub would be nice. You can just see the hint of the bay from the corner. And no neighbors to worry about seeing you in the tub."

She glanced from the window to the shower. "Or the shower," she said.

He coughed a little, clearing his throat. "Right. We'll put up window treatments later, probably last. But they'll be something unobtrusive. The natural light in here is just too good to cover up."

"Too good to cover up is right," she said.

He quirked a smile. Yeah, this was gonna happen.

No drunkenness. No deals made for a do-over. No morning after trying to make it right.

Just straight-up I-wanna-jump-your-bones sex.

He reached behind him and turned the water warmer. A cold shower was no longer needed.

Hot and steamy was on the menu for lunch.

She took a step closer to him, reaching out. Her fingers were cool and smooth along his chest.

"Do you have a change of clothes in that gym bag over there?" she asked. Her eyes left his chest and reached his. The corner of her mouth turned up in a soft smile.

"Yes," he said. Her smile turned wicked, and his dick went even harder. "Do you still keep a change of clothes in your trunk?"

She nodded, her gaze already back on his body. "During the

summer, I basically live out of my trunk I'm back and forth so much."

He snaked an arm around her waist and tugged. "Good. Because it's been a very dirty morning, and I think we both need to get clean."

She squealed when the water hit her, and Reilly turned it warmer. It felt good to him, but he'd been sweating all morning.

And was about to get another workout.

IT WAS SLOW AND EASY. They took their time touching each other. Peeling their wet clothes off while exploring. He took her the first time with her back to him, her hands against the shower wall, head bent, hair under the waterfall.

But the second time, they faced each other. And kissed. More kissing than they'd even done in her studio. Reilly couldn't taste her enough. If this truly was the last time, he had to store up the taste, the memory of Sarah's body.

How her breasts were exactly the right size for his big hands. And how her nipples pebbled and hardened as much from the water as from his mouth on them.

The sounds she made as she got near her orgasm. Like she almost didn't want it to come. But how her body eased into it, then shuddered in his arms, her hands sinking into his ass.

Jesus, to think they'd been missing out on this exquisite pleasure for all these years.

He let that thought go as he released into her soft body, pushing her against the shower wall, one of her legs hitched high on his hip.

It wasn't time to think about the past. And he probably shouldn't even dare to think about the future.

Too complicated.

But for right now—as Sarah took her hands from his ass and wrapped them around his shoulders and hung on as he pumped the last few times into her—Reilly would keep his mind on the present.

The rainfall turned from warm to cooler. Shit, they'd probably been in there over an hour.

"You need a bigger hot-water heater," Sarah said into his ear.

Then she hugged him to her, his dick still buried deep inside, and they laughed together.

Nineteen

Eight years ago
Age twenty-one

SARAH STOOD IN LINE AT THE KEG, STAMPING HER feet to get warm. If she'd gone to the University of Michigan or Michigan State, she'd probably be wearing a cute little skirt, sleeveless top, and slutty, strappy sandals to a Saturday night party in mid-April.

Probably even have a tan.

But at Michigan Tech, Sarah had to pull out her winter jacket and big, warm boots to attend the Spring Fling.

It wasn't a formal, just a big outdoor party that a frat had every spring to commemorate midterms being over. Some years it was nice enough to wear shorts, but most years it was jeans and sweaters.

Tonight it was layers and wool-lined snow boots.

Ah well, life in the Copper Country.

She reached the front of the line and held the cup under the tap, fumbling with the plunger with her wool mittens on. Finally getting the cup full, she stepped out of line and almost ran into Reilly.

"What's that? You're drinking?" he asked, eyeing the cup in her hands.

There was no judgment in his voice, only curiosity.

"It's not mine. I'm just getting it for Kip."

"He can't get his own?"

"He's going to the bathroom. I said I'd get it."

"You're back with him?"

She shrugged, not really sure herself. "Who knows?"

Starting to move toward the other side of the large field that made up the back area of the frat, Reilly slid in front of her, stopping her.

"Pfft," he said, then knocked the plastic cup out of her hand. It landed in a snowbank to their side, the snow swallowing up the liquid, making it look like some guy had taken a leak.

"Dude, waste of good beer," somebody from behind her said.

Reilly grunted. "You don't need to be getting that asshole's beer for him."

Sarah huffed and started to move to get back in line.

"I get a refill for you all the time, Reilly. It's just being polite."

She had no cup now. Did she have to pay for another one? Was that how these things worked? Or was the five bucks at the door enough to get her a clean cup? She always brought her own pop or water, since she didn't drink, so she wasn't really up on what all admission fees covered.

Reaching the end of the line, she took her place. They really needed to have more than one cup-filling station.

Reilly still stood by the side of the keg, about ten—no, eleven—people away from her.

He was wearing jeans and work boots, probably his winter ones. His blue ski jacket had a season pass for Mont Ripley hanging from the zipper. A blue knit cap was pulled low on his head. All you could see of his curls were a few poking out the back, but those were mostly obscured by the high collar or his jacket.

Guys. Sure, they could completely dress for the weather. Whereas Sarah, and probably every girl there, had spent quite a bit of time figuring out what pommed knit cap looked best and how to arrange her hair for maximum showing while still trying to not contract frostbite.

Not for the first time that night did Sarah think things weren't fair.

Reilly gave her a look, and she could see his sigh from where she stood, now nine people away from him.

For one, his breath was obvious in the cold night as he let out the big sigh. Also, his shoulders heaved in an overly dramatic fashion.

Reilly was not dramatic—which could not be said for the girls he dated.

When she got to four people away from him, he held up his arms and let them drop.

"Reilly, it's no big deal. I'm just getting a beer for a friend."

He walked the five steps to her, getting close to her face. "He is not your friend. Do not say that."

He was right. Friendship wasn't what she was looking for with Kip tonight.

"Whatever."

"Jesus, Sarah," he said.

"Look, I want—" The breath for speaking was gone from her because her stomach was on Reilly's shoulder. He'd squatted, placed a shoulder in her gut, and lifted her up, letting her dangle with her legs down his chest and her head at his ass. An ass covered by his ski jacket, which was actually quite soft against her cheek.

"Reilly! What the hell are you doing? Put me down!"

"Not yet," he said. He walked through different groups that were gathered around the various bonfires the frat boys had hurriedly put together when they'd been dumped on with snow all week.

When Reilly reached the edge of the field, they came to large snowbanks where a plow had moved all the snow to clear off the field. The snowbank was right at her waist, which she realized when Reilly set her down. They both slipped as he released her, and they grabbed for each other as Sarah fell backward into the bank. It was hard and not at all fluffy. And pretty damn cold. And she'd get the hell off it as soon as Reilly got the hell off her.

"Sarah, listen to me," he said. She looked up at him. His hands were in the snow beside her head, one arm sunk into the bank. That was going to be really cold on his arm. It was starting to seep through her back already. She pushed at his chest, but he didn't move. She spread her legs to scooch out from under him, but it just made his weight fall deeper into her.

Trapped, she sighed. "What?"

"Kip? Really? After New Year's Eve?"

"That was months ago," she said. Not much conviction in her voice.

"Like three months ago," he said.

"Three and a half," she countered. But her voice had lost its steam.

"There is a field full of guys here, Ess. Why him?"

She tried to push at him again, but he shook his head and continued to lie on top of her. "Because it's easy with him," she said.

"What?"

She looked away from him. She could see the bonfires in the field behind him, make out the students clustered around the flickering fires.

They were far enough away from the party that nobody would notice them out there. If it were any other man than Reilly lying on her in a snowbank far from the group, Sarah would be panicking and wondering if her voice would carry over the music that was blaring outside.

Instead of panicking, she listened to the music. "Bad Romance" was playing. She loved that song.

"Explain, Sarah," he said, moving his body on hers to get her attention.

"Kip is easy. I know what I'm going to get with him. The sex was always good. He'll be easy to walk away from in the morning. And his body is amazing."

Reilly's head shot up. "So you're just looking to get laid?"

"Something wrong with that?" she asked, ready to defend

herself.

"No. Hell no. Endorsed and encouraged when it comes to that ratfucker. Use him and walk away with my blessing."

"Well, that was the plan," she said. It was mostly true. Kip had come on strong from the moment she'd walked into the party. She was pretty sure he had more than a one-night stand on his mind. But she couldn't deal with that thought right now. And certainly not that she'd just told Reilly she was only looking to get laid.

Which was also true.

It being easier with Kip was half a lie. It would be easier to end up with him that night but not so easy to walk away the next morning.

But Reilly seemed to think her capable of it. Because he hefted himself off her and held a hand out. She took it, and he lifted her so she stood next to him.

"We really panked the hell out of that snow," he said. She looked down at the deep indent they'd created in the bank.

"You betcha we did," she said, her Yooper accent sliding out.

They both laughed and turned to walk back to the party. As they neared the first bonfire, they caught some curious glances from those gathered around it. Not crazy curious. The small student population of Tech was used to seeing Reilly and Sarah together.

The bonfire beyond them was where Kip stood with some of his hockey teammates. Her steps slowed a bit, as did Reilly's.

There were a couple of girls with the two other guys, their arms slung around the girls' shoulders. Kip stood alone. Ostensibly waiting for her.

Easy. So easy.

"Okay," Reilly said beside her. "Catch ya later." He started to turn in the direction of the field's edge and the shoveled walkway that led to the parking lot at the side of the house.

"You taking off?" she asked.

He turned back to her, stopping. "Yeah. I'm tired. And cold.

You have a good night. I'll talk to you on Monday."

"Okay. You want me to drive you?" she asked.

"No. I walked here."

So had Sarah. It wasn't that far from the house she shared with four other girls. But it was quite a walk from Reilly's house on the other side of Houghton.

She looked back at Kip, who still hadn't seen her. He was laughing at something one of his buddies said. He really was gorgeous.

She thought about the good sex they'd had when they were together. And how long it'd been for her lately.

But then she thought about either having a conversation with him in the morning or trying to sneak out without waking him.

Neither choice was attractive to her.

"Wait up," she said, and turned in Reilly's direction.

He stopped, and when she joined and then passed him, he caught up to her.

They didn't say a word the entire walk to her place. Reilly crashed on the couch, something her roommates didn't mind. In fact, they liked waking up to a sleeping Reilly on the couch.

But he was already gone when Sarah got up the next morning.

Twenty

"SO IT SEEMS THAT THE DO-OVER HAS HAD, UMM, A little spillover," Sarah said to Reilly.

"Yeah, it's really *showering* over," he said.

She snorted while she shook her head. "No. Just no."

"Yeah, all right. That was lame. But at least we can laugh about all this now. Talk about it."

They were in the Seafarer a few nights after the day she'd visited him at the Dollar Bay house.

The shower day.

Sarah's body tingled from thinking about it. Basically she was experiencing perma-tingle, because she hadn't been able to stop thinking about it.

Or the morning in her studio.

And sometimes the night before that—though that was in a different category.

What she *didn't* think about any longer was that first night when a drunken Reilly had crawled into her bed and they'd had really bad sex.

Which was the whole point of the do-over—to put that night out of the picture.

And she sure had other pictures swimming around in her mind, which achieved that goal.

"So yeah, let's. Talk about it, I mean."

"Is that why you wanted to meet here early?" he asked.

They were meeting Jess, Zeke, Petey, and Alison for dinner. But Sarah had asked Reilly to meet her at the Seafarer a half-hour before the others were due to arrive.

Tessa had the night off, so Sarah had Reilly all to herself for a bit.

She took a deep breath then let it out. Huh. She thought she'd be more nervous about this, but she found she really wasn't.

"What is it?" Reilly asked. There was more curiosity on his face than concern.

"I'm just wondering if…"

A flash of understanding crossed his face. And if she wasn't mistaken, a bit of panic too. "Is this the 'what are we' talk?"

"What are we?"

"The whole 'where are we headed' thing? Because I'm—"

"Whoa, whoa." She held up a hand, then dropped it to the bar. "That's not what this is."

Relief? Was there relief? She wasn't sure, and she could usually read him so easily.

"Sarah, just say it. You know you can tell me anything."

She could. She absolutely could.

"Well, it was supposed to be one and done, right?"

"The sex? Yeah?" he said.

She took a drink of her pop, nodding. "Yeah, and then, of course, there was the spillover."

"Right?"

"So I was wondering if we'd want to spill over…over again."

"Over again? Or over and over again?" He took a drink of his beer, not breaking eye contact with her while he did.

She shrugged. "Whichever."

He turned more fully in his stool so they were completely facing. Their knees bumped, and he widened his feet on the base of the stool so both his legs were outside of hers.

The movement suggested he might be on board with her idea. She relaxed fully. Yeah, you couldn't fake the kind of physical satisfaction they'd had in her studio and his shower. He wanted more of that too.

They'd both had great sex with someone they'd been in love with. That wasn't what this was. Hopefully, they'd each have that again with someone and it would work out that time. But until then…

"To be clear, you are talking a full-blown friends-with-benefits situation."

Another shrug. Another sip of Diet Coke. "Yeah, I guess I am. I mean, it's not—"

"I'm in."

"—something I'm thinking would last long. It's—"

"I'm in."

"—probably a bad idea, even. But—"

"I'm in."

"What?"

He put his hand on her leg, his thumb on the top of her thigh, palm along the side. "Sarah, I'm in."

Know when to take the yes.

It was sales advice that she'd learned at a seminar she'd gone to for small-business owners. When you've made the sale, take the order and get the hell out.

She sat back in her stool, which edged her legs closer to Reilly. And his hand closer to the edge of her shorts.

They weren't short shorts, but they weren't Bermudas, either.

"Well, good," she said. Reilly grinned, his thumb moving across her thigh, his fingers tightening on the underside of her leg.

Just when she thought his hand would disappear up the leg of her shorts, he sat back, taking his hand with him.

Damn him.

He took another long swallow of beer. Had she ever noticed how his throat moved when he swallowed? Had she ever noticed that men's necks were attractive in the first place?

Reilly's was. Strong and tan, with his towhead ringlets framing the back.

"So, okay. Do we need, I don't know, some ground rules or

anything?" he asked.

"Um, I don't know. Do we?"

"Shit, Ess, I don't know. We're obviously making this up as we go, right?"

That was for sure. Then a thought came to her.

"Well, you know there was that do-over episode of *Seinfeld*," she said.

"Yeah?"

She nodded and excitedly leaned forward. "But wasn't there also an episode where they got back together for a while?"

"Oh, yeah. Yeah. Right. Because they wanted this, that, and—"

"The other," they said at the same time. Then both laughed.

"So, we really are using *Seinfeld* episodes as our life coach now," she said.

"What the hell is a life coach?" Reilly said.

Sarah laughed, the weight she'd been feeling since driving away from the Dollar Bay house completely lifted.

"Anyway. They did ground rules. Like I remember staying over was optional. Stuff like that," he said.

"But staying over is always optional with us," she said. "What else?"

He started to say something, his eyes lit with humor, but then stopped. Instead, he shrugged. "I can't remember."

Sarah racked her memory, then got it. "Oh, yeah. They ended their friendship in that episode, right?"

He rolled his eyes. "It's a show. It's not us. Besides, they were pals again at the end of thirty minutes."

"Let's throw out the ground rules. Except for one major one," she said.

"Which is?"

"A time limit. Do we want one?"

He gave her the universal "what's wrong with you?" look. "Why would we want to put a time limit on having good sex?"

She was about to answer, but then heard him mumble to

himself, "Very good sex. *Great* sex."

She patted his knee. "Very great sex, Riles. How about that?"

"Damn straight. So why the time limit?"

She sighed. "Because it would be too easy to let it go on. And that hurts both of us."

"How?"

Did she bring up Paula? Would her name cause the whole thing to come tumbling down? Which was fine, but Sarah was hoping to get a few more weeks of very great sex before those two got back together.

"Well, you still have a possible future with Paula. You don't just live together for a year and then leave it so unresolved."

"Sarah, couples do that kind of shit all the time."

"Yeah, I suppose. But *you* don't, Reilly. There was something there with Paula. Or there must have been for you to ask her to move in with you in the first place."

His expression went blank, and he rubbed a hand across his face.

Damn. Why couldn't she have listened to the seminar's advice a little longer? Take the order and get the hell out.

"I'm not thinking about getting back together with Paula."

There. See. She wasn't getting in the way of true love by suggesting this arrangement. The thought of that had been on her mind.

"Right now," he added.

She nodded. Yeah, it was still on the table for him.

And that was fine. If he and Paula ended up together, married with kids, Sarah's involvement in Reilly's life would diminish anyway. Not disappear, never that. But it would be so much less.

So at least she'd have this very lovely parting gift of having Reilly in her bed for a little while.

"And you," he said.

"Me what?"

He did a hand wave that encompassed her whole body. "Who knows when some single-guy tourist who's up here for a fishing charter stumbles into your candle shop?"

"Single men don't make a habit of going into candle shops." This she knew all too well.

Another hand wave. "Maybe he's buying a candle for his mother."

"So now I get a guy with mommy issues?"

"Okay, the candle's for his sister."

"Better."

"He gets one look at you. You get one look at him. Blammo."

"Blammo? The love of my life and I experience blammo?"

He shrugged and then took a long drag from his beer. "I don't presume to know your heart, Sarah."

They both burst out laughing.

"Jesus, can you even believe we're having this conversation?" he asked.

"No," she said, the laughter quieting down.

He leaned forward, his hand going back to its previous position on her thigh. Higher. And definitely under the hem of her shorts.

"But I'm glad we are. Having this conversation. Glad we're doing this," he said. His voice was soft, and there was humor there, but no laughter.

"Me too," she said. She placed her hand on his arm, loving the feel of the springy hair and strong muscles.

"So. Time limit. A month? The summer?"

She shrugged. It was mid-July. Summer was the busiest time for both of them. So who knew how often they'd even get to be together. A month didn't seem long enough if they could only carve out one night a week.

"The summer sounds good," she said.

"Okay. The summer. Or whenever blammo walks into your shop. Whichever comes first," he said, smiling.

Or whenever Paula comes around, wanting you back.

But she didn't say it. It was certainly more likely than blammo, but she'd just keep her trap shut.

Maybe she did learn something from that seminar after all.

"The summer. Or blammo," she said. She held up her pop, and he joined it with his beer.

"The summer. Or blammo," he repeated while they clinked glasses. They both took sips and put the drinks down on the bar. Their other hands were still on each other.

"So, are we telling people?" Reilly asked.

She studied him, trying to read if that was a good or bad thing to him. He wouldn't want it getting back to Paula. Or would he? Would that be a warning shot to her? Something to make her jealous enough to want to get back together with Reilly with no ultimatum?

"Probably not. If there's a time limit on it, doesn't make much sense, right?"

"Right. And we're together all the time anyway, so it's not like people will think something's up."

"Right. So. It's under wraps."

"Under wraps."

They both looked down at their hands on each other. Reilly squeezed her thigh, his strong fingers deliciously digging into the back of her leg, causing her to lift it slightly off the stool.

"Under wraps in about thirty seconds," he whispered, moving closer to her.

They were early to meet their group. Early for the dinner rush. And only a few people were in the bar area. None of whom they knew.

"Fast," Sarah whispered as Reilly's mouth moved to hers.

"I thought too fast was what got us the do-over in the first place," he said.

She couldn't even laugh because his mouth was on hers. He tasted of beer, smelled of the outdoors, and felt so frickin' fantastic.

He tilted his head, and the kiss grew deeper. She clutched his forearm and slid up his bicep (which flexed at her touch!). Then she wrapped her fingers around his neck.

She started to move closer, wanting to touch more of him as

their tongues tasted each other.

"Holy wah!"

Sarah and Reilly bolted apart. Reilly whirled in his stool, and Sarah looked beyond him. She didn't even need to. She knew that voice.

Petey and Alison walked toward them, everyone in the bar stopping and staring at the loud—and huge—man who'd joined them.

"Un-fucking-believable," Petey said when he and Alison got to Sarah and Reilly.

The shock on his face made Sarah start laughing, which caused Reilly to smile.

So, not *completely* under wraps.

Sarah's cousin looked at the two of them.

"You're early," Reilly said.

Petey snorted. "Yeah. And you're busted."

Twenty-One

"All right. One question. No, wait. A million questions. Obviously. But a quick one before Jess and Zeke get here," Petey said.

They'd moved to a table, and Petey and Alison had received their drinks. Reilly was shocked he'd even waited that long before diving in with the third degree.

At least, Reilly hoped it would just be the third degree and not end with him getting the shit kicked out of him by a former NHL bruiser.

"Shoot," he said, then inwardly cringed at his choice of words. Petey didn't own a gun, did he?

"Okay. Does Jess know? I ask now so if the answer is yes, I can pump away all night."

"Babe, maybe change the verb," Alison said.

"Yeah, ha! Grill 'em. Grill 'em all through dinner." He looked at Alison, who gave him a nod.

"Jess doesn't know," Reilly said.

"*Nobody* knows," Sarah said. "And we'd like to keep it that way."

"Keep *what* what way?" Zeke asked from behind Reilly. Petey gave a shit-eating grin. He'd known Zeke and Jess were coming up behind Reilly and Sarah.

"Oh, nothing," Petey said.

Reilly relaxed a little, but Sarah still stayed tense beside him.

Shit. She knew Petey better than Reilly did.

"Just that Sarah and Reilly are bumping uglies."

Sarah hung her head, shaking it. Alison swatted—no, it was more like a healthy punch—her husband's bulging arm. "Petey! What are you thinking!"

"What? I don't have patient/client privilege in my life. I can say whatever the hell I want."

"Clearly," Sarah said.

"Ha!" Petey barked.

Jess and Zeke took their seats at the table, across from each other. Jess next to Reilly, Zeke next to his best friend Petey.

For some crazy reason, Reilly felt like he had when he and Sarah were little kids and her older cousin Petey would come home for the holidays. Like he and Sarah should be sitting at the kids' table, but there was some kind of mix-up, and they had joined the adults.

But no, they were all adults now. All in relationships. All having the very great sex.

"Is this okay?" Jess said softly to him. "We can head out. Grab some food to go."

"No, it's cool," he said to his business partner. Jess hadn't seemed very surprised at Petey's proclamation. Alison hadn't seemed too surprised either.

Did everybody see something that Reilly and Sarah themselves never saw?

No. The look of shock that had been on Petey's face. The look of bewilderment that was now on Zeke's face.

The men had never seen it coming. Reilly sure hadn't, either.

"Wow," Zeke said, confirming to Reilly that he'd had no clue. "That's kind of a big deal, right?"

"No," Sarah said quickly. Reilly looked at her, raising his eyebrows in question. She patted his arm. "Not like that. I mean, yes, it's…good."

Good? Good? It felt fan-fucking-tastic to him that he was going to have a summer full of Sarah. And not just best friend

Sarah, but Naked Sarah, who was quickly becoming his favorite kind of Sarah.

"It's just that we're trying not to make a big deal out of it."

"Roger that," Zeke said. He picked up a menu and started looking at it. "So how long you guys been a couple?"

"We aren't a couple," Sarah said. Again too quickly. Again too vehemently. Reilly gave her another look, and she sighed, shaking her head. "It's just..." She looked at him for help.

Oh, no. He'd been in these situations too many times not to know that whatever he said next would be the wrong thing.

Best to just let Sarah handle it.

Besides, he'd like to know what label she'd put on it for their friends.

He nodded at her to take up the reins. She rolled her eyes at him, or possibly at everyone.

"It's just, you know, we found ourselves at a place in time where neither of us is seeing anyone. We're adults. We decided to..."

All four of their friends answered at the same time.

"Get it on," Petey said.

"Take it to the next level," Zeke said.

"Finally act upon your feelings," Jess said.

"Explore long-suppressed attractions," Alison said.

Sarah pointed at Petey. "Ew. But yes." She pointed at Zeke. "Yeah, I guess. Sort of." She pointed at Jess. "No. Not really."

And the last point was at Alison. "No. Not even close."

Alison nodded slowly and leaned back in her chair. Reilly got the impression a lot of Alison's patients probably got that look. Understanding, compassion. But maybe not *quite* believing. A passive-aggressive way of calling bullshit.

"She's right. It's more about timing than anything else," Reilly said.

"You both had some time to kill, so you decided to bone my baby cousin?" Petey said.

"I feel like there's no right answer to that," Reilly said.

"There's really not," Petey said, glowering.

"This was a mutual decision," Sarah said.

Her cousin sat back in his chair, arms crossed. A posture not unlike that of his wife, and yet entirely different.

The waitress—Heather, one of the high school kids Tessa employed for the summer tourist season—took Jess and Zeke's drink order and scurried away.

Reilly was both happy and bummed that Tessa wasn't working tonight. Bummed because she would have been a great diffuser for whatever was about to play out. Happy because he didn't want her to see her baby brother get his ass kicked by a former NHL star. And also maybe by a former Navy fighter pilot, if he was reading the look Zeke was giving him right. He'd set down his menu and was taking up the same pose as Petey.

"We're just hanging out for the summer. Maybe not even that long. Nothing more than that," Sarah said.

Well, it was something a little more than that, Reilly thought, remembering their afternoon in the shower. And how unbelievably glad he'd been a few minutes ago when Sarah proposed making their do-over an extended engagement.

Jess made a snort/laugh noise next to him. "You want to get in on this?" he asked.

She shook her head. "None of my business."

"That's not stopping me," Petey said.

"It's not stopping *anyone*," Sarah said.

Heather arrived and gave Jess and Zeke their drinks. The men were drinking beer, Alison and Jess wine, and Sarah Diet Coke.

After taking their dinner orders, Heather gathered up the menus and hurried back to the kitchen. Reilly wasn't sure if she was trying to hurry because she knew he was the boss's brother or because she saw the big, dark, ready-to-burst storm cloud that surely was hovering over their table.

Nobody wanted to get caught in the downpour about to hit.

"Cute kid," Zeke said, nodding at Heather after she left the table. "She's dating my nephew, Stevie."

Petey looked at Heather, who was just ducking into the kitchen. "Yeah? I thought she was dating Twain's kid, Matty?"

Both men looked at each other, then smiled. "All right, Heather. Way to go," Petey said.

Reilly didn't really want to spend time talking about the love lives of teens—especially one who worked for his sister—but if it took them off the scent of his relationship with Sarah? Way to go, Heather.

"It's just that…" Jess said, getting everyone's attention.

Right. She had something she wanted to say.

"Go ahead, Jess," Sarah said in a much different voice than she'd been using with her cousin.

"Oh, only that Zeke and I had a stopwatch on us too, in the beginning."

She looked across the table at Zeke, who nodded solemnly. "Yep. Sure did." Then he looked at Petey and added, "Until my undeniable charm wore her down."

Another snort from Jess. "Yeah, right."

Laughter from the table. People took sips of their drinks.

"All I'm saying is, sometimes we have the right intentions in the beginning—we don't want to hurt the other, we don't want to string them along when they're looking for something, or someone, different."

"Nobody different. Never. Couldn't happen," Zeke said softly to Jess. Reilly, being next to her, heard it, and also heard Jess's soft sigh in return.

"My point, I guess, is we go into something with a set of intentions, but sometimes things change. We change. And it'd be silly to deny something good, something great, because it broke your ground rules."

Ground rules. Hadn't they actually used that term just a half-hour ago?

Could something like Jess was describing happen to them?

"That wouldn't happen with us," Sarah said, setting Reilly straight.

Jess put her hands up in a surrender motion, then sat back, taking her wine glass with her.

"No. It's fine," Sarah said. "It's just that, with you and Zeke, what changed was you getting to know each other better, loving each other."

Zeke and Jess nodded, sharing a look. Reilly had known that Jess was a goner for her flyboy, but it was nice to confirm that Zeke was in just as deeply.

"But with Reilly and me, we know each other so well. And we already love each other. Just, you know, not like *that*."

"Sounds kind of like Zeke and me," Petey said. "Except we haven't secretly wanted to fuck each other for years."

Zeke said, "Speak for yourself," and everyone laughed.

Alison moved, leaning forward, and Reilly braced himself for some kind of hard truth. Some tough love or whatever therapist trick she had up her sleeve.

Sarah must have felt the same thing was coming, because she headed her off at the pass. "And what you said, Al, about long-suppressed attractions or whatever. It simply wasn't that way with us."

Reilly took a drink of beer and nodded. "That's true," he said, then let Sarah articulate it better for the both of them.

"It wasn't years of only missed timing or longing, stolen looks at each other. No wondering 'what if' or anything like that. It was always a friendship. Nothing sexual or romantic. Ever."

Yeah, best to let Sarah handle it. She said it so much better than he could have.

Brutally, that was how she'd said it.

Really brutally.

"I mean, really, if anyone should get it, it would be you two." Sarah pointed between Petey and Alison. "You guys weren't as close friends as Reilly and I are, but you've been in the same friend group for a ton of years. And then one day, you just saw each other in a different light. Mainly because Petey was staying with you after he hurt his knee. Timing."

Petey and Alison exchanged a glance that told Reilly there was much more to their story than everyone knew.

Interesting.

But not relevant.

"Well, cuz, let it not escape your attention that Alison and I are now married."

Did Reilly actually hear Sarah gulp? He looked at her. Yep, but she had her glass to her mouth, so that was probably all it was.

"Reilly and I aren't getting married," she said once she set the glass down. "If he's marrying anyone, it's Paula Westin."

Everyone at the table looked at him with accusation in their eyes, like he'd just fucked Paula on top of the table in front of Sarah. He held his hands up. "Nobody's talking marriage. To anyone."

The accusation eased a little bit, but the glower was definitely back on Petey's face.

Reilly continued, "Hell, it's more likely that Sarah marries first. Some tourist that wanders into her shop." He looked at Sarah, who was smiling at him and nodding.

"You looking for that, Sarah?" Zeke asked. "Because I get single guys on my plane for fishing trips all the time. Lots of times I'll bring them here for a beer after the charter is over. I could arrange for an introduction or two. I am a pilot, you know. A professional wingman."

The women groaned at the joke, and Zeke and Petey did a fist bump. Reilly did neither.

"We're good, thanks," he said to Zeke.

"I don't know," Sarah said softly to Reilly. "Whichever comes first, right?"

"You know what?" Sarah said after a long sigh. "It's really new—Reilly and me—and it's only for the summer, so there's really not much sense in dissecting it. We're just going to have some fun, that's all. Really, that's *all*."

Reilly nodded at her, put his arm around her, and squeezed. He noticed none of the other couples were nodding in agreement with them.

Heather came with their food, and they all started digging in.

"How's the house coming?" Alison asked in the general direction of Jess and Reilly.

"Good," Jess said. Reilly nodded his agreement as he chewed his burger. "The master bath is complete. We'll be drywalling the bedrooms next week."

"I saw the bath the other day," Sarah said. "It's amazing. I love the tub. I hopped right in it, clothes and all, didn't I, Reilly?"

"Yep," Reilly said. He felt his face burn and kept eating his burger, not meeting anyone's eyes.

"I loved that too," Jess said. "I'm so glad we were able to keep it. It goes so well with all the other stuff we did, like the rainfall showerhead."

"Yes, that's a great feature," Sarah said. Her voice cracked at the end, and she grabbed her pop and took a deep swallow.

"I still say you need a bigger hot-water heater," Zeke said.

Sarah and Reilly both froze. They both looked at each other, then at Zeke. Zeke, who was being kicked under the table by Jess. "Hey," he said. Jess looked at Reilly with the guilt he was feeling mirrored on her face.

"You were on the island. No chance of you walking in. And I cleaned the whole bathroom afterward," she said.

"*You* were on the island," Reilly said. "And I scoured that thing until it glistened."

There was a moment where no one spoke, and the two couples just stared at each other. Alison and Petey looked at them all and then at each other, shrugging.

First Jess smiled, then Reilly. Then the four of them burst out laughing. Alison got it first, smiled, and took a bite of her salmon. Petey looked around at Jess, Zeke, Sarah, and Reilly all laughing. Then he looked at his wife, who only had to raise one brow at him.

"Ooooh!" he said. The laughter made another wave before it

died down, everyone returning to their meals and drinks.

"Babe," Petey said to Alison, "we have got to check that place out. Sounds like a fucking awesome shower."

Sarah choked on her Diet Coke, doing an actual spit take. Reilly patted her back while all of the couples cracked up.

Twenty-Two

"HOLY WAH, THAT WAS INTENSE," REILLY SAID. HE ROLLED off her, pulling the sheet up to cover them both.

It was too hot for the sheet. Too hot for sex, even. Well, no, never that hot. But Sarah felt like her body was made of molten lava—heavy, hot, and oozing all over the place.

That dinner had taken a lot out of her. She'd taken the brunt of explaining their situation to the group.

Stupid Petey.

Stupid Reilly for not helping her out.

Stupid Alison for making Sarah think for the rest of the night.

Until she and Reilly had gotten to her place and practically ripped each other's clothes off. Glancing at her shorts thrown on the floor, she thought that perhaps there was an actual rip around the waistband. Worth it, if there was.

But now, with her body spent and sweaty, Jess and Alison's words came floating back through her mind.

"Fuck, it's hot in here," Reilly said.

"I can turn on a fan," Sarah said, starting to get up.

"How 'bout a swim instead?"

God, yes. That was what she needed. She nodded and scooted out of bed. "Let me grab a suit."

"Screw the suits," Reilly said. "No one will see us."

She'd gone skinny dipping at her place before. Her tiny strip of land didn't have much waterfront footage, but it was completely private. Trees on one side and a bend in the shoreline prevented her closest neighbors from seeing into her yard, and there was only forest on the other side, her business being the last one in town.

"Towels, then," she said. She grabbed a couple of her nicest beach towels while Reilly went to the fridge.

"Water or Diet Coke?" he asked.

"Water," she replied. He took a bottle of water and a couple bottles of beer from the fridge.

He was still naked, and with the refrigerator light shining behind him, he looked like some sort of Nordic god, his curls disheveled from battle, his body glistening with sweat. Victory had been his.

He was beautiful. Her Reilly. Reilly, who always had dirt under his nails as kids. Who inevitably had some kind of amphibian hiding in his pocket.

A child no more, in any sense.

A beautiful, godlike man. And he was naked in her kitchen and at her disposal for the summer.

Heaven.

She wrapped one of the bath sheets around herself and found her flip-flops. When she got to him, she took the beer and water bottles from him and handed him his towel. At the door, she slid the bottles into a tote bag that she kept at the ready for just such an occasion. Although she'd been alone the other times.

"What's in the bag?" he asked.

"You'll see," she said, and led them out the door.

They circled the small cabin and walked across the narrow lawn to the water. Dew was already forming, and it felt cool on her feet. Reilly was barefoot, so it was probably even better for him.

When they reached the beach, she handed him the bottles and then started pulling candles out of the tote.

They were larger pillars, mostly burned down. Some were

rejects, others were ones she'd really liked. But they were all wide, so they stayed in the sand when she wedged them in. After a couple, Reilly put down the bottles and offered his empty hands. "I'll do some."

She gave him three, took the remaining ones herself, and they placed them in the sand in no pattern, just randomly dotting the shore area. She took her lighter out, tossed the now-empty tote near the bottles of beer and water, and lit each of the candles while Reilly went to the water and waded a few steps in.

"Not too bad," he said.

The harbor she lived on was on Lake Superior, which, because of its depth, stayed very, very cold all year. In late August, you could stay in maybe a half-hour. But the harbor got a little warmer, and they'd been having a hotter-than-normal summer, so her little area was bearable for longer than a quick cooling off.

Not a lot longer, but longer.

"Holy wah," Reilly said from the water.

Sarah turned toward him to see what he was looking at. A boat beyond the harbor? Something in the water?

No, he was looking at the candles, now all lit and glowing in the sand. And her. He was looking at her.

"Drop the towel, Ess," he said softly. She did. A soft sound came from him. Not a gasp or a groan. Something in between.

She wondered if the candlelight did for her what being backlit by the fridge did for Reilly.

Not Norse god material, but maybe a Valkyrie? She spread her legs and put her hands on her hips. Wonder Woman, perhaps?

"Jesus," he whispered.

She laughed and ran for the water, taking three long strides into the harbor and diving in.

The cold water sliced over her body. Any languidness from the burger at the Seafarer and the two rounds of sex was gone, startled from her with the burst of cold.

"Crap, that's cold," she said when she broke the surface. She took a few strokes out so just her head would be above the surface as she half stood on the sandy bottom and half trod water. It was her "spot."

Reilly threw the towel back onto the beach and strode into the water, following Sarah under, coming up mere inches away from her.

"We haven't done this yet this summer," he said.

She shook her head. "Not for a while, actually," she said. Last summer, Paula had just moved in with Reilly, and he hadn't spent much time at Sarah's place in Copper Harbor.

"And never naked," she added.

"Feels pretty damn good," he said. "I was really roasting in there."

"Me too. No breeze at all tonight."

"Nope," he said. They both looked up at the night sky. No clouds, making all the stars unbearably bright. They hadn't even needed the candles.

"But they look really cool," Reilly said, reading her mind.

"Yeah, I love how they just seem to be part of the sand, like they grew out of a candle garden or something."

He grunted in agreement and swam a few yards away from her. His head went under, then his ass broke water, so much whiter than the rest of him. He executed a perfect somersault.

"Whoo!" Then he quieted his voice. "Sorry. Is that going to wake your neighbors?"

Sarah looked back to the shore. From where they were, she could see the front deck of the Mastersons' house. No deck light on, which meant they weren't there.

"I think they said they were going to Chicago this week. Their deck light would be on if they were here. So whoop it up."

He did another somersault, white ass still glowing in the moon—a double moon—and yelped again when he came up.

"Hey, do you remember when we'd absolutely rule in chicken?"

"Yeah," she said. Kids at the beach, playing chicken on each other's shoulders until the lifeguard would get on them.

"We were good," he said as he swam back toward her.

"We were."

He was at her side, and he stood facing her. Taking his hands out of the water, he laced his fingers together, creating a cradle. "'Member this?"

She laughed and nodded.

"Still got it in you?"

"In me? You're the one who does the lifting. Still got it in *you?*" she said.

"Hell yes."

"I'm not a scrawny seventh grader anymore."

"Pfft."

He dropped his hands, fingers still laced, under the water. Sarah lifted a leg, putting her hands on Reilly's shoulders to steady herself as she glided her foot into his waiting hands.

"On three?" he said, and she nodded. "One, two…three."

He threw her high, and she arced through the dark night, feeling like a soaring owl. She cleared her whole body from the water before diving back in.

Almost as good as the sex they'd just had.

Well, maybe not.

She broke the surface to see Reilly grinning, his white teeth showing in the soft moonlight. "Again?" he said.

"Again."

He threw her three more times, until they were both breathing heavily. When they were kids and got to this point, they'd rush to the shore, grab some money hidden in their shoes, and run to the beach concession stand for a pop or some ice cream.

Now, she swam to Reilly and pressed her naked body against his. He immediately banded his arms around her, pulling her closer.

"Better than concession-stand ice cream sandwiches," he said.

She licked the droplets of water from his neck. "I was just thinking the same thing."

"Sarah," he whispered. She took her mouth off his body to look up at him. The moonlight and candlelight from the shore gave enough of a glow to see the blue of his eyes. "Ess," he whispered, and then his mouth covered hers.

His lips were wet—everything was—but firm, and she met him in his insistence, his need to taste.

His tongue tangled with hers, pulling her in, sucking. She felt him start to get hard, and she moved into it, wanting it.

Sliding his hands down her back, he grabbed her ass, pulling her up. The water helped, and she easily stayed at just the right position, wrapping her legs around his waist.

Her breasts needed relief, but he had his hands full keeping her afloat, so she rubbed herself against his chest. Mostly smooth, with just a sprinkling of baby-fine blond hair.

"Shit, Ess," he hissed.

"Inside me, Reilly," she replied, then leaned her head the few inches needed to get back to his mouth.

He did a mean balancing act to keep her ass in one hand while taking his hard cock in the other and guiding himself to her. She sank down onto him, causing him to lean his head back in a long sigh.

She took the opportunity to nuzzle his neck, the tendons taut from his pose. A small nip from her—a mere graze of her teeth—brought his head back down and his mouth to hers.

She started to rock, not able to gain much traction with her feet locked behind Reilly's back. The water did its magic, creating a swell that moved her body. Reilly moved his hands to her hips and gripped her, catching the wave, bringing her up and down on top of him.

"Holy wah," he said through a soft groan.

"I know, eh?" she said. Both of their Yooper accents came out strongly.

The water was cold, and they'd been in longer than was probably wise. But she delighted in the prickles against her skin—a counterbalance to the heat rising inside her.

The wave they created built, its ebb and flow becoming faster as Reilly rose and drove her hips into himself.

"Reilly, I'm…"

"Yes, Sarah," he said.

As in most things, they were thinking alike. She buried her head in his neck as she came apart, her arms wrapped tightly around his shoulders. Her inner muscles spasmed, and she cried out.

"Let it go, Ess," he said, pumping her hips faster. His ass clenched beneath her legs, and she dug in with the heel of her foot. "Fuck, that's good." He pumped one last time and released into her.

She bit down on his neck as he did, eliciting a deep moan from him.

He held her that way, the water slowly calming around them. When she had her breath back, she started to unwrap her legs from around him, but he stopped her.

"Hang on," he said. She did, with both her arms and legs. He walked them out of the water, showing more balance and grace than Sarah thought possible with the cold water and a wet woman draped around him.

"Keep hanging on," he said. "Tighter." She did and was glad, because she was almost upside down when he leaned over to snag both of their towels.

He unfurled one and let it drift to the sand. With the other one in his hand, he dropped to his knees and laid Sarah on her back, coming down with her. They rolled so that Reilly ended up on his back with Sarah nestled into his side.

He pulled the other towel over them both like a blanket.

She hadn't had this exact scenario in mind when she'd splurged for the extra-large, extra-plush beach towels, but was glad that she had.

"Big Dipper," Reilly said, and Sarah looked up. Easy to find, the constellation shone brightest in the star-filled sky.

"Amazing," she said.

"I'll say," Reilly said. Sarah didn't ask if he meant the stars or the night they'd just had.

It could apply to both.

She started to shiver from the wet and the cool night. "Wanna go inside?" he asked. She shook her head, and he pulled her closer, giving her what warmth his body had. It was enough.

The candles continued to flicker, and Sarah watched the glow as they burned. She wasn't sure who fell asleep first.

SHE KNEW WHO WOKE first, because Reilly was waking her up with kisses along her neck. "Ess, check out that sunrise," he whispered.

She rubbed the sleep out of her eyes. "Beautiful," she said. The horizon was an explosion of pinks and golds, the sun creeping its way into sight.

He kissed down her body, pulling the towel away from her. "Beautiful," he repeated.

But his eyes weren't on the sunrise.

And his mouth most definitely wasn't pointed in that direction.

Twenty-Three

REILLY PUT THE DIRTY PAPER PLATES IN THE TRASH CAN. The pizza box from the Commodore went in the fridge with the leftover pizza in it.

Sarah sat at his kitchen table looking like she wasn't quite sure what to do next.

Which was odd, because in the two weeks since the night at the Seafarer (with that fucking Petey!), they'd entered a very easy pattern of dinner in Sarah's cabin and then moving over to her bed (with that fucking!).

It hadn't been every night—their schedules hadn't permitted it—but when they'd been together so far, it had always been at Sarah's cabin in Copper Harbor.

All of Reilly's ranger shifts were able to be moved to either the Harbor or Isle Royale, and he'd catch a ride to the Harbor with Zeke and Jess afterward.

On days he wasn't rangering, he'd work on the Dollar Bay house. Most of those days, he'd still drive up to the Harbor afterward to see Sarah, but not always if he and Jess were working later, or Sarah had something going on.

When she was in town, she stayed at her mother's. It was the entire bottom-floor walkout with its own entrance, and Reilly had crashed there a hundred times, but he still felt weird about going to Mrs. Ryan's house with the express intention of sleeping with her daughter.

They'd sworn their dinner companions to secrecy that night, but Reilly knew they had to tell Tessa, lest she find out some other way.

And because they ate at the Seafarer a lot and Reilly couldn't keep his hands off Sarah when they were around each other.

At first nervous about telling Tessa, thinking she'd disapprove, Reilly was shocked when she'd burst into tears.

And then even more shocked to learn they were happy tears.

He'd held Sarah in his arms that night and felt something shift.

He just wasn't sure what.

But the next morning, Sarah had shooed him out of the cabin so she could get to her candle making, barely acknowledging him when he said when he'd next be available.

And he knew they were firmly back in Whichever Comes First territory. Which should be a relief—and it was. But it was also a little unsettling.

The very great sex continued, though, so apparently Sarah hadn't been affected by Tessa's tears like Reilly had.

Maybe something still remained from his feelings of unease that night, because he'd been adamant that Sarah come to his house tonight.

All night.

She'd been to his little house a million times. She'd crashed in his guest room a million times. Before Paula. During Paula, she'd been there for dinner a few times, but there'd been no more crashing in the guest room.

And she wouldn't be sleeping in there tonight.

Like every night with Sarah since the do-over, it was all so familiar and yet all so different. Because normally Sarah would be up getting rid of their trash with him, not sitting at his kitchen table watching him.

Waiting for instructions.

"Want to watch a movie?" Sarah said when Reilly didn't offer up anything.

"Sure. Go on in. I'll grab some drinks. Popcorn or anything?"

She shook her head. "No. I'm stuffed, thanks." She rose from the table and disappeared down the hall to the living room.

He cleaned up the table, washed his hands, and grabbed a beer and a bottle of water from the fridge, then took one more look around the tiny kitchen to make sure all was in its place.

When he'd graduated from Houghton High School, his father had put their house on the market, as they'd agreed two years prior when Reilly was sixteen. Reilly was never sure what deal Tessa had pulled with either her father or her husband Elden, but she had given Reilly enough money to buy a tiny house in a neighborhood not far from where they'd been and to pay for tuition to Tech. He'd worked jobs all the way through to pay for books, food, and household crap. But the house was his, as was the Tech diploma.

When he came into the living room, Sarah was already in the chair she always used when they would watch TV. Remote in hand, she was clicking through his movie channels.

Reilly moved to his beat-up recliner, set his beer down on the side table, and moved to bring Sarah her water.

Walked right past the big, empty couch to get to her.

"Hey, you want to watch on the couch?" he asked, waiting by the side of it.

She looked at the couch and at her lap in the chair. Confusion crossed her face for a second, and then she got it.

"Oh, yeah. Sure." She left the chair and joined him at the couch. He set her water on the coffee table and retrieved his beer, setting it down by the water.

"You have a particular side you want?" she asked. A weird look crossed her face.

She was thinking of him and Paula on this couch.

Yeah, they'd used the couch sometimes, but typically when they'd watch TV together, he'd be in his recliner and she'd sit in one corner of the couch with her legs curled up under her.

"Nope. Don't really use it all that much," he said. "I'm always over there." He pointed to his recliner.

"Well, we don't have to—"

"Sarah, it's only a couch," he said. Wrapping an arm around her waist, he pulled her to him as he sank down. No sides needed to be chosen. They were both sprawled all over the couch.

He stayed on his back, loving the weight of Sarah on top of him. She shifted around, finding a good position, half on top of him, half behind him, wedged into the back of the couch.

Her head was on his chest, arm around him, and they were both able to see the television.

"Oh, I love this movie," she said, her hand with the clicker dropping. "Are you up for a sappy romcom?"

Shit, with her draped all over him like that, he'd watch a frickin' marathon of sappy romcoms.

"Yeah, that's fine. Is that Drew Barrymore?"

"Yep. It's *Never Been Kissed*. You haven't seen it?"

"I don't think so."

"You'd know if you had. Okay, it's only about ten minutes in. So, here's what you need to know."

She got him up to speed on the movie, which wasn't hard—pretty easy setup.

He watched it, he really did. And it was cute. But his attention was more on the woman whose body fit so well with his on the couch.

At one point, he reached behind them, grabbed a throw off the back of the couch, and covered them both. The movement made Sarah burrow around him more. When the blanket was settled, he wrapped his arm around her and left it on her hip. He slid it just under shirt, so he could feel her warm skin.

She did the same, placing her cool hand on his abs underneath his tee.

They'd watched a hundred movies together. But they'd never watched one *together*.

The feeling he'd had the night they'd told Tessa crept back while Sarah sighed and giggled throughout the movie.

This was good. It was right.

Could it last? Could they *make* it last?

And if it didn't, would things ever by this right between them again?

"I *love* this part," Sarah said.

Reilly pulled his thoughts from a future with Sarah. A future with Sarah? He'd never put it in such framework before.

Was it possible? Could this very great sex last? Could their friendship with very great benefits become a long-term, committed relationship?

"I don't know why, but I'm just a sucker for this ending. Always have been," she said.

This time, he really did pull his thoughts away and pay attention to the movie.

It was the Grand Gesture part. He'd watched enough romcoms with Sarah over the years to know that much.

A baseball field. Crowds of people waiting expectantly for our man to show up. But he was late. Of course he was going to show up, people!

Drew Barrymore, looking cute as hell, feeling like shit on the pitcher's mound.

"Excruciating," he said.

Sarah laughed. "Don't worry, Riles, it ends well."

"I know that. Of course it ends well. But God, it's like a worst nightmare. All of that, that…"

"Emotion?"

"Emotion out there in front of everyone. I mean, everyone. The whole damn cast of the movie is there."

She laughed again. He felt the reverberation against his chest and thought it one of the nicest things he'd ever felt.

"That's the point. She's declaring herself in front of everybody. So is he. When he shows up."

His worst nightmare.

"I know, that would be your worst nightmare," she said. He pulled her closer to him, pulling at her hip so she lay fully on top of him.

"It's sometimes spooky knowing someone shares my brain," he said.

She pushed herself up so she could look down on him, her hair falling to the side, creating a curtain around them.

"I know," she whispered. "It used to really freak me out."

"And now?" he said just as quietly.

"And now, we're sharing not only our thoughts, but our bodies."

He waited for more, sure he read her thoughts but not wanting to be the first one to say it.

Didn't want to be the one standing on the pitcher's mound with the town feeling sorry for his lonely ass.

She smiled. He smiled back.

"It's pretty great," she said.

"Yeah," he agreed.

She leaned her head down the three inches it took to kiss him. It was soft, sweet, no rush. He heard the crowd cheer from the television.

He deepened the kiss with Sarah, wrapping his arms around her back.

Drew and her guy had nothing on Sarah and Reilly.

He kissed Sarah again.

And again.

THEY STILL HADN'T had sex in Reilly's house.

It was the first thought that came to Sarah when she woke up next to him in the morning.

In his bed, yes. But she was still fully clothed. And tired as she'd been, she would have remembered having sex with Reilly and then getting dressed again before falling asleep next to him.

Damn it. For some reason, she'd been both dreading and anticipating finally taking their new relationship to Reilly's house.

It wasn't to be a fuck-you to all the women he'd dated or who had moved in. Really, it wasn't.

Okay, it was a little bit.

And really, only Paula had moved in for any length of time.

All her stuff was gone, but her touches remained. Because no way would Reilly have picked out the high-thread-count sheets Sarah was on right now.

Reilly didn't even know what thread count was.

They'd made out during the closing credits of *Never Been Kissed*. Just when he was about to roll Sarah over on the couch, the announcement came from the television that *Total Recall* was about to start.

Reilly popped his head up with a mischievous look. "If I have to watch a romcom, you have to watch Arnold for me."

She'd huffed but agreed, and they'd settled back into their movie-watching positions. Reilly had always loved Schwarzenegger movies when they were kids. Sarah didn't get it, but she indulged him. Even tried to stay awake.

But no, that wasn't happening.

She'd woken to find Reilly carrying her upstairs. "What time is it?" she said, curling her arms around his neck.

Was he even strong enough to carry her up the stairs? Apparently so.

"Late," he said. "Sleep."

It was an easy command, with Reilly's arms so strong around her, his scent so familiar, his body so warm.

He put her down in his bed and pulled the covers up over her, not even bothering to pull off her shirt and shorts.

She felt the weight when he got into the bed and felt his arm snake around her waist, pulling her close. She wanted to turn to him, finish what they'd started on the couch, but her mind was losing traction and her body seemed too heavy to even roll over.

She slept.

And now, Reilly slept and Sarah had to get going. She couldn't even wake him for a little somethin'-somethin' before she got on the road to the Harbor.

It was Maya's day off, and Sarah needed to open the store

herself.

She snuck out of bed, made a quick pit stop in Reilly's bathroom, and headed downstairs.

Her bag of clothes and toiletries that she always kept in her car was still out there. She'd meant to bring it in last night, but went to the living room right after dinner and then never left the couch.

She grabbed her shoes from the living room floor by the chair where she normally sat and went to the kitchen.

Should she leave a note?

She never had before when she'd crashed at Reilly's place. But those times she hadn't slept in his bed with him.

What was the proper etiquette for their situation? Whatever that was.

For a moment last night, she'd sworn Reilly was wondering the same things she was. That what they were doing was so good, could it possibly last? Could they actually turn their deep love for each other, and the passion they felt for each other's bodies, into something lasting?

Forever?

She shook the thoughts from her head. The Harbor. The store. These were the things she needed to worry about right now.

A possible future with Reilly would have to wait.

An hour-long drive ahead of her probably wasn't what her racing mind needed this morning. With no time to make coffee, she grabbed a bottle of water from his fridge and decided against the note. He knew she needed to open the store this morning—she'd mentioned it over pizza.

Pizza.

She went back to the fridge and grabbed the Commodore box. Sadly, cold pizza for breakfast on her drive to the Harbor was not something foreign to her.

After grabbing her car keys from the table, she went out the back door from the kitchen and walked down the four steps to the back driveway.

And ran into Paula Westin.
Blammo.

Twenty-Four

SARAH CAREFULLY UNWRAPPED THE CANDLE FROM THE bubble wrap.

"Oh my God," Alison said. "Sarah, that's *amazing*."

"I'm sorry it took so long."

Alison waved her words away, coming over to the coffee table in her office where Sarah had placed the candle.

"I had the one we talked about, the outline of the U.P., all set, with the baby's name and date carved in the bottom. In fact, I brought it for you too, in case you'd rather give her that one."

"I'm sure it's great, but my God, I can't *not* give this one to Katie, it's so beautiful. And so them."

Sarah smiled. She loved the candle too. She'd started working on it that day in her studio after she and Reilly had told Tessa about the new twist in their friendship.

It was probably her most ambitious work so far. She'd started with a large rectangle that stood almost a foot tall when on a table. Four wicks. And seven layers of coloration. The carving was what took the longest.

"I mean, it's like a sculpture, isn't it?" Alison exclaimed. She sat on the floor, legs crossed and under her coffee table, getting close to the candle, shifting the wax paper that it sat on to see the different angles.

Sarah had carved a family of four into the wax. Each one was at a different depth, allowing for a different layer of dye to show through. The effect was a father in red, mother in navy, toddler in pink, and baby in powder blue. They were all standing together, hands entwined on a bed of green grass.

"It's like one of those family stickers on the back windows of cars, but 3-D," Alison said.

"Yeah, exactly," Sarah said, admiring her work with Alison.

"But much, much more intricate and beautiful." Alison looked up at Sarah, who had taken a seat in one of the two chairs that faced the single chair Alison probably sat in during her therapy sessions. "This is so lovely, Sarah. Katie is going to love it. Thank you."

Sarah smiled, pleased Alison liked it. It was one of Sarah's favorite pieces, if not her *most* favorite. "I took a bunch of pictures of it, and if you don't mind, once you give it to Katie, I'd like to ask if it's okay if I put them on my website. As an example of my custom work. It can be a one-of-a-kind, though. I wouldn't repeat it."

"Oh my God, is that a golf club? It is. That's so perfect!"

Sarah nodded and pointed to a few more of the details she put in. "Here's the hole, over here, like the green they're standing on is a golf course. This is a steno tablet in Katie's hand, like a journalist would use. And those are peaches around the feet of the little girl."

"Peaches," Alison said. Her eyes were misty when she looked at Sarah again. "I can't even express how wonderful this is. Thank you so much, Sarah."

"Of course," Sarah said.

Alison climbed off the floor and sat in her chair, facing Sarah. She continued to study the candle from her new angle. "And I'll ask Katie about the photos, but I'm sure she won't mind. It'd be like bragging rights. She got the first candle in the new Sarah Ryan Family line."

Sarah laughed. "She did. And you may have something there,

a new line of candles."

"Great market—baby gifts."

"I've done a couple of wedding cake toppers that people wanted to have as a candle."

"Exactly. Get them all through the phases. Wedding shower, wedding gift, baby shower, baby gift. Believe me, with my besties going through all the phases the last few years, I know what I'm talking about."

Sarah laughed again and sat back in her chair. She thought better of it and sat forward. "You probably have someone coming in? I'm actually surprised to find you alone."

"My last appointment for the day was an hour ago. I'm free and clear. Sit back, talk to me. What's been happening since I last saw you at your mother's for Ryan family dinner?"

That had been Sunday. Monday, she'd stayed over at Reilly's. Tuesday morning she'd seen Paula. It was now Friday, and she hadn't seen Reilly since.

Granted, he'd been on Isle Royale since Wednesday and unable to be reached. Still.

"Not much new since Sunday," Sarah said. "You?"

Alison shrugged. "Not really. I keep shorter hours in the summer when I can, so I can get out and enjoy the good weather while we have it. Petey's on the golf course when he can be. At the driving range when he can't. Life is good."

The woman radiated a quiet happiness that Sarah both recognized and was envious of. She was happy her cousin—who had been like a big brother to her after her father died—had found love and was married. Happily.

"Things good with Reilly?" Alison asked. "Must be a weird dynamic at times, having just been friends so long, eh?"

Sarah looked around the little office. It was cozy and welcoming, with neutral tones and soft furniture. But it was very much a therapist's office.

"I feel like the clock is about to start on my session," Sarah said.

Alison smiled. "I know. Occupational hazard. Whenever one of my girlfriends comes to hang out, she inevitably says she thinks I'm in shrink mode." She shrugged. "Maybe I am. Hard to turn off sometimes."

"I'll bet," Sarah said.

"But if you don't—"

"Reilly's old girlfriend showed up on his doorstep the other morning, and he and I haven't spoken since," Sarah blurted out.

"Wow. Okay. Umm…"

"Not that I'm saying I want you to be a therapist about it or anything. I just…"

"No. I know. I asked as a friend. I'm curious as a friend. If you want to talk about it, let's do that."

Sarah nodded, sitting back in the chair. She slid off her flip-flops and curled her legs under her on the chair, letting her skirt fall over her legs.

"Want something to drink? I always have some Diet Coke here, for after hours," Alison said. She got up and went to a corner of the room that housed a mini-fridge, a small sink, and a coffee pot. Taking a Diet Coke out, she looked at Sarah, who nodded. Alison grabbed another can of pop and returned to her chair, handing Sarah one of the cans.

Sarah popped the top and took a sip, holding the can with both hands on her lap.

"So, you haven't talked since then? Not at all? That doesn't sound like the two of you."

"He sent a text Tuesday night saying he wasn't going to make it to the Harbor because he'd be leaving on the *Ranger II* from Houghton next morning to go to Isle Royale."

"And that was a change from the plans you made previously?"

"Not really. I knew he was leaving Wednesday for a few days on the island. He didn't know Monday night where he was leaving from. If he'd be taking a shift on the Ranger or just getting to the island on his own. With Zeke or one of the other boats."

Alison nodded. "So his text was to confirm where he'd be leaving from."

"Yes. We already knew we wouldn't see each other. And that I probably wouldn't even see his text for a while, being in the Harbor."

"Right. That must be so frustrating, having such spotty service up there."

Sarah shrugged. "I'm used to it. And it's kind of nice. Most of my friends are slaves to social media, but I'm barely on that stuff. Except for the shop."

"So, what did Reilly say in his text about Paula stopping by?"

Sarah took another sip of pop and straightened her skirt. "Nothing. I'm not even sure he knew that I saw her. He only would have if she told him."

"Would she have told him?"

Sarah cleared her throat, fearing it might close up on her. Many people had probably cried in the chair she now sat in, facing Alison. Sarah did not want to add to that tally.

She knew Alison wouldn't mind, but Sarah was *not* going to cry over the ending of an arrangement with Reilly that had a time limit on it from the beginning.

Blammo.

"I don't think she'd mention it because…"

"Because?"

This part was hard, admitting the truth. "Because Paula would not see it as relevant, that I spent the night at Reilly's."

"She wouldn't care that you slept together?"

Sarah shook her head. "No. That's not it. It wouldn't *occur* to her that we slept together. She'd just think, did think, that I crashed at his place."

Which, actually, was exactly what happened. That night, at least.

"Oh," Alison said. She got it. Got how much that stung,

unreasonable as it was.

Sarah was not seen as any kind of romantic threat to Paula. A woman who had been sleeping with Reilly for over a year. A woman who had lived with him, shared a bed.

And not for just a "with benefits" situation.

"What did she say to you?" Alison asked.

"Not much. She asked if Reilly was up yet. I said no. She said good, because she wanted to make him breakfast. She was holding a couple of bags of groceries. I'm sure I saw a package of bacon. As an afterthought, she asked if I wanted to stay."

"Asked if *you* wanted to stay in *Reilly's* house while she made a breakfast he didn't ask for."

"Yes."

"As Petey would say, she's got a set of brass balls, that one does."

Sarah laughed, able to hear her cousin's voice in Alison's words. "She does, at that."

"Safe to say you said no," Alison said.

"I did. Got out of there as fast as I could. Went to the Harbor, worked. Got Reilly's message later. And here we are."

Alison nodded. "Must have been a shitty few days for you."

They had been. Awful. But Sarah shrugged. "Oh, you know, not that bad. We knew we were only going to hook up for a while. That it would be over after summer. So it's a few weeks earlier. That's fine. We'll just—"

"Wait, wait. Hold up just a second," Alison said, raising a hand. She looked stunned, and Sarah guessed she didn't say that to her patients much during therapy.

But she barreled through. "Are you saying you're ending it with Reilly? Does *he* know that?"

"Well, I'm assuming he does because of Paula's reappearance and the lack of communication since."

"You said yourself he's been on the island."

"Right. Sure. I guess there will probably need to be an actual conversation when he gets back, but yeah, that part of us is over."

"To be clear, it's *you* making that decision."

Sarah took a sip of pop, then put the can on the table next to her, her fingers cold from holding it. "So I guess I'm more Reilly's type than I thought," she said with a little chuckle.

"What do you mean?"

"Reilly usually lets the women in his life make the decisions. I think his policy is less fight, less strife."

"Petey would call that happy wife, happy life. And he wouldn't be wrong." Both laughed. Alison sobered first. "But by making that decision for Reilly, you're taking that choice away from him."

"And I'm sure he's good with that."

"Are you? Because that could be an awfully big gamble."

Sarah shook her head. "It's not."

Shifting in her seat, Alison looked intently at Sarah. "Let me ask you this: are you in love with Reilly, Sarah? I know you love him, care deeply for him. But are you romantically in love with him?" Sarah didn't answer right away. Alison pointed at the candle Sarah had dropped off. "Do you want that someday? A partner? A family?"

"Yes," Sarah said, without thinking. "Someday."

"But you don't see having it with Reilly?"

She hadn't. Not growing up. But had things shifted since they'd been sleeping together? Had her vision of what Reilly and she could be to each other changed?

"It doesn't matter," she said, as much to herself as to Alison.

"There you go, making another decision for Reilly. Why not give him the chance to decide for himself?"

"He's had twenty-nine years, Alison. It's not like an opportunity never presented itself. We've been single at the same time lots of times over the last ten years. He doesn't think of me like that."

"But you didn't think of him like that for those ten years

either, right?"

The word stuck in her throat, but she answered, "Right."

"And your feelings, attractions, seem to have changed. How do you know Reilly's haven't?"

Alison made a good point. Sarah looked at the candle again. Was there something to it that this candle, that of a family, poured out of her once she and Reilly became more than friends?

Or was it just turning thirty this year that was majorly messing with her?

"I don't want to stand in his way," she said. "I love Reilly and want him to be happy. A few months ago, he was really happy with Paula. She wanted more and told him so—which, in a weird way, I respect—and he freaked. But they were happy."

Alison shrugged. "Maybe they were. Or maybe Reilly just let it happen. It doesn't matter."

"But I don't want to stand in his way. He would never do that to me."

"Making an ultimatum about only remaining his friend if he isn't with Paula would be standing in his way. You'd never do that."

"No," Sarah said. "I wouldn't."

"Letting him know he has options on who to be with. That he can make his own choice. That's not standing in anyone's way. It's letting them *make* their way."

"Yeah, I guess," Sarah said, wondering at Alison's words.

"I believe our time is up," Alison said in what was obviously her therapist voice.

Sarah looked over to see her friend—because Alison was now more to Sarah than just her cousin's wife—laughing. "I'm just messing with you. Why don't we get out of here and go find your cousin? We've got some steaks that are ready to throw on the grill tonight. Petey's steaks will make you forget men even exist."

"Even Petey?" Sarah teased.

"Especially Petey," Alison said.

They gathered their things and walked to the door of the office. When Alison turned back to turn off the lights, Sarah saw her gaze return to the candle.

"Amazing work, Sarah."

"Thank you."

"You can create whatever you want," Alison said, and turned the light off then locked her office door.

Sarah wasn't sure if she was talking about candles or something else.

Twenty-Five

Eight and a half years ago
Age twenty-one

Reilly looked around the crowded fire hall for Sarah. And her date, Kip.

There. She was wearing a new dress. New to him, anyway, though he didn't have a close inventory on her closet.

It was gold and shimmery and cut low.

Definitely a New Year's Eve dress.

Her hair was down, and it looked like she'd put some curls in it, but Reilly couldn't be sure. She looked good. Cleaned up nice for the big night.

Looked a lot better than she had three days ago, when he'd last seen her. She'd been wearing sweats and a baggy Tech hoodie as they watched their hockey team on TV play at a holiday tournament in Detroit.

Sarah's new boyfriend had scored the winning goal. Been named MVP of the tournament.

And had returned to the Copper Country in time to take his girl to a New Year's party at a tiny fire hall way out on the Houghton canal road.

A pretty fucking great Christmas break for Kip Goodrich.

Reilly's had been spent working as much as he could at his job in the forestry department and talking on the phone to his girlfriend Jody, who had gone home to Grosse Pointe for the three-week break.

He really liked Jody, had been dating her since just a few weeks after classes had begun. He was sorry to be apart from her for this long.

And the sex was pretty good too. He'd *really* missed that since she'd been gone.

So, Sarah's month-long thing was going to ring in the New Year right, but Reilly would be going home alone to call his girlfriend at midnight. Which was still a couple of hours away, so he grabbed a beer and looked back through the crowd for someone he'd want to talk to other than Sarah.

Her thing with Kip was still new enough that Reilly didn't want to be their third wheel for the night.

Except…

His eyes went back to Sarah in her gold dress. She was not happy. No party joy in her expression. She wasn't pissed off, either.

Sarah was scared.

Kip leaned over to whisper something to her, since the small building was packed with locals of all ages. Then he left her, heading toward the john.

The scared look didn't leave Sarah's face.

Reilly made his way through the crowd, greeting people he knew and nodding at those that he only recognized. When he reached her, he was happy to see that whatever look he'd read in her face was disappearing with his approach.

"What did that colossal douche say to you?" he said when he got to her.

She laughed, the sound coming like more of a sigh of relief than actual humor.

"Nothing. He didn't say anything. I mean, nothing like that. And he's not a douche."

"He's a hockey player." Enough said.

"My cousin was a Tech hockey player," she said. Reilly gave her a pointed look. "Before he was a Detroit Red Wing," she added.

"Yeah?" Reilly said. "You're kind of making my point for me, Sarah."

She laughed, and this time, it was genuine. Reilly felt the tension leaving his body. Sarah's laugh could always do that. Even if her earlier look was what caused his tension in the first place.

"So if he didn't say anything, what did he do?" Reilly asked, more gently than his first question had been.

The truth was that Kip had a couple of inches and thirty pounds on Reilly and could probably kick his ass if it came down to it. But if an ass kicking was what it would take for Sarah not to have that look, Reilly would gladly take it.

He didn't spend too much time thinking about how a fight would help the situation. He was a guy, after all.

Sarah took a deep breath and let it out, glancing the way of the bathrooms. "It's just…he's drinking."

Reilly looked around the crowd. Everyone had a drink in their hand. He had a beer in his own. It was a New Year's Eve party. Their first as twenty-one-year-old people.

"I mean, he'd already been drinking before we came. I didn't realize it when I got in the car with him. And it's starting to snow pretty hard out."

There was a window behind them, and Reilly took a glance. Shit, he'd be wiping off his car for forty minutes with the amount they were getting.

"You drive his car home," Reilly said. Simple. Sarah never drank. She was a great permanent designated driver.

"That's just it. It's a stick."

He rubbed a hand through his hair. "Jesus, Sarah, how many times are we going to have this conversation? Learn to drive a damn stick shift!"

"I know, I know. And we haven't had this conversation lots of times. Like, twice. Maybe."

"Three times. In high school, when I said it'd be good to learn it, and you said you'd never need it. That day we were at the party after smelting that one time."

"Yeah, I remember."

"Two was freshman year, when you were buying your car and there was that Honda that was such a good deal."

"That car was so cute," she said, remorse in her voice. "That's only—"

She stopped herself because she remembered the third time. Reilly continued, "And three was up at the Harbor two summers ago, when Tessa asked—"

"Me to move your car while you were on Isle Royale for that forestry thing. Yeah, yeah, three times. You're right."

"Right about Kip being a douche too, but I guess it'll take years before you concede that one."

She snorted and took another glance in the direction of the bathrooms. Kip was heading their way, but being stopped by most of the people at the party. Everyone knew who he was. The Tech hockey team was the closest the Copper Country got to celebrities. Except for when Sarah's cousin Petey was in town. Reilly watched as Eddie Tuisku, a man in his sixties, stopped Kip to talk to him.

Reilly had a little more time alone with Sarah.

"So you both ride home with me," Reilly said.

"He would never do that," Sarah said. Reilly could understand that. He wouldn't want to ride home with another dude when he had a date for New Year's either. But he just added it as another strike against Kip.

"If he stops drinking now, it'll be okay. There are still two hours until midnight, so I think he'd be fine. I mean, he's not falling down drunk or anything," Sarah said.

She was trying to convince herself, not Reilly. And Reilly would agree with any other person's logic in the same situation. But not Sarah, and not when it came to anything remotely close to possible drunk driving.

Her father. Of course. He'd been killed by a drunk driver on New Year's Eve.

"Okay, well, you're not getting into a car with him, Sarah."

A tiny shake of her head. Good. She wouldn't. "But he shouldn't be driving." She waved her arm around the gathering. "Nobody should on these roads anyway, let alone tonight."

It was snowing, yeah. Heavily. But it wasn't anything Yooper drivers weren't used to. And hopefully, everyone here either had a designated driver, had carpooled, or knew when to stop drinking.

Sarah's hand was shaking as she held a glass of punch. Unspiked, of course, since there were kids in attendance. Reilly took the glass from her hand and set it on the windowsill behind them. He kept her hand in his, lowering them to their sides, trying to convey a sense of calm.

"Listen, here's what you do. Kip stops drinking. You spend the next two hours dancing. Get your big kiss in at midnight and then get out of here. Beat everyone off the roads. If Kip isn't okay to drive, then we make him ride with me."

"You won't want to leave that early," she said. He noticed she didn't outright nix his plan. Just the part that would jam up Reilly's night.

"Why not? I told Jody I'd call her at midnight. I was going to leave before then anyway. But I'll stay and check back in with you then, yeah?"

"Oh, you don't have to—"

"Yeah?"

She nodded, and he squeezed her hand.

"You mind not holding my date's hand?" Kip said. Damn. Reilly hadn't kept good tabs on his approach.

Sarah pulled her hand away from Reilly's. "Just hanging out until you got back," Reilly said, holding his hands up in mock surrender.

Let Kip think Reilly was scared of him. He didn't give a shit. This was all about Sarah.

"Okay. I see an old friend of my mom's who looks like she wants to dance. You guys should join us on the dance floor," Reilly said, starting to move away from Kip and Sarah.

"Not hardly," Kip said. The disdain was dripping from his voice.

"Check in with you later," Reilly said to Sarah, who nodded in return.

He started to walk away, but the crowd moved just then, and his pathway was blocked. He was still in hearing distance of Sarah and her douchebag boyfriend. (And if Reilly hadn't thought of Kip as a douchebag before, he sure did now.)

"You don't want to dance?" Sarah said to him.

"Nah, I'm good here. Don't need a bunch of Yooper yokels stomping on my feet. I've got to skate tomorrow."

"Oh!" There was hope in her voice. The pathway opened up, but Reilly stalled in moving forward. "Well, if you have to skate, you might want to switch to punch. It's pretty good, actually."

A small, derisive laugh from Kip. "Babe. It won't be the first time I've skated hungover. Shit, I've practiced still drunk."

"Oh," Sarah said. "Well, maybe if—"

"Babe, the john was pretty big. I'm thinking it'd be the perfect place for a quickie."

"Kip. Knock it off." There was warning and yet a little teasing in her voice. It seemed to Reilly that it was a tone she was used to using.

"How about a blow job, then?"

Reilly made his way through the crowd, found his mother's friend, and delighted her by asking her to dance.

At eleven thirty, he stepped off the dance floor and went to the bar for a water. Kip was there, regaling a few older men with his feats of strength on the ice. Reilly was happy to note that the men didn't seem all that impressed. Yeah, all Yoopers had good douche radar.

Except women when it came to guys like Kip.

Or maybe they did, he thought as he saw Sarah walking toward them, her coat in her hand. Reilly's coat as well. But not Kip's.

Reilly tried not to smile too broadly as Sarah approached

them and flipped his jacket to him.

"I'm leaving," she said to Kip.

Kip didn't seem surprised, so they must have had whatever conversation they were going to have about their departure.

Reilly noticed that Kip had a beer in his hand.

"Just relax," Kip said. "Don't be so emotional."

Reilly and the two men Kip had been talking to turned their eyes to Sarah. They all knew enough that you didn't tell a woman she was being emotional.

Especially when, as in Sarah's case, nothing could be further than the truth—calm, focused, and trying not to let the disgust show through.

She ignored Kip and turned to Reilly. "Are you okay to drive?"

He nodded. "I stopped drinking right after we talked. I'd only had two beers before that."

"You can't leave before midnight," Kip said, his voice growing louder. "That's stupid."

Reilly took a step toward him, but Sarah put a hand in his chest. "Reilly needs to get home before midnight to call his girlfriend."

"Ha! Phone sex? That's what you're going to get on New Year's Eve?"

"That's more than you're going to get," Sarah said as she pulled on her wool coat. The men with Kip and Reilly all jumped to help her with it, but she already had it on before they were able to get to her.

Reilly held out an arm for her to lead the way, and she did, never looking back at Kip.

It did take forever for Reilly to clean the snow off his car, but Sarah helped even though she was in heels and he'd told her to wait in the car.

The roads were bad, but he'd driven in worse. Still, he took his time driving the twisty canal road, making sure Sarah was not white-knuckling it.

"I'm fine," she said. He wasn't sure if she meant about Kip or being on the road. Maybe both.

"I know," he said. They didn't say another word the rest of the drive.

When he got to her mother's house, where she was staying during the holidays, he put the car in park but kept it running.

"Thanks, Riles," she said. It was for more than the ride, and they both knew it.

"Anytime," he said. It was for more than the ride, and they both knew it.

She got out of the car. Just before she shut the door, he said, "I'll pick you up at ten tomorrow morning."

"What for?" she asked.

"Driving lessons."

Twenty-Six

"YOU'RE A HARD PERSON TO TRACK DOWN," REILLY SAID from behind Sarah. She'd heard him approaching down the pebbled path that led from her store, cabin, and studio to the beach where she sat.

She'd brought down the same tote bag of candles and set a few of them around her, liking the glow they gave off as she listened to the waves slowly break on the shore.

"How was the island?" Sarah asked as Reilly sat on the blanket next to her. He was still wearing his ranger uniform. He untied his boots then took them and his socks off and rolled up the legs of his pants. Then he sat back, his arms behind him, legs crossed at the ankle.

"Good. Regular stuff. Nobody stealing greenstones. Nobody got lost. Saw a moose."

"Cool," Sarah said.

"How are things on the mainland?"

"Good. Regular stuff. Nobody stealing candles. Nobody got lost. Saw a stray cat."

"Cool."

They smiled at each other. Reilly leaned in to kiss her.

Sarah leaned back.

"Reilly, we need to talk," she said. She hadn't wanted to start like that—so clichéd. But she didn't want to kiss him either, or the resolve she'd had since talking with Alison was sure to leave her.

And she'd feel even worse in the morning.

"I've never liked conversations that started out that way," he said.

"Oh, you won't mind this one. Pretty straightforward, I'm thinking."

He nodded, drew his feet up, and leaned forward, putting his arms on his bent knees, hands dangling down.

"Whichever comes first has come?" he asked.

She nodded. "I'm thinking yeah, it has."

"You saw Paula at my place that morning?"

"I did, but it's really not about that."

Reilly looked at her. The night was cloudier than the first time they'd been out here skinny dipping and she'd lit fewer candles, so his expression was harder to see. Maybe that was just as well.

"I'm not back with her," he said softly.

But you could be. If you were free to be.

She didn't say the words, didn't want to put him on the spot, making him declare exactly what he felt for Paula versus what he felt for Sarah.

Because Sarah was guessing she'd win in the friend division, but not in the passionate love part.

"She made me breakfast. We talked, which was good, with the way she left. But we didn't... I didn't say that—"

"It's okay. Like I said, it's not really about Paula. We were just biding time. We both said that."

"Yeah, but that was before."

"Before what?"

Reilly was watching her, but she guessed he could see her no better then she could see him. Now would be a great time for that reading-minds trick they did from time to time.

No such luck. Reilly shrugged and looked out at the water. "It doesn't matter. If you're ready for it to be over, then it is. I'm the one who started the whole thing by climbing into your bed. You get to put the brakes on whenever you want. Blammo or not."

Fight for me!

But he wouldn't. Not go-with-the-flow, laid-back Reilly Turkonen. Sarah had made the call, and he was happy to go along with it.

Even this time.

Even ending things with her.

"It's going to be weird, eh? To be together and not touch you. Not kiss you."

"Maybe at first. But if you'll remember, at first touching and kissing was weird too."

He chuckled, his warm voice sending a tingle through her. "That didn't last long."

"No. And this won't either. We'll be back to where we were before in no time."

"Right," he said, still looking out at the water. "Just like nothing ever happened."

"Exactly," she said.

He let out a long breath and ran a hand through his curls. Even though Sarah couldn't see them, she knew the curls would flop back into place, forming corkscrews that framed his face. The face she'd kissed. The mouth. The mouth that had kissed her on every part of her body.

And never would again.

But she had always loved Reilly as her dear, dear friend, and she would not stand in the way if he wanted a future with Paula.

Maybe that would happen, and maybe it wouldn't. Time would see to that.

But she did know it was less likely to happen if he was still sleeping with Sarah. Paula wouldn't wait around forever, and probably not at all if she found out that Reilly had been sleeping with Sarah ever since the night she and Reilly had broken up.

And yeah, that tourist *could* walk into her shop any day now looking for a candle for his sister. Or Zeke could meet the perfect guy for her on one of his charters. Or both!

Why not blammo for her? She deserved it.

They both deserved to find their happiness, and stalling with a continued hookup wasn't going to help them get there.

Besides, it was almost August. They only had a month more of the very great sex anyway. Maybe longer if you counted Labor Day as the end of summer, as all those in Michigan who made their living via tourism did.

God, she would miss the very great sex.

He had his boots back on now, pant legs rolled down, and was standing. Apparently his plans had changed when sex was no longer on the schedule.

"Not exactly. Because Sarah, something *did* happen," he said.

Before she could say anything, he left. It was a long walk back to the cabin. She could shout something out at him, and he'd no doubt hear it, but what would she say?

It was a great parting line, and she'd let him have it.

She stayed on the beach for a long time, until the candles were down to nubs. Just like the last batch when she and Reilly had fallen asleep in each other's arms.

She'd have to replenish her tote bag. No hurry, though. She didn't expect to come back for a night on the sand anytime soon.

She snuffed out the candles, shoved them in her bag, grabbed the blanket, and walked back to the cabin.

There was no sign of Reilly—not that she'd expected it.

But still, it stung as she entered the empty cabin.

Twenty-Seven

MRS. RYAN OPENED THE FRONT DOOR TO HIM. "REILLY, why are you using this door and not the kitchen like you always do? And why did you knock?" she said, as she stepped aside to let him in.

"Just felt like a change," he said. She didn't seem surprised to see him, just at where he'd chosen to enter the house for Sunday dinner at the Ryans'.

"Well, your timing is excellent. We're just sitting down to dinner."

"I'm sorry I didn't get here sooner to help out," he said.

They passed the formal living room—a room he and Sarah were not permitted to play in as children. They'd been relegated to the family room in the finished walkout basement. The floor Sarah now inhabited in the winter months.

"Not a problem, Reilly. You know you're always welcome here. It's good to see you. It's been a few weeks."

"I've been on the island a lot lately."

"Yes, that's what Sarah said."

So Sarah hadn't told her mother that their relationship had taken on a new twist.

"Let me just grab a place setting for you, dear. Sarah said you wouldn't be joining us today."

Or maybe she had.

Mrs. Ryan turned and smiled at him. No—same warm smile

he'd known all his life. She waved him toward the dining room while she went into the kitchen from the hallway.

"Hey, Young Turk," Petey boomed when Reilly walked into the room. "Help us get closer to even odds. Dad and I are outnumbered."

"Hello, Reilly," Petey's mother Ellen said.

"Reilly," Dan Ryan said, nodding in Reilly's general direction. He was already loading mashed potatoes onto his plate.

All seemed normal.

And then he looked at Sarah.

Pain.

Aww, crap. His being here caused her pain. Not what he wanted. Not what he'd *ever* want.

But why should it? She was the one who had called it quits. The one who had wanted to go back to the way things were before.

No benefits.

"Have a seat," Petey said, pulling out the chair next to him. Which was across from Sarah. It was where Reilly always sat when he came to the Ryan family dinner. But today, he would like to be on the other side of the table, next to her. Alison had that seat, with Dan next to her. Ellen was next to her son, and Mrs. Ryan—Yvonne—sat at the head of the table.

The other end was left empty. Always. It wasn't a creepy "this is where Peter would sit if he were still with us" thing, but nobody ever sat there.

"Here you go, honey," Yvonne said, coming through the swinging door to the kitchen, a place setting in her hand, which she set down in front of Reilly.

"Thanks," he said, taking the linen napkin and putting it his lap. A flash of Yvonne teaching him to do that many years ago whisked past him. He looked at Sarah again. Her eyes were coming back to his, like she'd followed the motion of his napkin placement. She gave him a soft smile.

He could tell that she remembered the first time too.

"I've loved you my whole life," he said to her.

The clatter of silverware against plates stilled. Bowls of food that were being passed froze in the hands of the passers.

A sheen of wetness came to Sarah's eyes. Oh shit, he'd given her pain by coming, and now he was making her cry.

"I love you too," she said.

It wasn't past tense, so that was good. But it wasn't quite right.

"We all love you, Reilly honey," Yvonne said from the head of the table. Her words were measured, and she was studying him closely. "You're like family to us. You *are* family to us."

A snort from Petey to Reilly's left. "Yeah, like kissing cousins. No, scratch that one."

"Eww," Petey and Sarah said at the same time.

"Petey," Alison said, warning in her voice.

"What?" he said. "You think I'm going to blow it again? I learned my lesson after the night at the Seafarer. Took three nights to get you back in my arms. My lips are sealed."

"Petey," his mother said, and swatted his arm.

Alison rolled her eyes at her husband. "It so didn't."

Petey laughed. "I know. But you were pissed. It just so happens that you can't keep your hands off me, even when you don't want to talk to me."

Ellen smiled at that one and put a roll on her plate. Dan scowled.

Alison sighed. "Heaven help me, but he's right."

The table all laughed. Grateful for the break in tension, Reilly took the basket of rolls from Petey, dropped one on his plate, and passed them over to Sarah. She took the basket with her eyes down, not looking at him.

Yvonne was still studying him, looking between him and Sarah, her head tilting like she was staring at puzzle pieces.

When you figure out how it fits, let me know.

But that was just it. Reilly *knew* how the pieces fit. How they were supposed to fit now. Maybe how they were always supposed to fit and they had just never paid attention, too caught up in their lives. Growing up. High school. College. Careers. Boyfriends. Girlfriends.

Maybe they'd just never noticed each other in the way they had the past month.

And, at least for Reilly, always would.

"Is that a new top, honey?" Yvonne said to Sarah. "It's very pretty."

Sarah nodded, swallowed a bite of food, and wiped her mouth on her napkin. "It is. Thanks. I saw it online, and it just jumped out at me."

He looked at the shirt. The soft cotton of a T-shirt, but long sleeves, peach, and a wavy neckline that seemed somewhat familiar to him.

"The neckline," he said.

She looked down at herself and adjusted it a little, though there was nothing wrong with it. "Yeah? They call it a scalloped neckline."

"It's like your prom dress," he said, surprised at his own words. Where had that come from?

She looked at the neckline again. "Yeah, I guess. Maybe that's why it jumped out at me."

"I can't believe you remember a dress she wore over ten years ago," Yvonne said. Sarah looked at him with the same thought in her eyes. Though in hers it was more of a question. "You were so kind to take Sarah that night. She wouldn't have been able to wear that beautiful dress if you hadn't stepped in."

He looked at Yvonne and smiled. "It ended up being a fun night." He caught Petey glaring at him, lifting his hand like he was going to cuff the back of Reilly's head.

Just like he had that night.

Holy wah!

Something rushed through Reilly, words bubbling up. Words that had no business being said at all, let alone at a dinner table with the elder Ryans in attendance. And especially with Petey next to him. And yet Reilly couldn't stop the words from forming first in his mind, and then out his stupid mouth. "I wanted to peel that dress off you that night," he blurted out to Sarah.

Sarah and the rest of the table.

A huge exhalation left his body. Like he'd been holding his breath since prom night twelve years ago.

But he hadn't. Not really.

Or had he?

"What?" half the table asked.

The other half stared at him, mouths agape, utensils frozen halfway to their mouths. And the cuff at the back of his head by Petey.

Sarah came out of her frozen position, dropped her fork to her plate, and pointed at Petey's hand, now returning to his own damn area.

"You did that prom night too. Why?"

"Because I knew he wanted to peel your damn dress off you."

"How?" Reilly and Sarah asked.

Petey rolled his eyes. "Jesus, you two. Does it matter? You're together now, right? Who cares how long it took for you to reali—"

"We're not together," Reilly said.

Petey whirled in Reilly's direction. "What? When'd this happen?"

"Friday," Reilly and Sarah said.

"When were you ever *together*?" Yvonne said. There was surprise in her voice, but not nearly as much as Reilly would have guessed.

"A month ago," Sarah and Reilly said, again at the same time.

"Did you really? Want to? That night?" Sarah said. She took a glance at her mother, probably seeing if it was okay to broach the subject of Reilly wanting to tear that gorgeous prom gowns to shreds.

Yvonne seemed cool with it.

"Yeah," he said, admitting it to himself as much as to Sarah.

"Why didn't you say anything?" she asked.

"Why didn't you do it?" Petey said.

"Petey," Alison and Ellen said, their tones similar.

"You mean beside the fact that you'd given me a stare-down like no other?" Reilly said.

Petey waved a hand, letting the huge mitt fall on the table. "That shouldn't have stopped you."

It wouldn't have. It was crazy, mixed emotions that had. The feelings came crashing through, scaring Reilly at their intensity. That night, he really had thought Sarah was the most beautiful thing he'd ever seen. And all he'd thought about was the neckline of her dress.

Pinning that corsage on had about killed him.

But then...

"You seeing Travis with Steph," he said. "It kind of..."

"Killed it," Sarah said.

Reilly shrugged. "I guess."

Sarah nodded and looked at her hand. She had a roll in it, halfway to her mouth, but looked at it like it was some sort of foreign object. She set it on her plate.

"So you guys are really done? Not"—Petey looked at his mother, perhaps the only woman who could shame him into some sort of discretion—"*that* kind of friendship anymore?"

"That's right," Reilly said.

"But we'll always be friends," Sarah said, looking at Reilly, not Petey.

"That's right," Reilly repeated.

"Well, um..." Yvonne, ever the hostess, tried to get things back on track. "Of course you'll always be friends. Nothing can break the bond—"

"That day in the bleachers," Sarah said.

Reilly whipped his head from Yvonne to Sarah. He didn't know exactly what she was going to say, but he knew by the tone of her voice that he did not want to miss a word.

"Yes?" he asked.

"The first time. The day you got me out of class?"

"Yes?"

"And you told me about your dad and brothers leaving?"

"Right?"

She looked at him, then away, around the room, like the answer to her unasked question was floating around them.

"I…I…wanted to lean over and lick your tears off your face."

The words were as shocking to her as they were to Reilly. She actually even put her fingers to her mouth, like something unintended had escaped.

Unintended and unknown. Until now.

"Dude, you cried? What a pussy," Petey said. Quietly, though nothing Petey did or said was ever really quiet.

"Watch it, tough guy," Alison said. "Seems like a lot of secrets are spilling at this table today. You want me to join in?"

Petey held up his hands in surrender to his wife, did a zipper across his mouth, and then crossed his arms over his chest, sitting back. Like he was waiting for the show to go on.

Not disappointing, Sarah continued, "I wanted to crawl into your lap to comfort you, yes. But also to lick your tears away. Not wipe them away. No, I wanted to taste your salty tears that day."

"Dan, maybe we should take our dinner into the kitchen?" Ellen said.

"Not on your life," Dan said, and then he dropped his fork and assumed the same pose as his son.

Yvonne had a soft smile on her face as she watched her daughter. Sarah was struggling, trying to find words, thoughts coming to her that she'd never truly formulated before.

He knew this because he was going through the exact same thing.

And yet Yvonne was smiling.

"And the day you took me to Maya's class?"

"Yeah," he said, leaning forward, arms on the table. Yvonne had taught him better than that, but today, manners be damned.

Sarah leaned forward too, but the table was too damn wide. "You gave me my life that day, Reilly. I didn't know it exactly then, but I knew something had changed for me. And you gave me that."

"You had it in you the whole time. You just needed to find it."

Her glassy eyes returned, tears pooling but not falling. "Thank you," she whispered.

"Ess," he whispered.

"No whispering," Petey said. "Ow," he added when somebody did what Reilly wanted to do and kicked him under the table.

"I wanted to kiss you that night. When you dropped me off," Sarah said. Laughter bubbled out of her, like she couldn't believe it herself.

Reilly was having a hard time too.

"I did. Holy wah, I wanted to kiss you that night. When you dropped me off. But then you reminded me to get my candle out of the back, and the thought just…" Her hand fluttered, like her thought of kissing him had that night. Fluttered away.

What if she had? What if he had peeled her dress off on prom night? What if…

"We can't," she said. "We can't what-if the past."

He nodded, not surprised she read his mind.

"Sometimes it's good to look at the past," Alison said. "To help you understand where you are today."

They all nodded. Alison's shrink voice had a way of doing that to people, making them mindlessly nod along with her. Mindless was one way of describing the info dump that was spewing from Sarah and Reilly.

She wanted to kiss him. Kiss. Kissing.

Another long-ago memory wafted up to him. Another beautiful dress.

"You were a golden goddess on New Year's Eve. And Kip did not deserve to even look at you, let alone be your date."

"Who was Kip?" Alison said.

Petey answered, "I don't know. I'm not even sure *they* know what the hell is going on. It's like they're speaking in tongues or something."

"I was hoping the drive home would take longer so we'd be together at midnight," Sarah said. "And not only so you wouldn't be able to call Jody."

"I didn't call her," Reilly admitted. "I called the next day and told her I'd gotten stuck in a snowbank."

"Is that what the kids are calling it these days?" Petey said.

Reilly turned to him. "Dude. Seriously?"

Petey rolled his eyes. "What? I'm no cockblocker, but she is my cousin, man."

"Petey," his mother said.

"Sorry," he said, then turned to Reilly and mouthed, "Not sorry."

"At midnight, I pretended you'd been my date," Sarah said.

Reilly didn't say what he'd been doing at the stroke of midnight. But the vision of Sarah in that dress guaranteed that there was a different kind of stroke going on.

"Baby, what do you call all this?" Petey asked his wife. "Purge? Repressed memories?"

Reilly and Sarah looked to Alison for answers. They didn't know what the hell was going on, either.

Alison shrugged. "I'd just call it good, old-fashioned denial."

"Even to ourselves?" Sarah asked.

"That's the best kind," Alison said. She looked across the table to her husband, and a very playful smile crossed her face.

"Aw, baby. What you do to me," Petey said.

Denial? Really? Reilly didn't think that was it. But if not? What could—

"At Spring Fling. When you were beneath me on that snowbank."

"Ooh, this one sounds like fun," Yvonne said.

"Or cold," Dan said.

"Both," Reilly and Sarah said, then shared another smile. He leaned closer to her, not wanting the rest of the table to hear. Yeah, right. Like that would happen.

As if on cue, the rest of the group leaned forward too.

"Let's just say," he said quietly, "I *really* wanted to make an interesting snow angel that night."

A bark of laughter. "I wanted to pull your chook off and run my fingers through those curls." She sat back in her chair, sighing heavily. "*Man*, have I wanted to run my fingers through those curls."

"They're pretty great curls," Alison said.

"You got that right," Ellen added.

"True that," said Yvonne.

"Hey," Petey and Dan said.

And suddenly Reilly realized—*really* realized—that their most intimate secrets—secrets that they hadn't shared with each other because they'd withheld them from even themselves—were being thrown on the Ryan dining room table like they were the second course.

No, this isn't how it should be. Crap.

He sat back, eyes moving back to Sarah's face.

Help.

She looked around at the group. Then she shook her head and threw her napkin on her plate. Rising from her seat, she shook her head again, covering her face with her hands.

"I can't do this anymore," she said, and ran from the room.

Leaving Reilly to face the Ryan family alone.

Twenty-Eight

"Took you long enough," Sarah said as Reilly climbed up the bleachers to join her. He got to her, sidestepping the candle she'd brought to the football field with her. Lit, so Reilly could find her.

Not that he couldn't find her anyway.

Reilly would always find her.

"The first two gas stations I stopped at didn't have tiger cookies," he said. A bottle of beer was in his hand.

"So you kept looking," she said.

He smiled, sat, and pulled a small pack of tiger cookies from his jacket pocket. "I kept looking."

She took the cookies and tore open the package. She slipped one of the cookies over her finger, like a ring, and tapped it to the long neck of his beer bottle in a toast. He took a swig, and she took a bite, careful not to break her ring.

"Thanks for pulling the running-from-the-room bit," he said.

She shrugged. "I should have done it sooner."

"Yeah, it was more than I wanted to share with your family."

She turned her head to face him, able to see him clearly in the glow of the candle and the clear night and bright moon. "I know. That's why I left. I would never want you to do that—make you run out through the crowd to the pitcher's mound with everyone watching. You would hate that. You hated *that*." She waved a hand to indicate the family dinner she'd stormed away from an hour ago.

Only Reilly realized it was a fake dramatic exit. It was to get him out of there. Have the conversation they needed to have alone.

"I'd do it, though," Reilly said.

"Huh?"

"Run through the stands, past the crowd, out to the pitcher's mound. I'd do it if you were there waiting for me."

"I know you would," she said.

He let out a deep breath. "But seriously, thanks for not making me go any further in front of everyone."

"I got you, Riles."

"I know."

He turned toward her, sliding a leg over the bleacher so he straddled it. "I just want to be really clear. I am not getting back with Paula. Not now. Not ever. I was *never* going to get back with her."

She mimicked his motion, bringing a leg over the bleacher as well so that they were face to face. "Good. Because I'd probably have to kick your ass."

"What? Why? I thought that's what you wanted. Why you ended things with us."

"What I wanted? No. That's what I thought was best for you. The person I love most in the world. But not what I wanted."

"Then why?"

She'd thought about nothing else since the day she'd dropped the candle off at Alison's office. Given the pent-up, long-forgotten memories that had just spilled out of her at her mother's dining room table, she had most likely been thinking about it long before the summer.

"Because it was scary, Reilly." A weight lifted from the chest. Yes, that was what it had been. She just hadn't realized it. "So scary. Even now. I think I'm the most scared I've been since my dad died."

"Ess," he whispered. He started to reach for her hand, but

she put it in the pocket of her jean jacket. He wasn't the only one who'd brought something. She pulled out two small tapered candles that she'd broken off, both only about four inches long. Leaning over, she lit one from the pillar candle she'd set on the bleacher beneath them. She handed the taper to Reilly and then lit his from her flame.

"That day. My dad's funeral. I lit your candle. You held my hand. You became my best friend. And I thought—just for a second—that everything was going to be okay."

They held their candles with their right hands. Reilly reached out and took her left hand in his, placing them on the top of his thigh. "It is going to be okay, Sarah. No matter what happens between us. I swear it."

"I know," she said. "I believe you." She did.

"Okay. And, just so there's no mistake, so no one thinks I let a woman—even one I'm crazy about—make my decisions for me."

"Again."

"Again," he said, giving her hand a squeeze. "I love you, Sarah. I will love you forever. And I am *in* love with you."

She started to answer him, to tell him how much she loved him too, but he held up the hand holding the candle, raising his finger in a "one sec" motion. "Damn," he said when the wax from the candle ran down to his hand. "You need to put those little shields on these things like they have at the church."

"I was in a little bit of a hurry," she said. "I didn't know how long it'd take you to get out of there and follow me here."

"Not damn long."

"Besides, a little burn won't kill ya," she said.

He smiled at her, a sweet, goofy smile that was all Reilly. "Oh, the burn is definitely killing me. But in a very good way."

"Reilly."

"But what I was saying? I love you—yep, said that. Oh, yeah. I am ready to put a ring on your finger today. Tomorrow. Whenever you're ready to say yes."

A lump clogged her throat. Holy wah, Reilly was proposing. And she hadn't made this decision for him. But still... "You don't have to do that with me, Reilly. I won't hold our relationship hostage. Waiting for a diamond-ring ransom."

"I know. I'm not saying this out of fear. Or guilt. Or because I think you want me to. Hell, I don't even know *if* you want me to."

"I do," she said.

He chuckled. "Those two words sound pretty good coming out of your mouth."

"Don't get ahead of yourself. It's too soon to talk like that."

His chuckle turned to a boisterous laugh. "Too soon? *Too soon?* Twenty-nine years is not too soon."

"You know what I mean," she said, but she was smiling too. Smiling at her beautiful, blue-eyed man.

"Okay. We'll go at your pace on this. Not because I'm indecisive. We're going ring shopping tomorrow. You can decide when you want to wear it."

"Reilly."

"And set a date. You can decide that too."

"Gee, thanks," she said, but she was laughing.

"I'm not dicking around here, Sarah."

He wasn't. She knew that. The laughter died down, and her smile faded. "I know you aren't. That's why I'm so scared, Reilly."

"Building a life together is scary."

"It is," she said.

"But a life without each other. That's even scarier."

"But..."

He shook his head. "I'm not talking about losing my friendship. You'll always have that. But we could have it all, Ess."

"This, that..."

"And the other," he said with her. "What do you say?"

"I say yes."

"Good," he said. "Now kiss me, because this candle wax is burning the shit out of my hand."

"See why I didn't want to bring it into the very great sex?"

"Good decision on your part," he said. He smiled at her and then blew out his candle.

She blew out her candle too and moved into his arms.

Into his kiss.

Twenty-Nine

"WHY WERE WE INVITED TO THIS AGAIN?" REILLY asked Sarah.

She handed him some more dishes to place in the dishwasher after she'd rinsed them off at the sink. "I think it was because of the candle connection. And the fact that Petey and Alison were hosting the party after the christening."

Reilly loaded the dishes she'd handed him. Finished, he closed the door of the dishwasher and leaned against the countertop. "Are you going to get invited to parties of all the people you make a custom candle for?"

Sarah shrugged as she turned off the sink and dried her hands on a towel. "Who knows? I hope not. Because if the line of new candles takes off, we'd be going to all kinds of weddings and showers and christenings."

"God help us," he said. But he smiled and held his arms out for her. She walked into them and wrapped her arms around his waist, resting her head on his chest.

"I think Petey and Alison just wanted us to get to know their friends better."

"We've got friends," Reilly said.

"All their couple friends."

"We need couple friends now?"

She chuckled and nuzzled into his chest. "Relax. No one's going to force you to do five-course dinner parties with all couples."

"Got that right," he said. She could hear the humor in his voice. He might have put up a mock stink about having to go to the christening of little Michael Luna, but he'd enjoyed himself at the party afterward at Petey and Al's house. The weather had cooperated, and the festivities had taken place outside.

Sarah looked out the window and saw Petey and Alison, Katie and Darío, Lizzie and Finn Hampton, Zeke and Jess, and Twain and Liv Beck all still enjoying the early evening. All of the other guests, including Katie's large family, had already left.

The five couples were gathered around a large picnic table on the lawn with some stray lawn chairs pulled close. Darío Luna stood behind his wife, holding his son and swaying back and forth. Katie held their daughter, Peaches, in her lap. Or tried to. The toddler kept reaching for Sam Robbins, Lizzie and Finn's son, who was sitting in his mother's lap across the table from Peaches.

Twain Beck also was standing behind the sitting women. Also swaying, as he held his daughter Faith, who had just turned six months old.

Lizzie and Finn's older daughter Annie came out of the sauna, ran to the end of the dock, and dove into the water.

Reilly turned to his side with Sarah still in his arms so he could also see out the window.

"It's a good group," he said. "I'm glad they included us."

"Me too," she said. They watched as Annie Hampton climbed back on the dock and dove in again. "I haven't been here since Alison's dad's funeral. Nice to see a much happier crowd."

"That was quite a day," Reilly said.

Annie got back on the dock again. The same dock Sarah had stood on that day and told Reilly that they'd slept together when he'd been drunk.

"Don't remind me," she said.

He ran his hands up and down her back and placed his chin on the top of her head. "I'm so glad you told me, Ess. Can you imagine if you hadn't? If you'd just kept that to yourself?"

"Yeah, you'd probably be engaged to Paula right now."

He snorted. "Not funny."

"Maybe not," she said.

"And I wouldn't have been. It was never going to be Paula."

"Maybe not," she said again.

"Definitely not." He hugged her tighter and kissed the top of her head. "Besides, I'm engaged to exactly the woman I want to be."

"Shh," she said. She pulled away and looked around the kitchen, making sure no party stragglers had found their way in. "I thought we agreed to wait to tell people."

"No. *You* decided to wait to tell people. I just went along with it," he said.

"That's right. And if you keep doing exactly that, we'll have a very great life together."

Reilly laughed, and Sarah smiled into his chest, hugging him closer. "We're going to have a very great life together anyway."

"I know," she said.

"So let's go down there and tell them," he said. "Let the very great life go public starting now. We'll swing by your mom's house on the way home and tell her. Tell Tessa tomorrow. You can finally start wearing your ring."

"I don't want to steal any thunder from Michael's christening," Sarah said.

Reilly nodded with his chin toward the group gathered outside. "I'm not thinking Mick is going to be put out or anything. In fact, the way Darío is slowing down his sway, I'm guessing the baby's out cold."

"Yeah, I guess we could go down there."

He heard the hesitation in her voice and leaned back to look at her. "You're not having second thoughts, right? We *are* going to go public. Aren't we?"

She rose on her toes and kissed him. "You bet we are. You're right. They won't think we're stealing thunder. It's just friends left. The party's basically over."

"Or just beginning," he said.

She nodded and kissed him again. About to turn toward the door, they both stopped when they heard a loud "whoop" from the group outside. Everybody was up and moving around the table. And they were all going to Alison for a hug. Her friend Lizzie had her hands over her mouth, and Katie was balancing Peaches while the three women hugged.

The men all went to Petey, shaking hands and patting him on the back.

"Alison's pregnant," Sarah said.

"Did you know that?" Reilly asked.

She shook her head. "No. I guess I knew they were trying. I think my mom mentioned it a while ago. But I wasn't sure how intently they were trying or how long or anything. I got the impression it wasn't something she wanted to talk about. At least not with me."

"Well, you just bought yourself a few more days of keeping our news private," Reilly said.

"Yeah, no way are we going to swoop in and drop our bomb now."

"It won't be a bomb. Probably won't even cause a ripple," he said.

"You're probably right. Besides, I really would like to tell my mom first."

Reilly nodded and leaned forward to kiss her. Longer, sweeter. Perfect.

"Let's go tell her," he said.

She nodded and took his hand as he led her away.

To start their very great life together.

Acknowledgments

Beta readers Holli Bertram, Liz Kelly and Patti Kearly were invaluable in their feedback. The editing at Word Wolfe and Editing 720 was, as always, top notch. And a big thank you to my last-look editor, Margo Burrage.

More WORTH books are coming!

In the meantime, try Mara's New Adult Romance Series

IN TOO DEEP
FRESHMAN ROOMMATES TRILOGY, BOOK 1

IN TOO FAST
FRESHMAN ROOMMATES TRILOGY, BOOK 2

IN TOO HARD
FRESHMAN ROOMMATES TRILOGY, BOOK 3

Mara Jacobs is the *New York Times* and *USA Today* bestselling author of The Worth Series

After graduating from Michigan State University with a degree in advertising, Mara spent several years working at daily newspapers in Advertising sales and production. This certainly prepared her for the world of deadlines!

Mara writes mysteries with romance, thrillers with romance, and romances with…well, you get it.

Forever a Yooper (someone who hails from Michigan's glorious Upper Peninsula), Mara now splits her time between the U.P. and Las Vegas.

You can find out more about Mara's books at
www.marajacobs.com

Mara loves to hear from readers. Contact her at
mara@marajacobs.com

Made in the USA
Middletown, DE
23 August 2023

37232962R00151